Comes

Barbara Maria Kelly

Copyright © 2017 Barbara Maria Kelly

ISBN:
ISBN-9781549928109

DEDICATION

This book is dedicated to my son, Charlie who
never stops encouraging me, never stops praising my efforts
and never stops saying, "Keep writing, Mom."
Thanks for helping me find my calling. I love you, Son.

TABLE OF CONTENTS

ACKNOWLEDGMENTS

Thank you, Charlie for getting me to the end and out there. Never would have happened without you. Thanks to Diana, who kept my writing flame fanned and alive, Debbie who suffered through that awful first draft who believed there was a story in there and Delaune, my friend and author who helped me far beyond with many hours of reading, offering great suggestions and getting me back on track. Thank you Paul for your early review that was a much needed lift. Lynn, thanks for reminding me each writer has a voice and I needed to keep mine. To my friends who read along as I wrote, Bev who said I was a good writer. Kippy, who told me to stop talking because she was trying to read a good book, mine. Eden who said she wanted to use my book as Christmas gifts, Jim who said it was amazing, Leslie who thought it sounded like a famous writer's work and to my lifelong friend, Dawn who said it was captivating. A special thanks to Betsy who did the first read edit.

St. Charles on the Missouri River in the year of 1800

CHAPTER 1

"I am going to kill him." Grace said in a very calm voice. She slowly raised the ax and swung it around high over her head then down with all her might. The ax landed heavily on the piece of fire wood. The splinter flew off the stump clattering to the pile of kindling beside it. At the same time the hen that was pecking for worms nearby squawked, flapped its wings and scurried toward the hen house, as though the ax had been intended for her.

There was no other sound except for the steady rhythm of the ax as the piece of wood became smaller and smaller while she chopped away at it. Grace finally stopped and turned from the wood pile holding the ax in front of her with both hands. She looked at her friend, Agatha who was standing by the wheel barrow patiently watching and listening for the time when Grace would be ready to talk.

Agatha Edwards had been Grace's friend almost from the moment they had met two years earlier when Alexander Monet had brought Grace to St. Charles a few days after their wedding in St. Louis. Grace and Agatha often laughed and said they had to be kindred spirits for it seemed they had known each other forever. There was some sort of mental connection that joined the two friends. Neither of them knew exactly what it was, but both accepted it and talked about it only between themselves. They knew how dangerous it could be to discuss such unexplained phenomena openly. There were still reports of people who had been murdered after they were accused of being a witch and working evil magic. Nonetheless, this unseen link that tied these two women together was the very reason Agatha had rushed to visit Grace today.

All morning while Agatha had worked through her chores the feeling that she needed to check on Grace would not leave her. She had known something was wrong. Finally, she had finished churning the milk and carried the butter down to the spring and put it in the spring box to keep it cool. She just could not wait any longer. Agatha had found her Papa in the garden and told him she was going to see Grace. She instructed him to fry up some ham to go along with the beans that were slowly simmering over the fire and the fresh bread she had made earlier.

Agatha had rushed to the barn, saddled up her horse and headed toward St. Charles. Normally she would have walked for it was not that far, but she had not wanted to take the extra time today.

Agatha had raced her horse passed the military Post and through the settlement to Grace's house, which was on the opposite end of St. Charles. She knew the people that had seen her would be wondering where in the world she was going in such a frenzy especially the nosey ones who would do more than just wonder. They would be asking, the first chance they got. Without a doubt the proprietress of the General Mercantile would be the first. That woman worked very hard at not missing anything that happened in St. Charles.

When she had reached Grace's house she quickly tied her horse to the fence and ran through the cabin calling for her until she found her out back. As she stood

3

looking at her now she could see the bruise marks on her face and neck even though Grace had left her long strawberry blond hair hanging loosely in an attempt to cover some of them up. This was not the first time Agatha had seen bruises on her friend. She knew there were most likely others hidden by her clothing.

Grace just kept standing there, holding the ax and looking at Agatha with those deep green eyes of hers. She looked confused as if she did not know what she was supposed to say or do next. Her eyes which usually sparkled with light had a dullness that scared Agatha.

Grace finally took a deep breath and said, "If I don't, Agatha, it will be because he has killed me first. It has come to that. There is a line drawn in the dirt and it can't be crossed ever again. I feel it as clearly as I see you. I know it's there because I drew it in my mind and if he hits me again it has been crossed.

"It's only a matter of time until he takes another drink too many and turns mean again. There never is any warning. It is like some sort of demon spirit has appeared, overtaken him and has brought a friend along just for me. The self I know and like as me is gone then and all I want to do is hurt him back. I cannot keep my mouth shut no matter how many times I tell myself I will."

Grace was pacing back and forth now and still holding the ax in front of her as she walked.

"The ugliness steps in me too somehow and I say every possible thing I can to hurt him. I accuse him of being unfaithful while he is off on one of his military missions. I am sure some of it might be true, but I suspect most could be imagined by me.

"I am afraid that one day I will not be able to rid myself of this ugliness that comes to me uninvited and seems to smother all the good I possess. Agatha, I am afraid that it will latch on and the Grace I always have been will be gone, lost forever and replaced by a woman I would not care to associate with much less be. I feel

4

myself diminishing a little each time it happens and I stay here until the next time.

"A line has been drawn in the sand. I know, because I drew it myself and if it is crossed again one of us could die. It would most likely be me. I am not willing to wait for that to happen. This insanity has to stop. I think I could have shot him if he had been here yesterday morning. I have to leave him and this place."

"Oh Grace, where will you go? What will you do? You know he will try to follow you."

Grace leaned the ax against the stump and started picking up the fire wood without answering. She began stacking it on the wheel barrow. Agatha bent over and helped her. Neither said anything. Together they pulled the heavy load of wood to the back porch and unloaded it near the door.

They went inside and Grace dipped water from a bucket sitting on her kitchen work table into a kettle. She very carefully sprinkled in a few tea leaves and set it on top of the stove. Agatha had sat down at the table and was patiently waiting for Grace to answer her question.

"Agatha," she said "you know I can't tell you my plan, because I don't know where I'm going. If I did and you knew, Alex would worry you until you might tell him. This way, you can tell him the truth and say you don't know. That when we talked I didn't have a plan, which is true. He will soon recognize the truth in your answer and leave you in peace. Just know that very soon I will be gone. I want to leave before he returns from this mission."

"Do you think you will eventually join your parents in New Madrid?"

"Of course, that is where I want to go right away, but that would be the first place he would look. I have to give this some deep thought."

Grace and Agatha found it hard to say goodbye to each other. Agatha was having a very difficult time in leaving Grace in the state she was in. They were both overcome with sadness, but despite this Agatha kept feeling like she was going to see more of her friend. Grace had promised that she would find a way to let Agatha know where she was after a sufficient amount of time had passed.

It was the middle of the afternoon when Agatha left for home. As she rode slowly through the settlement she was deep in thought and hardly noticed the two children playing in front of one of the houses as she passed. She unconsciously waved at them.

They both shouted in unison while energetically waving back, "Hello Agatha."

Agatha could see the bell tower of the Catholic Church over the roof tops. The Catholics were the first to build a church in St. Charles. They had constructed it out of logs that stood in the upright position. These soon rotted and Governor Blanchette had replaced it with a new framed building on Second Street.

Agatha could hear a ruckus coming from the Canard Inn just up ahead. It was the one of two taverns in town and the only one with sleeping accommodations. She figured it was most likely some trappers that had imbibed a little too much before continuing their trip on to St. Louis with their load of furs. Suddenly the swinging doors flew open and Francois came running through them with Hannah right behind him. He was holding a fellow high up in front of him by the nape of the neck and his pants seat. The man looked almost like he was sitting in an invisible chair as Francois sent him flying through the air. He landed on his behind in the middle of a big mud hole right in front of Agatha's horse. A second woman was right behind them.

She threw a coon skin hat out after the man while shouting "You no pay, you no play! Oh mein Gott! Agatha." She shouted.

All the while Hannah was hollering, "Merciful Heavens! Hold him, Agatha, hold him."

Agatha's horse had been terribly frightened just as she was. It was taking all she could do to control him as he reared up on his hind legs pawing with his front hooves. The man in the mud hole seemed to be too inebriated to know the perilous situation he had literally been tossed into.

Francois rushed into the street and grabbed the halter of Agatha's horse to help hold him until he was under control. He then led him over and tied him to the hitching post. He turned and looked up at Agatha.

"Agatha", he said. "I'm awful sorry. Are you alright? You look mighty pale."

"Jiminy crickets, Francois! When in tarnation are you going to start looking out to see who might be coming down the street before you throw your esteemed patrons in it?"

"Agatha, you are as pale as a sheet. You need some whiskey after that scare. As far as that goes, I do too." said Hannah.

"I think my horse and I both might. I don't know about him, but almost killing some fool drunk in the middle of the street has made me a little light headed."

"Francois help her off the horse."

The other woman said in her heavy German accent, "Is alright, Agatha. No more person drink in bar. Francois pour. You drink. Come."

Agatha was not much of a drinker, but today she felt like a swig or maybe two of some whisky might be just what she needed. Hannah and the other woman watched Agatha closely as Francois helped her to the ground. From the paleness of her face, they knew she might be unsteady on her feet. Agatha was glad for the help. Her legs did feel a little wobbly. She thought how amazing it was that a few moments of fear could have so much effect on a person's body.

Before they went through the swinging doors the other woman turned, took a couple of quick steps toward the man and spit on him while muttering what must have been German cuss words, Agatha thought.

The trapper was still in the mud hole, but had managed to clamber around and get in a sitting position. He slowly stood up, staggering and sloshing around. Every time he would start to bend over and reach for his hat, he would begin to lose his balance and have to plunge both hands in the water to keep from falling. If they had not been so concerned for Agatha they would have had a good laugh watching as his butte weaved in the air while he fought to keep from going head first back down. He finally managed to pick up his hat that had also landed in the hole. When he plopped it on his head streams of muddy water ran down his face. He started spluttering while stumbling around blinded and promptly fell back down on his behind with another big splash. The blacksmith across the street had seen it all and was chuckling to himself at the scene.

Agatha finished her two shots and visited with Hannah for a little while. She then went outside, untied and mounted her horse. Agatha nodded her head in greeting when the blacksmith looked up at her from his work. She knew he most likely had seen everything and would have a good time sharing it with his wife who would share it with someone else. It would be all over St. Charles by this time tomorrow.

The blacksmith had given up his life as a trapper and settled down at the request of his new bride. He was busy banging away at a piece of metal and whistling a tune. Agatha wondered if he would be able to stay in St. Charles and out of the wilderness. To hear her brother describing the clear rivers and most especially the Rocky Mountains made it sound mighty appealing to a man once he had been there. He had even told her that the majority of white men who experienced the beauty and majesty of that country could not stay away from it long.

When Agatha passed the Watkins General Mercantile, she half expected to see a face pressed up against the window pane. No one was there. The mercantile offered food staples and a variety of merchandise for the villagers who preferred to not have to travel to St. Louis as before. It used to be the only option unless a supply load came in on a boat or the Post had made a supply trip. Agatha had noticed that the variety of merchandise had increased significantly in the last couple of years. It was nice to consistently see necessities such as coffee, sugar, tea, flour, rice and beans in stock.

She remembered as a child when her father would go with some of the soldiers on a supply run all the way to St. Louis to get these items. He was always gone at least overnight. Sometimes it would take longer if streams were flooded and an alternate crossing off the trail had to be found. The trail was an extension of the Kings Highway which ran all the way down the west bank of the Mississippi to New Orleans. Agatha remembered standing under the black walnut tree in front of their cabin anxiously waiting for him even though he had not been gone overnight yet. He had always managed to bring her some candy sticks back with him no matter how long the trip took.

Before Agatha knew it she was passing the military Post. She was only about a mile from home now. Agatha's mother and father were among the first settlers of St. Charles which was founded in 1769 by Louis Blanchette, a French Canadian explorer. The post and village were situated on the Missouri River and about twenty miles west of St. Louis by land. The Missouri River flowed over two thousand miles before merging with the Mississippi River just a few miles east of St. Charles. In the past three decades the settlement had grown from three or four scattered families to a small little village. Napoleon had just this year regained control of the land from the Spaniards. Grace noticed the French flag had replaced the Spanish flag that had always been there her whole life. St. Charles was the westernmost semblance of civilization before entering the wilderness.

Agatha didn't look for her husband, Edmond. He was not there. He, Alexander and some others had been sent out yesterday morning early on a peace keeping mission with some of the Sioux south of St. Charles and would be gone several days. She did see one of the Indian scouts she was particularly fond of and waved. His name was Hawk Eye. Agatha thought it was a mighty fitting name for an excellent scout. She didn't know if she would have favored him so over the other scout if it hadn't been for what Edmond had told her about a mission they had been on a couple of years past.

Edmond had been among the soldiers on a hunt for some renegades that had killed a family of five, except for an only daughter who was fourteen years old. They had burned everything down to the ground, taken the girl and the horses, but not before slaughtering a cow and taking a small portion of the meat with them. A neighbor had seen the smoke and rode hard to get to the cabin. What he saw when he arrived made him sick. He headed for the Post to get help. He had ridden that afternoon and a portion of the night before reaching St. Charles. Edmond, Alex and Hawkeye were among the men sent out before daybreak to rescue the girl.

Edmond had said that when they were still a good distance from the cabin the stench of burned flesh had been nauseating. He had heard some of the men gagging. The first thing they had found was a hound lying in the trail with an arrow in him. It looked like he had been trying to get to the cabin, because he had managed to crawl quite a ways before collapsing. When they had followed a slight turn in the trail they had seen what they thought the hound had been trying to reach. A little boy had been lying on the ground who looked to be about five or six and close to him was a big bone. Most likely he had been hunting for the dog when the Indians attacked. The little boy had been clubbed in the head by a rider judging by the wound on his head and the horse tracks beside and near his body. Just outside what had once been the cabin was the body of a man and another older boy who had been shot and scalped. Both had been castrated. In the midst of the smoldering ashes was an iron bed frame with a woman's badly burned body whose legs had been spread open. They had been partially hanging over the end of the bed. Her head had been tilted toward the heavens and her arms stretched straight up from her shoulders toward the top of the bed. From the position of her body it was obvious she had been tied at the wrists and raped.

Edmond said they had left a detail with orders to bury the bodies and catch up with them afterwards. The rest of the soldiers headed out following Hawkeye. One of the soldiers who had stayed back on the burial detail had a particular fondness for dogs. He had buried the dog at the feet of the little boy. By the time the burial detail had caught up with the search party they had already covered a good bit of territory and had made camp for the night.

The next morning Edmond had been sitting on a log in front of the fire drinking his first cup of coffee. Most of them had been sleeping still or pretending to be. There had been no noise except what little the cook was making in preparation for breakfast. From behind him he had heard a sound of something heavy falling. When he jumped up and turned around he had not seen anything, but Hawkeye had called out as he had come through the trees toward the fire. Edmond had figured Hawkeye had shot them a buck. It had been a wild buck alright, but two legged. It was one of the killing party.

Hawkeye had told Edmond it had been bothering him about how careless the Indians had been about leaving a trail. He had known that was partly because they had not expected any soldiers to follow them so quickly and also because they had been traveling fast. He had left a couple of hours before daylight and with a full moon had discovered fresh horse tracks of a lone rider headed in the direction of the camp. He had found the rider's horse tethered to a tree close by.

Hawkeye had carefully worked his way back toward the camp. He had found the Indian with his bow in hand raising it to shoot Edmond in the back. Hawkeye's arrow had reached him before he could. He had been certain it was a scout the Renegades had sent back to see if they were being followed yet. A good scout would have done only that and reported back to the group, but this bunch was into killing for the enjoyment of it and Edmond was just too good a target to ignore. Their thirst for killing had made them reckless. The soldiers had caught up with them and rescued the girl.

Agatha was always glad to see Hawkeye, but when Edmond was on a mission she was happier when he was on it too. Both scouts, according to Edmond and Alex were extremely good but Hawkeye's skills went beyond that. They agreed that he had an extra sensing of things few men possessed.

CHAPTER 2

When Agatha reached home her father, Matthew was sitting on the porch in a rocker with his best friend sitting beside him. He loved that dog to silliness Agatha often told him. They were constant companions. When she brought the then puppy to her Pa it seemed to instantly put a little life back into him. Her mother had died eight years earlier and her father had gradually declined in health since her death. He was now at the point that he could do very little manual labor. He was still able to help with the milking and feeding of the cows and chickens which was a tremendous help to Agatha. She sold milk to the Canard Inn and two more families living in St. Charles. She also supplied them with fresh eggs.

Agatha had two older brothers she seldom saw. The older one had established a very successful fur trading business in St. Louis. The younger one had fallen in love with the wilderness to the west. He seldom came home. When he did it was to spend one night and then head on in to St. Louis to sell his furs.

"Hello Agatha. How was your visit with Grace? Hope you remembered to tell her to come and see me. Since you taught her your cooking secrets, we don't see her nearly as much. How is she doing anyway?"

Agatha did not like lying to her Pa, but in this case she knew she had to. "Oh Papa you know how Grace is when we get together. She nearly talked my head off. That is why I am late."

Agatha walked her horse to the stable, took off his saddle then she watered and fed him before joining her father on the porch.

"Papa, where's Frantz?" she asked.

"He told me he was carrying a load of hemp to the dock. Said he would be back by supper."

"Well, how about some of those pork chops tonight? I will make some red eye gravy and biscuits with some rice and greens." Agatha knew this was his favorite meal and was hoping it might inspire him to eat better. His appetite had been steadily decreasing and she was beginning to really worry. He looked at her and smiled.

"You don't want me to start drooling on myself now do you?"

Agatha was in the kitchen busily working on the supper meal. She had cooked for so long it was something she thought she could almost do with her eyes closed. Her mother, Anise had put Agatha to work in the kitchen at a very early age. Their time spent working together were some of Agatha's favorite memories of her mother. Sometimes while they worked Anise had told her stories about their coming to Missouri and things that had happened to them along the way. Even though it had been eight years since she passed, Agatha missed her terribly. Anise had patiently shown Agatha how to run the house. When she was old enough to manage by herself, Anise had worked along with her husband and two older brothers in the fields.

Unlike her brothers who took after her mother's side of the family and were big boned, tall and full bodied, Agatha was petite and pretty in her own right. She had black hair and dark brown eyes like her mother, but there the resemblance stopped. Matthew was a dark haired average sized man and stood just under six feet.

Anise had equaled him in height and had been described as beautiful by many.

She and Matthew had made their way to St. Louis down the Ohio and then to the Mississippi after leaving Virginia. After a short rest they had traveled further north and found this spot. They knew St. Louis was going to grow rapidly and wanted to be in an area with less people. They had found their land about twenty five miles from St. Louis and started clearing as soon as they had a basic log structure to protect them from the elements.

Matthew and Anise's first real friends had been a small group of Osage Indians. They had lived nearby for several years on the creek that bordered the western edge of their land. The Osage had long since moved further to the south in the Arkansas area and joined with a larger band of their people. Agatha was too young to remember them, but her older brothers remembered quite a bit about the Indians.

Her father and the dog came in from the porch.

"Got any of that coffee on the stove?"

Agatha was expecting this. She tried to make sure she always kept him a cup handy when he was in the house. She sat the cup in front of him at the table and went back to her cooking.

"Papa, tell me again about the time Mama first met the Indians." She thought it might help take her mind off of worrying about Grace. She never tired of hearing this story.

"Well, I had made a trip into St. Louis for supplies and was gone a couple of days. She had just told me our first child was coming and I really did not want to leave her, but she insisted that I go and get our supplies. She kept telling me she would be fine.

"The Post was making a supply run and she was afraid if I didn't go with them, she might run out of sugar before they made another trip. Her sweet tooth sure did act up when she was with child.

15

"Anyway, she loved the woods and would go and explore around the creek whenever she got a chance. I asked her to not do that while I was gone and stay close to the cabin."

Matthew took a sip of his coffee, scratched his head and kept going. "Anyway, I got back the next day in the late afternoon and put the horse and my mule in the lean to. When I opened the door to go in the cabin I almost had a heart attack. I was looking at one of the tallest Indians I had ever seen sitting at the table as pretty as you please. He had shaved all his hair off except for one spot that was long and hung down in the back. He also had a set of bear claws hanging around his neck. I tell you Agatha, you could have knocked me over with a feather.

"Your Ma looked at me smiling and said, 'Matthew, I would like for you to meet our new friend and neighbor. Have a seat while I fix us all some coffee. Matthew, please shut your mouth. It's hanging open so far, you might catch a fly.' I knew it was too, so I shut it and sat down."

"I had been wondering when I would see my first Osage Indian, but I sure wasn't expecting to see him sitting at our table. Well, Anise poured us all some coffee with lots of sugar and some cream. That Indian took one cautious sip, smacked and then guzzled the rest. He then stood up, said something we didn't understand and was out the door and gone before I hardly had time to blink.

"Before that Indian could get the door closed good, I lit into your Ma. Anise, I said, have you completely gone mad on me? How in the world could you let a wild Indian in this cabin? I kept thinking he could have kidnapped you, had his way with you or worse had his way with you and then scalped you. Haven't I told you at least a hundred times to not let any strangers in this house and most specially a wild Indian?

"She walked over and took my face in her hand gentle like and told me to hush before I worked myself up too much. She then went on to explain why he had been there. Your Ma had that look on her face that told me I better not be asking too many more questions, before she got to talk or I would sorely regret it.

"She then went on to tell me this story. She told me she had been exploring along the creek that early afternoon hunting for some greens to cook with supper. The creek seemed to be no more than twenty feet at its widest point and in spots was filled with some big flat rocks you could use to easily cross to the other side. Anise was always mesmerized by running streams. Cool clear ones were her favorite. She liked to go to the creek and quietly sit and watch the animals that came to drink. Anyway, she was walking along thinking about how there should be some good fishing in some of the dark pools she had passed earlier. You know your Mama. She loved fish caught from the creek.

"As she meandered along the creek bank she kept hearing a dog barking and thought how odd it was as we have no close neighbors. The barking dog was getting closer and seemed to be coming toward her. The barking was getting louder and louder. Anise became frightened and had found a tree she had hastily started climbing. She had just made it to a limb and perched right before the dog reached the tree.

"She said she sat there looking at that dog barking and carrying on and wondering what in the world she was going to do. She knew I would not be back until late afternoon. The dog finally stopped continually barking and changed to a few barks at a time. There they were the two of them. The dog sat staring up at her and her staring down at him wondering what in the world they were supposed to do next. Anise because she did not know about getting down and the dog because this was his first treed human. At this point of the story she would always laugh and say, 'That was the way the dog looked to be thinking to me anyway with that head cocked to the side and one ear sticking out.' Matthew laughed as he always did at this part of the story.

"She suddenly could hear wild thrashing through the bushes. Bursting through the undergrowth running was a young Indian girl who said something to the dog and it hushed any barking. She looked to be about eight years old. She walked over and stood by the dog. There they were. The child and dog staring up at Anise now in that tree and she was staring back down at them. She had not heard anyone else approaching, but an Indian man stepped into view. She felt certain he was an Osage Indian as he was very tall. He saw the situation and did not try to hide his laughter. Anise said she didn't see one danged thing that was funny about a frightened to death treed pregnant woman. Not at that time anyway."

Matthew yawned, took another swig of his coffee and continued.

"She said the Indian man made a motion for her to come down. Anise wasn't sure why, but she did not hesitate and climbed down to the ground. She had become quite a sight. She told me her bonnet was stuck over on one side of her head. Her hair that had been tied in a bun in back was half up and the rest scraggly and hanging down. Her dress and apron were all stained with tree sap where she had shinnied up that tree so fast. She stood there trying to tidy herself up a bit. As she was brushing the front of her dress she realized her hand was bleeding where she had gouged it. So she was then a real messy sight with her dirty, stained, blood smeared apron and dress, her hair every which way and her bonnet still cocked to one side. In addition to that her cheek had started stinging where she had a long bloody scratch. She said she thought she probably looked like she had been wrestling with the devil himself. I can sure see your Ma standing there in that condition and not thinking to be afraid just aggravated with her appearance and the Indian's laughter. You know she liked to be as neat and clean as possible always.

18

"The Indian came up to her and very slowly reached for her hand and turned it over. It wasn't a big gash, but seemed to be pretty deep as it kept bleeding. He spoke some words and pointed at her hand. Then he motioned for her to come with them and made some motions toward her hand. She somehow understood it was to treat it that he wanted her to go with them. She was a little uneasy, but was also very curious as to where they were going. Your Ma always said one of her greatest fears about living in the wild was being kidnapped by savages.

"She followed with the dog leading, the little girl behind the dog, she behind the little girl and the tall Indian was behind her. The four of them crossed the creek and walked away from it a little distance then turned away from the direction of the cabin following a path that ran perpendicular to the creek. After walking close to an hour they came to a clearing where the Osage village was.

"Anise told me she hadn't noticed while they were walking but they had come back closer to the creek. Near its bank stood cone shaped dwellings made of what looked like tree bark, mud and vines. She said she had counted nine of them. They were sitting in a circle. In the middle was a scaffolding over a fire pit with what appeared to be two deer hanging over the flame cooking. It smelled delicious she told me. There were men, women and children standing in the open area with curious eyes watching their every step.

"The women were dressed in skins that looked very soft, most decorated with colored beads. They all wore tunics, leggings and moccasins. Some of the women had their hair braided and others let it hang freely."

Matthew reached down and patted his friend on the head and then continued, "After they had passed two or three of the dwellings they stopped in front of one. He motioned for her to wait and he went inside. She could hear him and a woman talking, but of course did not know what they were saying.

"In just a moment he came back out followed by one of the most beautiful women Anise said she had ever seen. Her hair was raven black and so shiny. It hung straight down her back to her waist. Her eyes were an almond shaped deep brown that looked black. The face was highlighted by high cheek bones, a straight nose and thick lips which culminated in a slightly rounded chin. Anise could not help but stare. The woman motioned for her to go in the dwelling, then turned and entered.

"Anise followed her. Once inside she noticed how neat and tidy everything was. It appeared that everything had its own place. An assortment of clothing made from skins hung from the support poles of the lodge, along with hanging bows and arrows stored in an animal skin case with a strap long enough to go over the shoulder. There were several and all made from animal skins in different sizes.

"She also saw bunches of plants hanging upside down to dry. Some of which she thought she recognized. She could see large furry animal mats on the dirt floor in one area of the dwelling where it looked like a large family slept. There was a small fire in a hole in the ground in the center and smaller skins arranged around it. Directly over the fire the smoke wafted to the top and out of a hole.

"The woman put her hand on one of the skins near the fire and indicated she wanted Anise to sit there. She then went to what looked like a storage area of some kind. Anise felt the warmth of the fire and was relieved to be sitting near it. She told me she guessed the excitement and fear she had felt had drained her somewhat and she was chilled. The woman returned and cleaned Anise's wound, then put some salve on it and covered it with something that looked sort of like mud. She then tied a piece of soft leather firmly around her hand.

"She drank some liquid that was given to her. It had a slightly nutty taste, but was good. Anise had no idea what it was, but said it warmed her right up.

"After a little time had passed the tall Indian came in and motioned for her to come with him. She got up, turned and thanked the woman again and followed him out of the lodge. The man led her back down the path, across the creek and continued on towards the cabin.

"When they arrived he turned and headed back in the direction they had come. As she reached the door on impulse she turned and called to him with an invite for coffee making motions with her hands as if she were drinking something. He walked back to the cabin and went in."

Matthew paused for a minute and lit his pipe.

"Of course I had come in shortly after they did. The next morning the tall Indian with his beautiful wife and the little girl were at our door with a skin tied up which the woman handed to Anise. It was filled with black walnuts. Anise beckoned for them to come in. They did and she served them tea and some fresh bread she had just baked with some black berry jam."

Matthew could tell that something was really bothering his Agatha. He also knew that she had heard this story several times over the years from Anise and now from him. He understood that it helped her for him to tell them when she was missing her mother. It helped him in the telling. He knew there was something else going on that Agatha was keeping to herself. She would eventually talk to him about it when she could.

He said, "We all became mighty good friends. With time both families learned enough of the others language that we could communicate with a few words and hand and body motions."

Agatha asked him, "Pa did you ever think about just leaving here and going back to Virginia."

"Well the first couple of years were tough and the winters were down right hard on us. Our Osage neighbors arrived ever so often with a big chunk of fresh venison.

"The first winter I was out hunting. It was a cold winter day. It just seemed that the air was filled with moisture from the cold river water. Anise had been hunkered down in the cabin with our first born. The sky was gray and heavy looking. The temperature seemed to be dropping instead of warming up a good bit as it usually did on toward midday. I had been hunting all morning and had wound up in some woods I wasn't familiar with.

"I hadn't seen anything to draw a bead on and kept going. The animals were way smarter than me and were holed up. They knew what was coming. I didn't. It started snowing lightly, but it was sure some huge flakes falling. I didn't think too much about it and kept easing as quietly as I could through the woods in hopes of finding something. We were getting really low on our supply of dried meat. Anise and I both were wanting something fresh. The snow was falling a little thicker than when it first started.

"I had kept going deeper in those unfamiliar woods knowing that I wasn't but a couple hundred yards from the creek and could find my way back home by following it. I finally decided that I had better start walking toward the direction of the creek. I did. At least, I thought I did. It turned out that I had been so absorbed in listening and looking for game that I had not marked my location well and paid enough attention to which direction I was going. I was lost. I told myself not to panic, because I would just go back to where I started from and go in another direction until I found the creek or something I was familiar with.

"By this time the snow was really coming down. I now clearly understood then why there were no animals to be found. It was getting hard to see very far ahead of me. I had brought my little hatchet with me, as I always did when I hunted and was thinking I had better start making some kind of shelter before I couldn't see well enough to do that.

"I saw some movement not too far in front of me but the snow was so thick I could not tell what or who it was. In another second or two I could see it was an Indian and he was followed by two more. Luckily they were our neighbors and took me to their camp site.

"It snowed hard all the rest of that day and well into the night. I knew Anise would be terrible upset with worry, but all I could do was wait it out. Even the Osage would not go out in this weather and they were familiar with this land. The next morning it had stopped and I headed back to the cabin.

"I tell you, Agatha I knew as I sat by that fire with the snow steadily covering the land I would have frozen to death if those people had not found me and give me shelter. The storm had turned into a blizzard which was very rare for this part of the country. It was strange that our greatest fear of coming to this wild land was the Indians and now they had become our dearest friends. Not only that, but they had saved my life.

"They of course were used to the weather here and could tell when it was going to be bad. With time I learned to read the signs as well "

Agatha interrupted and asked as she was starting to put food on the table, "Pa, do you want some wild plum or grape jam with your biscuits?"

"No thanks, I am just going to do some serious gravy sopping with my biscuits tonight.

"You know your mother learned an awful lot from the Osage women. The first thing they taught her was how to fish the creek in winter with baskets. They showed her places to dig for roots and gather black walnuts and hickory nuts. With their help she soon knew where the wild plum trees were along with the blue berry bushes and fox grape vines. Afterwards, they taught her how to clean the small pelts and make them soft to use for you young'uns clothing during the cold winters. She learned how to make clothing for me and her using the animal skins that I killed.

"We often laughed and said it was a wonder we had not been mistook for Indians and shot. We would change into our regular clothes when we went into St. Charles. We found that the skins were mighty warm in winter and easy to work in. The truth of the matter was that most of the people that were not associated with the French or Spanish government who came through St. Charles at that time were fur trappers. Most all the men dressed pretty much the same way."

Agatha had put all the supper on the table. Frantz came in and sat down at the table.

"Oh my goodness Agatha, you have out done yourself tonight." He said.

Frantz had appeared at their door several years ago asking for work. He could not have chosen a better time as her brothers had taken off for an extended trapping trip. It had become hard on her folks to keep everything going on their own. Matthew had told him they could only offer him food and a place to sleep in the loft until the harvest was in. Frantz had eagerly agreed.

He turned out to be a mighty hard worker and the Stones were grateful for his help. He didn't talk about his past much except to say he was from New Orleans and his parents were dead. He was an only child. Only Agatha knew the truth.

After the hemp was harvested and sent to the dock and sold, Matthew paid Frantz. He asked him if he would like to stay on for a while. He could pay him a small salary he told Frantz. Frantz said he would stay.

They ate their supper pretty much in silence. The men were busy enjoying the food. Agatha was mostly shoving her food around on her plate. She did not feel like asking Frantz about the load of hemp which would lead to a conversation. She forced herself to eat, because she knew she would need it for the work ahead tomorrow. Unlike the men, there were no second helpings for her.

CHAPTER 3

After Agatha left Grace went back inside and sat the rest of that afternoon by the fire drinking tea, crying and trying to formulate her plan of escape. She could go to St. Louis and be welcomed by the Devereux family. Grace was born and grew up in their home. Her mother was governess to their children. She also knew that would be the very first place Alex would look. Besides it was too close to St. Charles. He would have no trouble leaving the Post and following her there.

"I have to get up and pack." Grace said out loud.

Yesterday had been a lost day. She had spent all of it in bed too bruised, sore and depressed to even try to get up and be productive.

Grace walked in the bedroom and got down on her knees and reached under the bed. She could not help groaning as she pulled two valises out and plopped them on the bed. It seemed that every bone in her body hurt. One valise was hers and the other Alex's. She planned to put as much as she could possibly stuff in each one. She remembered Alex telling her that if you rolled clothing you could get more in. She started rolling the pieces she had selected from the stack on the bed. Grace knew the two valises would hold enough clothing for almost a week. She also knew she could handle the weight even with them stuffed. They would be awkward, but she would manage.

Over and over she asked herself where she should go long enough for Alex to decide she had not gone to New Madrid to her parents. She did not pray in the sense that church people prayed. She talked to the Creator of All silently mostly, but sometimes out loud. She reasoned that if she was made in his image, she should talk to him like a person. Grace was not religious, but had a deep feeling for the spirit of goodness and a wariness of the spirit of evil. She did go to church, but found little comfort spiritually there. She did enjoy meeting her friends at church and usually attended each time there was a meeting. She read her Bible almost daily and had memorized some of her favorite verses.

This one came to her now and she quoted Isaiah 30:21 saying, "And thine ears shall hear a word behind thee saying, this is the way, walk ye in it. When ye turn to the right hand and when ye turn to the left."

Grace finally decided she would go to her gypsy friends in St. Louis. She remembered a story they had told about one of their group. It was about a man who had been wrongly accused of stealing from a merchant. The gypsies had kept him hidden a few days until they could make arrangements to get him safely on a boat headed for New Orleans.

Alex would not think of looking for her there right away if at all. Grace knew they would take care and hide her if it became necessary. She would talk with her friends about staying with them until Alex had had enough time to search St. Louis and rule out New Madrid.

He would look first at the Devereux family's home in St. Louis as soon as he had a chance to search for her. Grace was certain of it. She had decided to stop there before going to the gypsy's camp. Mr. Devereux held a sum of money in his bank that her parents had left for her. They had given it to him for Grace to have in case of an emergency. That emergency had come.

She did not want to involve the Devereuxs in an outright lie by asking them to say they had not seen her. She would tell Mr. Devereux this: She had decided that starting over would be too hard here or in New Madrid with her parents. She wanted to go back east where there would be nothing to remind her of him. Life would be easier there and she would stay with one of her cousins. She promised she would write once she was settled and felt Alex was not looking for her in St. Louis. She would say those words to Mr. Devereux and that way she would be the only one lying. Only she would know for certain that she was going straight to her parents as soon as possible.

Grace's ears did not hear a voice behind her telling her this was the way, but she did get an immense sense of knowing that it was the right plan to take. She would keep her mind focused on it. Trying to do so was a little harder than she thought.

She had finished all the packing she was going to do except for a little food she would prepare in the predawn hours and had gone back and sat down at the table. Try as she might she could not stop her mind wandering. She kept returning to the scene from night before last. Her mother had taught her that if something was bothering her to think about it. If there was nothing to do to change it then let go of it and not think about it again. Instead think about something that made her happy. Grace decided to go ahead and let her mind take her back to the night before last. She would relive it this one last time and then let go of it forever she hoped.

Grace remembered she was washing her dishes from supper. She had waited for Alex almost two hours and finally gave in from hunger and ate without him. She wondered if maybe he had been ordered out on a mission and didn't have time to come home and tell her. Usually if this happened someone would have come by before now to let her know.

She heard a horse neighing. It sounded like it came from the direction of their stable. She then heard footsteps on the back porch.

Alex opened the back door and called, "Grace".

Grace turned from her pan of dishes, grabbed a rag and was drying her hands. She knew immediately he was drunk. Try as she might she could not keep the look of disdain from her face nor the disgust from her voice.

"Alex," she said, "your supper is on the stove. I have already eaten. I am going to bed. Goodnight." She shook the towel out to dry and laid it across a drying rack Alex had built for her. She had only taken a few steps toward the bedroom door when he had grabbed her arm and was dragging her back to the table.

"Alex stop." she said.

He yanked a chair out and roughly forced her into it. In the scuffle she had hit her knee on the table leg. He was still holding her arm tightly.

Grace shouted, "Alex stop it! You are hurting me!"

"Hurting you no, I am not hurting you." he said, as he staggered to the other side of the table and sat down. "I am putting you at the table where any loving and dutiful wife would be happy to sit and talk with her husband while he eats. Now get up and serve me my food and then sit back down, Grace."

Grace knew by now it was best to not say anything more that might escalate this madness, but her knee and arm were throbbing and her Irish temper was boiling.

She did manage to only say in a very low tone, "Alex, you are drunk. I am going to bed." If Alex had been sober he would have realized how mad she was. He had only seen her this angry a few times. When Grace was terribly angry her voice became almost a whisper when she spoke.

She stood up and started for the bedroom again. Just as she was entering she heard the scrape and fall of his chair as he jumped up from the table.

"Oh no you are not, Grace." he shouted. "Not without me!"

This time he shoved her so hard from behind that her head snapped back. She landed half on and half off the side of the bed. He lunged and landed on top of her.

"You are mine and will obey me, Grace Monet. I am fixing to help you remember just what being a good wife is about."

His breath was so strong from soured whiskey that Grace was almost gagging. She was slapping his face and pulling his hair with her free hand. Alex slapped her across the face on one cheek and back handed her on the other. He grabbed her dress and chemise at the neckline and ripped them off to the waist in a couple of tugs. When her breasts were exposed he began to suckle them roughly and loudly just as a starving animal would do.

Just as quickly he stopped and jerked her all the way on the bed. He pinned her arm again over her head with one hand while he undid his pants. He reached down and pulled up her skirts. He pushed her legs apart with his and pinned them spread.

Grace's legs felt like they were going to break. He had put his legs on top of hers. He still held her down just below the chin. He took his arm that was holding her down and put it to the side of her head. He lifted his chest up a little to brace himself to penetrate her. In that moment Grace took the advantage and punched him in the nose. He growled and grabbed her around the throat strangling her.

"You will obey me, Grace Monet. I am your husband. This is my right."

Grace remembered in a flash her father telling her that if she was ever attacked and possibly could to poke the assailant in the eye with a finger. She knew she was going to pass out from lack of oxygen soon. She managed to get her fingers straightened and stiffened on her free hand. She aimed for his eye, struck and saw blackness.

When she came to the house was silent and he was gone. It was cold in the cabin. She crawled under the covers and drew up into a small thing lying on her side with her knees drawn up to her chest. She could not bring herself to get up. She hurt all over and the horror of what had happened was almost more than she could bear. She did not leave her bed all day except when absolutely necessary. No fire was made or lamp lit when the day ended and night came. Grace slept little through the night. When the birds started announcing a new morning, she got up.

She made a fire, heated some bath water and bathed. Her body was covered in bruises and ached all over. She made a little food for nourishment and ate. She was moving slowly, because it hurt to do so. She removed all the bedclothes, took them outside and put them in the wash pot. As she was removing the quilt she noticed a few drops of blood on it. She had not seen any blood on her while she was bathing, so it must be Alex's, she thought. She filled the wash pot with water from the porch well and got a fire going underneath. The water was hot before she realized she had not remembered to wash the blood stains out of the quilt in cold water.

With a deep sigh she said "No matter, I won't have to see it again."

Grace walked back in the house and started cleaning the kitchen while brewing some coffee. She told herself to keep moving no matter how much it hurt. She went outside and emptied the slop bucket in the hog trough. Next she caught a chicken, grabbed it around its head and spun it around a couple of times instantly breaking its neck. She threw it to the ground to keep from being scratched as it flopped around from muscle contractions. Grace waited until there was no movement then chopped its head off and hung it up while she got a fire going under the scalding pot.   A bucket of water from the well was enough. Once the water was hot, she unhooked the chicken and holding it by its feet she dunked it in hot water for about a half a minute and then started plucking the feathers. The stench made her slightly nauseous as it did each time she slaughtered a chicken. She knew it was necessary, but she hated the whole process.

As Grace worked through each chore she forced herself to concentrate on what she was doing. It kept her from thinking about what was breaking her heart. After she had gutted, cleaned and cut up the chicken, she decided to go ahead and bake a couple of loaves of bread, so there would be enough for her trip. While it was baking she would boil some eggs and fry the chicken. She knew she would eat very little between now and leaving in the morning.   After feeding the chickens and gathering their eggs she went to the wood pile. That's when Agatha had come to check on her and found her chopping wood.

After Agatha left her she had made it through the rest of the day by continuing to stay busy. Grace cleaned the windows and then made the bed. She took all of her remaining clothes, folded them neatly and placed them in her trunk. Grace wrote a note to Agatha telling her to take any and all the clothes she wanted. If there were any she did not want, she asked her to give them to Hannah. She folded it unsealed and placed it in the trunk. Next she wrote one to Alex.

> Alex,
> Please do not waste your energy and time trying to follow me. Even if you did, it would not matter. I will never live with you again. By the time you read this I will have made arrangements in St. Louis to start divorce proceedings and be well into my return journey back east. As you know I have some family there also. The farther away from you I am the better.

There is a note for Agatha in my trunk about the disposal of my clothing. I hope you will honor it. I will be getting rid of the clothing I am carrying with me as soon as possible. You see, Alex, I want nothing that can possibly remind me of you.
Grace

She folded the note, wrote his name across it and laid it on the table. She took off her wedding ring and placed it on top of the note.

Occasionally she could not help but stop to gaze at her face and neck as she passed by the mirror. The black eye was not too prevalent, but it was noticeable. She had a slight bruise on the other cheek. Her neck was really bruised. She would have to cover it with a scarf. Now she realized she would need to be at the dock before daylight, not just because of avoiding nosey people's questions about why she was leaving, but to conceal her face. She just could not bear the thought of people knowing the truth. It was hard enough that Agatha knew.

All of night before last started coming back to her as she waited for this night to end. She wanted the morning to come, so she could leave. She was now pacing back and forth in the kitchen vacillating between tears of hurt, anger and confusion.

"All right Grace," she said out loud, "enough of this. You did not come on this earth to spend it in tears. Crying buckets full won't help this. It's poison to you. Let go of it."

She sat back down and took a few deep breaths just as her mother had taught her to do when upset. She then closed her eyes and took a slow deep breath.

"From now on when my mind wanders to you, Alex Monet, it will dwell only with the good days and nights we had together. No longer will the evil that comes to me from your drunkenness be allowed." She then took another deep breath and said, "Leave my presence demon spirit and return no more."

Immediately a calmness and peace came over her. Grace was smart enough to know this would not keep the horrible memories from creeping back in, but she made a conscious decision that when one of them did, just as her mother had taught her, she would immediately replace it with a good memory of her life. It wasn't five minutes before the ugliness was trying to push its way back in to her thoughts. She had to stop pacing again which she knew was not helping, so she made herself stop and breathe deeply again. She knew she was not ready to think of Alex with anything but malice right now. But she also knew she had to be strong and was determined to do what she said. She decided to let her mind take her back to St. Louis. She was very happy there. She sat back down and drifted to St. Louis.....to her life there when she first met Alex.

It was in the summer of 1796. Grace had been sent to the market to do the daily shopping. She had finished her purchases as quickly as possible, so she would have some extra time to meander a bit.

Grace loved the noise of the people as they haggled with the vendors. She sensed an energy here that she did not feel in other public gatherings. She didn't know why, but she enjoyed it immensely and always tried to make extra time for her market trips. There was always someone interesting who would catch her eye. If she didn't see anyone new that interested her there was always the knife thrower she could watch.

Grace never failed to look for the Indian woman who made baskets from willows and grasses. She found her sitting on her fur mat. As always she was wearing her native dress. Grace loved to look at her bead work she had sewn on her clothing and her moccasins. It was the work of an artist. Today she was not weaving but painting one of her grass baskets. She and Grace had talked a little before and had become casually acquainted. She was married to a trapper and spoke English. They visited a few minutes while Grace admired her work.

She heard music and followed the sound. It was an elderly couple who were singing in their language of Romani. The man played a violin quite well. Grace knew this was a couple from the small band of Gitans as the French called them and gypsies by the Americans. They were camped on the edge of town.

They had placed a worn round basket on the ground in front of them. There was a small crowd gathered around. She wondered what their history was as they sang for the passersby. Maybe they were professional performers in their younger years for many of the Romani were. She could sense there was a deep love between the two.

As she stood there letting her imagination run away with her something caught her eye to the right. It was an orange being tossed toward the basket. Because the sides of the basket were low it simply landed in the basket, rolled around the side and back out again heading straight toward her. She bent over to pick it up.

At the same time another hand reached out and grasped for it. She looked up from under her bonnet and straight into the eyes of the most handsome man she had ever seen. His eyes were a soft brown and they were filled with tiny sparkles of light. It felt as though she was looking into a space she had been to before.

Grace could do nothing but stare. She could not look away. She could hear no noise of any kind. There was only these penetrating eyes. She knew she must have gasped for she did not remember taking a breath. He too seemed to be drawn into her gaze as they both slowly stood up. He was smiling and Grace knew her mouth was hanging open.

As she seemed to come back to her senses, she opened her hand holding the orange out and stammered, "Is this yours?"

"It was", he said. He took it and proceeded to walk over and place it in the basket along with another orange he took out of a coat pocket. "Now it is theirs, but I am glad it decided to take a detour before that happened otherwise I might never have met you. I am Lieutenant Alexander Monet", he said.

Grace extended her hand and said, "How do you do Lieutenant Monet. My name is Grace Wells."

Grace later learned that Alexander had joined with the United States Army ten years earlier when he was eighteen. The Army was fighting for control of the Northwest Territory against the Native Americans and the British. The Northwest Territory included the land from the Mississippi River east to Pennsylvania and from the Great Lakes in the north down to the Ohio River.

The territory had been ceded to the United States by the British in the 1783 Treaty of Paris that ended the American Revolution. However, in reality some of the British showed no desire to release this territory and consequently continued to maintain forts and keep policies which supported the Indians.

President George Washington wanted the hostilities between the Native Americans and the settlers to end therefore he directed the United States Army to strive for that goal along with attempting to enforce sovereignty over the territory.

In 1789 President Washington wrote to the governor of the territory, Arthur St. Clair. Washington asked Governor St. Clair to determine if the Indians living on the rivers of the Wabash and Illinois were "inclined for war or peace" with the United States. Governor St. Clair replied that they were inclined for war. In the five years previous the Shawnee and Miami Indians along the Ohio River in Kentucky had fought with the settlers encroaching on the land and approximately 1500 settlers had been killed.

Unfortunately the majority of soldiers and militiamen serving with the United States Army were untrained. As a consequence there were many battles fought over several years with heavy losses of soldiers and militiamen. In short the Indians were winning the war.

Alexander had lived through two of the most devastating battles fought with over 1,000 soldiers, militiamen and settlers including children that were killed. The last of these two battles became known as the St. Clair Defeat. Alexander never talked about the St. Clair battle and spoke little of the previous battle.

Shortly after the devastating defeat of the Army at St. Clair, President Washington called General "Mad" Wayne Anthony into service to form a group of highly trained and organized men known as the Legion of the United States. Alex was selected for this group and was given the rank of Lieutenant.

Four years later the Confederacy of American Native Indians were forced to cede extensive territory. This was done at the signing of the Treaty of Greenville in 1795 and thusly ending the Northwest Indian War.

After the war Alex decided he wanted to go further west. He and another soldier, Edmond Edwards who had fought with Alex, joined with some other soldiers who no longer wished to be a part of any military organization. They decided to head west. After a while of traveling through untamed wilderness they finally decided to follow the Ohio to the Mississippi River.

From there they were able to get a ride on a keel boat headed for St. Louis. Alex had met the governor in St. Louis a few days after they arrived. Blanchette was very impressed with Alex and Edmond's military history and offered them a position at the Post in St. Charles with a decent pay rate.

Truthfully, Alex did not talk about it, but he had missed the structured part of his military career and was tired of traveling. He was ready to put some roots down somewhere. He knew along with Blanchette that St. Louis was growing and opportunities would be limitless in the not too far distant future.

He agreed to join with Blanchette and so did his friend Edmond. He immediately proceeded to purchase the cabin for sale in the village and Edmond gave him a small sum each month to stay with him rather than at the post quarters.

Edmond had not decided if he would stay longer than the three years they had agreed to. However, it was not any time before he had met Agatha. He was in love with her and intended to marry her as soon as she would agree to it. He told all this to Alex at supper one evening only after meeting her that very morning at the trading post for the first time. Alex had told him to slow down and take a breath. He needed to spend some time with this girl and get to know her and her family.

Edmond just looked at him like he was crazy and said, "Alex, there are times in life when that is exactly what you should do. I mean slow down and look at things from all angles. My friend, this is not one of them. I am not taking a chance on losing this girl."

Alex, tried to talk to him further, but Edmond would not hear any of it. He laughed about it now, because that is exactly what happened to him and Grace. He knew the moment he looked into her eyes that there would never be another woman for him. He sometimes teased her and asked if she had put a gypsy spell on him. Grace would smile and always say, "Alex my love, life is a mystery and so is that." Then without fail if their location permitted, she would kiss him on the cheek and ever so softly blow in his ear.

Grace came out of her reverie and realized the fire was almost out again. She grabbed a shawl and threw it around her before going outside and collecting more wood. Once she warmed up a little it came to her that for the first time Alex had not chopped and gathered extra wood for her before he left on a mission.

Grace was glad he had not been around this morning either. The emotion of anger that had kept changing to degradation and back again to anger still held her strongly in its grip. She had not been sure what she might have said or done if he had been in her sight or reach.

She lit another lamp and force fed herself with a cold biscuit and a small bowl of deer stew. Grace looked at the clock and it was almost midnight. It would be daylight in about five hours. She knew she should rest a little, but just could not face the thought of lying down with her mind in a constant whirl.

She made the decision that she would definitely leave for the dock before daylight in the morning. She knew if she waited any later everyone would be busy about starting their day. Nearly always there would be at least one flat bottom or keel boat headed for St. Louis at daybreak. She would go to the dock packed and ready to go.

There would be no way of making it through the village after sunrise without encounters followed by questions about her journey. She had to leave real early. She also did not want anyone she knew asking her what happened to her face. It would be obvious she was going somewhere as she would be lugging two valises. Grace did not want to have to deal with it if possible. If she did by chance see anyone that questioned her she would simply tell them she was going to visit friends in St. Louis to do some shopping. It would be dark and they would not see her face clearly. That should appease any nosey neighbor mulling about at that time of the morning.

The clock chimed once for eleven thirty. It had been a wedding present from the Devereuxs. She thought about her parents and how they had not even considered the idea of matrimony for her. At least not before she was to leave St. Louis and join them in New Madrid. There had been plenty of want to be beaus around before she met Alex, but she had not had the least bit of interest in any of them. She had found most very boring and the rest too focused on themselves to even consider getting to know her.

She was glad her parents had the foresight to leave her with some money in the bank. Alex knew she had it but did not know the amount. He might possibly believe her lie to Mr. Devereux that she did go back east.

Since Grace could remember, all she really ever wanted out of life was to fall in love and be a good wife and mother. She always thought that her marriage would be as strong and loving as her parents. Not once had she thought it could be anything like this nightmare it had become. Now she would be facing her parents and telling them she was going to divorce Alex. Mr. Deveruex had the necessary business associates to help expedite this process. She felt the weight of it all starting to smother her.

Grace laid her head down across her folded arms on the table and closed her eyes. Almost immediately she was back in the nightmare. She sat back up.

She was going to concentrate on her parents and her childhood. She could hear her mother's voice again telling her about how they had met and their life in St. Louis. Grace closed her eyes and let her mind take her back to one of those rainy cold St. Louis days when she had talked her mother into telling her again about meeting her father, Charles Wells.

CHAPTER 4

Grace heard Catherine saying, "It was 1786 and the ship had left Dublin over two weeks ago. It was well out in the Atlantic Ocean. If all went well, we had been told we should be reaching Virginia in about five more weeks. Your father was working as a deck hand on board the ship. I was traveling with my parents who were migrating to the states to get away from the turmoil in Ireland. People were starving to death. There was rioting, pillaging, fires and death in the streets of the cities. Even though we were in the country and away from the cities he feared the violence would reach us.

"It was fate that your Papa and I met. The larger ship my father had originally booked for us had much better accommodations. However, it had suffered damage on its last voyage and was being repaired. Only with some connections of Papas were we able to get this passage. If we had not taken it the trip would have been delayed several months. The few poor and mostly middle class people who could were all struggling to get out of Ireland. The rich had no need to leave. They were simply buying up the land as fast as it became available at a price that would never have been acceptable in better times.

People were desperate and literally starving to death. We were some of the very lucky ones and knew it.

"Unfortunately, the seas had been rough at the beginning of the trip and I had not fared well as a sea traveler. I had already spent several days at the ship's railing emptying my stomach. The ship was tilting from one side to the other. The bow was hitting the water so hard after being lifted by a high wave and falling in the empty space under it to the trough below, that each time it hit I was afraid the ship would break. I knew it was dangerous to be on deck, but I had to get outside and breathe some fresh air. The hatch which was usually kept closed during rough seas had been left open. I did not know, but suspected the crewman who had brought our food had simply forgot to close it.

"I was not the only one that was sick and unfortunately the ones who had been using buckets beside their berths weren't always able to hit them fully every time. In addition the chamber pots from last night had not been emptied. It was too rough for any of us to locate the crew and get something to clean the floors with or get fresh water to clean ourselves for that matter. This was the third or fourth day of the really rough seas but this day was the worst of them all.

"As I fought my way to the ladder I was being knocked from one side of the ship to the other and slamming into buckets and berths. I made it to the ladder and started to climb up and out to fresh air. This time while climbing the ladder I lost my grip with my left hand. In a rapid motion I was turned around and no longer facing the ladder but hanging in the air looking back at the people in their berths and the buckets and pots sliding across the floor. This time a few of the trunks people had been using to eat on and write letters were also sliding. Everything and everyone was tilted and I wondered how they were managing to stay in their berths. I was holding on with one arm and reaching back for the ladder with my feet. The ladder was no longer behind me. Because of the ship leaning so far the ladder also was at an angle and I simply could not get my feet anchored. I could not reach it. Just as I was really starting to panic and afraid I might lose my grip the boat started to right itself again and I was able to get my footing and turn around on the ladder and grab it with my left hand.

"I knew it was insane to go on deck now, but I felt I might go mad if I did not get out of that putrid, foul smelling area to the fresh air. I was being driven and could not turn back if I had wanted to. I had no clue that my destiny was being put into place.

"I made it to the railing looking like a drowned ragamuffin, reeling like a drunk, my face the color of split pea soup with spittle running down my chin while I hung on and heaved. The ship was rolling so, I could not let go of the rail to clean or even wipe my face for fear of falling over or under the railing and into the sea. I had one arm wrapped under the railing and the other over. The sea seemed to be getting mighty close to my face when the ship rolled to the side I was on. Then before I knew it I would be holding on for dear life when it rolled to the other side. I would lose my footing sometimes when the bow raised in the climb of another huge wave. I realized that I should have listened to the words of the captain. Safety was below deck. I was afraid I might not make it back to the hatch and my berth below. The thought of being washed or slung into the dark sea terrified me so and I began to scream.

"Suddenly I felt someone come up from behind me. They grabbed the rails on each side of me. I could tell it was a man who had a hold of me.

"I heard him shout to grab his right arm with both hands and hold tight. Then he told me when the boat starts to right itself I was to let go of the rail. Don't be afraid I have got you. When I tell you now, you turn to the left with me. We will head for the galley hatch very quickly. He made sure I understood and told me to get ready?

"Yes, yes." I shouted. I grabbed his right arm with both hands as he told me to. I did not know who had me and did not care. For the first time since I knew how much danger I was in I felt safe. The boat had dipped perilously close to the water again.

Just as it had almost leveled itself and was starting a slow rise in the bow, the man shouted, "Now." We ran for the galley hatch. My feet were slipping and sliding on the wet deck, but we made it to the hatch. I noticed the man had no shoes on and I wished I did not either. He grabbed a hand rail beside the hatch just as the boat started its downward drop for the trough. I let go of him and grabbed it too with both hands. He took his free hand and encircled me again just as he had at the rail. He put his left foot down a couple of steps in the galley and braced them in the opening for the jolt that was coming when the bow hit the trough.

"Before I realized what was happening he dragged me through the hatch and down the ladder into the galley. He seated me at a big table. I was certain this is where the crew ate. In spite of everything I could not help but think of how much I missed sitting down at a table for a normal family meal. The passengers were forced to eat wherever we could find a spot in our living and sleeping area. It consisted of berths on each wall of the ship and our so called living area was the space between the berths.

"He told me he hoped I didn't mind. He had asked the cook to prepare some ginger tea. He said it would help with the sea sickness. He sat a mug in front of me and placed my hand around the handle to keep it from sliding off the table. The man took a seat across from me. It was the first time I had taken a good look at my rescuer. Even in my weakened and sickly condition it was impossible not to see how handsome he was. I knew how I must have looked and wished it had been differently.

"He sat with me until I managed to get a few sips of the tea down then aided me in returning to my berth. When he went up the ladder and out, he closed the hatch. It wasn't but a few days later and with the help of ginger tea and time I had managed to get some sea legs.

"The rest of the voyage we spent together on deck when he had some free time. There was nowhere to go and nothing to do but talk. We had become well acquainted by the time we were approaching Virginia's coast line. He told me that he had inherited a small farm in Ireland and had been lucky enough to sell it to a land grabber. He did not get what it was worth, but with the state of things he knew it was his only chance to get to the New World and make a fresh start.

At this point Catherine would laugh and say, "Charles told me he had not planned to take a wife so soon, but he said when he saw me trying so hard to stand on deck that day and not be thrown overboard, he knew I would become his wife. We were married a few weeks after landing in Virginia and immediately made arrangements to go west to St. Louis."

When Charles and Catherine arrived in St. Louis he had managed to get work at a saw mill and Catherine was hired by the Devereuxs, a wealthy French Canadian family. Her duties were to assist with the family's children in the learning of the English language and European history. She was fortunate enough to come from a family that was able to see that she received a good education.

Since Catherine was married, she had managed to negotiate a salary that included room and board for herself and Charles. The salary was low they thought, but once they calculated living expenses for food and quarters in the least expensive area of town, not to mention the undesirable conditions existing there, the salary did not seem so low. It was actually quite generous.

Both felt they would be able to save most all of their income. With what they had in Charles' land sale and Catherine's dowry within a few years they would be able to purchase some land somewhere and start their own business. They had spent hours talking about it and both knew they did not want to buy land to farm. They wanted to find a place somewhere that was just starting to grow, establish their business and grow with it. Neither of them knew where that was going to be just yet, but they kept their ears open for information.

Catherine was quite learned in other subjects and extremely well read. Once the Devereux's realized this her teaching duties were expanded. She was given an increase in salary.

Only a few months after she was hired Catherine discovered she was pregnant with Grace. She and Charles were overjoyed, but Catherine was worried about not being able to find work. How would they live and save money too if only he was working. Charles had assured her that they would realize their dream, he just wasn't sure how right then.

Once she was absolutely certain and knew she would be starting to show any day, she went to Mrs. Devereux and told her of her condition and gave notice. She told her that she would start looking for other quarters immediately.

Elise Devereux had said in her heavy French Canadian accent, "'My dear Catherine, please. This is not news to me. I have been seeing it in the changes in your face and your body. You can't possibly expect to leave me now that I have finally found you. My children adore you and in this short time you and Charles have been here, I have become quite fond of you both myself. Don't worry about where we will put the baby. We will figure something out that will work for you three."

Catherine's eyes had watered as she replied, "Your generosity and kindness is appreciated far more than you can ever know, Mrs. Devereux."

"There, there Catherine. Dry those eyes and let's have some tea and cake to celebrate this good news. I love babies and will be anxiously awaiting the arrival with you. While you are at it, please call me Elise. I feel that we are family and we need to start making plans to add a small addition to the house because I think we might be having another baby arriving ourselves," she beamed.

Grace had been born shortly after an addition had been added to the two story house. There were three additional bedrooms and another quite roomy sitting room with a small library that connected to her parent's bedroom. This was given to Catherine and Charles strictly for their use.

Catherine had talked to Elise and asked her if she could take a small space of the sitting room and use it as a family dining area for their evening meals at times. She explained while they thoroughly enjoyed being with the staff at meal times and the occasional dinners with the Devereuxs, they needed more family time and having it over an evening meal was very conducive to everyone's schedule. Elise had immediately agreed and said she wished she had thought of it sooner. She took Catherine shopping the very next day for a suitable table and chairs to put in there.

Grace remembered sitting at that table with her parents while they were making plans for their future. They would exchange any new information they had learned about what was happening on the Mississippi and Missouri Rivers. She remembered the first time they talked about building a boarding house. She could still see their animated faces filled with anticipation of their future venture.

Growing up Grace had very few chores to do as there were servants to take care of their daily needs. Her days were spent pretty much as the Devereux children spent theirs. The older children were in class with her Mother a big portion of the day. Grace along with the younger Devereux children was supervised by a new live in governess when Catherine was in class or preparing for the next day's lessons.

There were quite a few times in those days when Catherine had extra time on her hands. Grace would want to play with the other children. The governess always encouraged Catherine to let Grace continue playing with them. She spoke often about how well behaved Grace was and how she liked having her in their company. On those days Catherine would go in the kitchen and beg the cook to let her help. That was the only part of being a wife she missed in her life. She had learned to cook from her Mother at an early age and thoroughly enjoyed it.

The cook would give her some carrots to scrape and some potatoes to peel. When she realized Catherine was going to be an asset and not an unwanted underfoot pest in her kitchen, she began to teach Catherine some of her recipes and tricks she had learned from years of experience. As a result Catherine took the basics she had learned from her Mother and expanded her cooking skills greatly with the things she learned in the Deveruex kitchen. Catherine dreamed of the day when she and Charles would establish their own business and she would be able to work and prepare in her own kitchen.

Grace was glad they had their boarding house built and open for business. She hoped their life in New Madrid was all they had dreamed it would be. It sounded like it was from her mother's letters. In the last one she had received from Catherine they had enough boarders that it became necessary to hire some help with the cleaning and laundry. Catherine had written that she was not letting anybody else in the kitchen just yet. It had taken too long for her to finally have her own.

Grace still sitting in her kitchen felt a heaviness settle on her as she thought about leaving her home. She had put so much into it. In all fairness so had Alex. She got up from the table, picked up a lamp and began to stroll from the kitchen to the other side of the big room. She set the lamp on a table and sat in her favorite chair and drifted back to the first time she saw it.

Alex and Grace had arrived in St. Charles late afternoon. When they stopped in front of Alex's log house with its big front porch all the way across, she thought how unloved and barren it looked with the bare windows, weedy unkempt yard and much needed fence repairs. Nonetheless, she also saw the potential and could not wait to get started.

She immediately went to work cleaning the yard. She planted some periwinkles in bunches along the edge of the front porch from seeds a neighbor had given them as part of their wedding gift. Next she and Alex had collected some rocks from the creek bed and bordered a walkway from the porch steps to the front gate. She planted more seeds along each side. While Grace was busy preparing for a yard filled with color, Alex was busy repairing the fence and gate.

The previous owners had planted some running roses along the fence line. She pruned and fed those. Some of the clippings she transplanted to other spots along the fence for they were easy to root. It wasn't long before there was color everywhere when you approached the house.

Grace then talked Alex into adding two more windows on the front of the house and one on each side. Mr. and Mrs. Devereux had given them a tidy sum for their wedding gift. They decided to use some of it to purchase the glass. She knew he had spent all he had to get the place. Grace hated to feel closed in and loved the additional light that streamed in through the four new windows.

When Alex had made the purchase with the previous owners he had talked them into leaving most of the furniture. Namely the kitchen table and four chairs, a bed that could sleep two people in one of the bedrooms, a rocking chair, a couple of lamps, some cooking utensils and enough mismatched dishes for at least two meals.

Grace had kept a diligent watch for any new arrivals of household goods at the mercantile store. She had managed to get the rest of the things they needed when a bit of merchandise not spoken for trickled into St. Charles. The other pieces of furniture they wanted were made by a wood craftsman who lived nearby. These pieces included her writing desk and chair that she cherished.

Grace looked at the window coverings she had taken so much pride in making. They had also received enough cloth at the wedding welcoming party that she was able to make them for the parlor and the kitchen. The parlor and kitchen extended the width of the house as one big room. The parlor being on the left when you were looking at the front of the house and the kitchen on the right. There had not been enough cloth to make six window coverings in the same material, but the colors of the two combined pieces of fabric complimented each other. She covered the four front windows in one color and the remaining three windows in the other. Once she had made some rag rugs from scraps and placed them around a coziness just seemed to seep into the house. Alex loved what she had done and did not hesitate to let her know.

They had both worked in the back yard. It was an even larger mess than the front. Grace cleaned and planted the vegetable garden. Alex repaired the chicken coop, hog pen and smoke house. He also had removed some of the boards from the back porch. He then dug a well and built a square enclosure for it that went from the floor up to about waist high on her. Grace could only remember seeing one well like this before. He said that way Grace would not have to tote water from the spring anymore. It was wonderful to be able to step out her back door on to the porch and draw water there. Especially when it was raining or cold. She had loved him even more for her well.

Grace did not know much about cooking, but that was not keeping her from trying. Alex never complained about anything she cooked. But there were many days she longed for some of the food from the Devereux house. Once the house was in order she started spending a lot of time with Agatha who was an excellent cook.

She had brought some writing books with her from St. Louis and used one of them to make notes on cooking and recipes Agatha gave her. She also included in this one the many other things she wanted to learn, such as canning, medicinal poultices and teas just like her mother had done. It even contained recipes for what to use on cuts and burns.

She really utilized her time when Alex was away and spent all she could with Agatha learning all there was to know about taking care of her home and husband. There was no market here to speak of yet. You could go down to the dock and occasionally get some fresh catfish or bream, some sugar cane, molasses and maybe some fresh corn. Nothing was for certain to be there, but she liked to go anyway. It wasn't the market in St. Louis, but there was activity on the river since the Northwest Indian War was over and more settlers were coming through St. Charles on their way further west. Some of them were stopping to stay and settle in or around the area.

Now Grace thought, I won't see St. Charles continue to grow. I will be gone. I don't know who will live in my home next if Alex sells it or remarries. I just hope they will love it as I have. There was love in this house for a little while, she thought and a lot of it, but something happened to Alex and he had begun to drink more and more. Grace tried hard to get him to talk to her but he would not. At first he only abused her verbally, but soon it became physical and then violent. She could not help it as tears slowly began to run down her cheeks. So much more living and loving we could have done together, but now it's over. She did not try to stop crying this time, but sobbed uncontrollably until there was nothing left in her to cry out.

CHAPTER 5

It had become quite late and Grace had finally moved from her favorite chair and was standing in front of the fireplace looking at the flames leaping about when someone knocked very softly on the door. She could not imagine who it could be at this time of the night that would be so timid with their knock.

She immediately reached behind the heavy mirror that sat on the mantle and brought out a pistol. The mirror had been secured at the bottom to lean back against the stones and made a great and inconspicuous spot to hide it for quick access.

She made no noise and stood tense and alert to see if she could hear any movement outside. The pistol was loaded. Alex had insisted that she keep it there because so many nights he had to stay at the post or was away under orders. He taught her how to load it, shoot it and take care of it.

Grace made not a sound as she listened as hard as she could to see if there was any movement outside. She silently thanked herself for remembering to close the curtains. At least whoever it was might not know she was alone. She heard the soft knock again. Grace moved close to the door.

"Who is it?" She said in as brusque a voice as she could manage.

"Grace, it's me, Alex."

"Go away, Alex. You know I have the pistol and it is loaded."

"Please, Grace let me in. I am not drinking and I need to talk to you. Afterwards, I will go back to the post. I give you my word that I have not had a drop of liquor. Please, Grace just for a few minutes and then I will go away."

As she stood there in confusion because she knew they had only been gone for two days, the knock came again just as softly.

"Grace, I truly will leave and go back to the post, I just need a few minutes to speak with you."

Grace could tell that he had not been drinking solely by the sound of his voice. She hesitated a few seconds and then slowly slid the top board and then the bottom board back that secured the door and opened it. As she stepped aside to let him in she could not keep her heart from doing a little skip as it always had with Alex when she first saw him after being parted for a while. Maybe this time it was because she had thought she would never see him again.

He reached down and took the pistol from her hand then put it back in its place behind the mirror. He walked over to the table and stood behind one of the chairs.

"May I sit down?"

It all seemed so strange to her. Here her husband stood acting as though he were an invited guest. Just hours ago she was telling Agatha she felt like she could have shot him. This was insane and the lingering anger was starting to surface. It was almost all she could do to keep from screaming at him to get out. She motioned for him to sit down for she could not speak.

Grace then busied herself preparing some coffee. She needed something to do to gather her emotions and obtain a place of calmness. She knew if she didn't she would never be able to sit and control the anger already starting to boil inside her. Even now she wanted to lash out at him and throw things.

Grace knew he was not going to hurt her, because he was not drinking. She knew that this was going to take more than a few minutes whatever happened. After arranging the cups, pouring cream and adding the sugar the way Alex liked it, she then sat down and waited for the coffee to boil.

Alex was sitting with the note from Grace in one hand and her wedding ring in the other. He had picked it up and read it while she was making coffee. His face was crestfallen but he said nothing.

Grace put her hands on the table, joined them and took a deep breath. She looked at Alex straight in the eyes and just stared. She was determined she would say nothing in anger. If she could not manage that, she would say nothing. After another deep breath she was ready.

"Alex I am going to leave you no matter what you have to say. The only way you got in here tonight is because I know you have not been drinking. For if you had been I might have shot you. Do you know that you raped me? These marks on my neck are from your fingers that almost squeezed the very life out of me. Do you have any idea what it feels like to have someone on top of you pinning your arms down with their knees and striking you across the face? Well, I do and I made a decision that I would kill you before that happened again or die trying.

She got up from the table to pour the coffee.

"I am glad you have come back before I leave in the morning, so that I can make sure you understand why I am leaving and so you won't follow me.

"You have often said the next morning after you have hurt me, that you did not remember it. I know you were telling me the truth by the look of surprise on your

54

face when you would see the marks you had made on my body.

"However, we never talked about it and what had really happened. We would not talk about anything for a few days. As time would pass we would get through the daily motions of living while speaking, but not really talking. You would not drink. The day would come when we could not stand being separated for another minute. We would make love and your tenderness shown would stay with me until the next time you drank too much.

"I am not sure exactly when the first time you hit me was. All I know is that you had just returned from an assignment. The violence since then has escalated and become more frequent right along with your increased drinking."

As Grace had talked Alex's head had dropped more and more until he had placed his arms on the table for support with his hands clasped together as if he was going to start praying. He raised his head where he could look her in the eyes while he spoke.

"Grace", he began "I do not blame you if you leave me. If you do I will not follow you. When I found myself in the stable where I had passed out as you said, I did not remember what had happened, only a sense that it was very bad. When I eased in the bedroom to get a clean uniform I walked over to the bed and looked at you sleeping.

"When I saw the marks on your neck my heart felt like it had fallen to my feet and my stomach rolled. It was as though I was eight years old again and was looking at my mother lying in bed after my Dad had beaten her the night before. Grace could not help it. Her eyes grew big and her mouth opened to speak.

Alex held up his hand, "Wait Grace, before you say anything. Just let me get these things said, please. If not right now there may not be enough courage in me to speak of them ever again. I had told myself over and over as a child it was all a bad dream. I did not have to talk about it and would not do so even when the nuns would try to get me to after I woke up screaming night after night.

"Eventually the nightmares stopped and I didn't think about it anymore. I know you have often wondered why I would not talk about my childhood more. I lied to you. Not about being from an orphanage, just about arriving there as a baby.

"I was eleven years old when my mother died. The doctors said it was from pneumonia, but I knew it was brought on by her unhappiness and abuse from my drunken father. It was not even a month later that he hanged himself in the study. I did not find him a servant did, but I saw him before they got him down.

"It turns out that it appeared not to be from his grief over the loss of my mother, but he had finally managed to gamble away all of the family holdings which went back several generations. When the magistrates were done and all the property was liquidated there was nothing left. There was no family in Canada and no money to send me back to France. Letters were written to try and locate family in France, but nothing was ever heard from anyone. "In the meantime I was placed in an orphanage and there I stayed until I ran away when I was fifteen. I worked my way south and wound up joining the Army.

"After seeing you lying in our bed and knowing what I had done or almost done it literally made me sick. I realized at that moment that I could have killed you in the night, found you dead yesterday morning and would not have remembered what happened. Living would not be possible for me if that had happened. I made a decision that I had to understand what it was that was driving me to this horrible and insane behavior.

"You know that I don't take to religion, but all the way to the Post I prayed that if there was a God or a Being that could help me understand to please do so. Really, I had no clue as to what it might be, because honestly I could not bear to think about hurting you and tried to bury it each time it happened just as I had my childhood.

"As we rode out from the Post my mind began to remember things shared by the other soldiers. The memories were coming in bits and pieces as the alcohol had not left my system yet and my mind was not clear. It is often said by some of the other soldiers that you have to keep the ugliness you see, the physical and mental pain you feel and the confusion that comes when asking why completely to yourself or you will go mad.

"Well that is what I have always done with my nightmarish childhood. I quit asking why when I was young and just kept it all to myself. You are the first person I have ever told this much about it. Always when it comes up, I just simply say I was raised in an orphanage. I have no family. That will instantly stop anymore conversation about my youth.

"Then there are others that say if you don't talk about all the horrors that come your way, especially the killing of your fellow man you will surely go insane. As we rode along hour after hour and only stopping for food and to rest and water the horses, I began to feel as though I was on the edge of getting an answer.

"We made camp yesterday late afternoon. I ate and went to sleep immediately. I awoke before anyone, except for the sentries and made some coffee. My head had cleared a lot from the booze and felt pretty near normal again. I know this sounds crazy, Grace, but it was almost like my mind was not being controlled by me. It was as though I had been placed in this state of complete mental relaxation and could only see or think what was being directed or given to me. From where it was coming I know not. I felt as though I was a part of everything, but at the same time alone. I knew something was reacting to my pleas for help and was intervening somehow through my mind. I have never felt that way before.

"As we sat there by the creek eating breakfast and by habit not talking loudly when out in the wilderness, I began to look at each man in the group. There were twenty of us. As I looked at the first one I thought, he talks about it. The second man I looked at I thought, he does not talk about it. As you know Grace, most of these men I have been with for several years and know them as well as you can ever know somebody you ride with. We all have been scheduled together for watch duty many times. It is something about being awake when it seems that the rest of the world is sleeping that can encourage a man to talk about things he would never dream of mentioning in the day light. When one of them shared a story of the personal horrors they had seen it might take a little time, but it always got around to everybody. Most times it would be the one that had seen something horrid and then told it again to someone else. Before long it reached us all.

"I know from firsthand experience it is not an easy pack to carry around that is filled with so much horror caused by the actions of human beings on one another. It can be very difficult and sometimes impossible for a man to empty this pack. If they are able to do so, even though new images of horror will be stuffed in it, they are the ones that seem to find the goodness and joy that comes with living life each day. Every man has to figure out how and when he empties his own pack. Grace, I never opened mine up, except to stuff more in and tie it back up again. It just gets so heavy sometimes and without even realizing it I turn to the whiskey to numb the feelings and forget the memories. It appears that it will work on some occasions, but the next time might be the time I have drank way too much and the craziness stored up in me comes out in a cruel and evil way. I hurt the one thing I truly love in this world, you. I can't explain why that happens, but I know this. Too much of the whiskey opens the doors to the gates of hell for some. I don't even remember what I have said or done.

"Anyway, by the time we had finished eating I had looked at each one of those soldiers and determined if they kept things to themselves or if they were talkers. We left that camp site and reached the river in the late morning. We set up camp and most of the men were working on cutting and trimming some trees to make rafts for the crossing. The cook had made us a bite to eat. As the rafts were being built, a horse approached camp. It was one of our scouts. He said we had orders to return immediately. It had been reported that there was a renegade war party spotted a couple of days west of St. Charles and we were ordered to ride with only one brief stop to rest the horses and eat a bite.

"As we rode back toward the post my head had cleared and I thought about the men who talked. They never discussed it when they were drinking with the exception of one who was a loud mouth drunk and liked to fight. Another thing I noticed is that it was a rare thing for any of these men to drink into oblivion. Oh, they drank and had a good time, but there always seemed to be a point where they would quit before becoming out of control. If they did drink too much they would usually just pass out, but I did not remember a one of them becoming ugly in any way except for the loud mouthed one. Maybe his pack was filled with horrors none of us had ever experienced or maybe he was just plain mean. He had no close friends that any of us knew about and his family was not with him.

"I then thought about the ones that did not talk about it. They were the ones who seemed to drink the most. In this group which was less than ten there were three men who did not drink at all. When asked why they would just say something like life seems to go better that way.

"So that left four more and me. Of those four I knew that one of them had a family but it was rumored that his wife had obtained a divorce. He never talked about it. There was another one that had a reputation of getting in fights when he drank, so it was common knowledge to keep the liquor away from him after a certain point.

"The third one had made the statement several times that the way to keep a woman in line was to give her a smack from time to time. We always thought he was kidding, but after I thought about it I vaguely remembered hearing about his wife talking to another soldier's wife who then told her husband about him hitting her. It was never mentioned again, so I had forgotten about it.

"The fourth man it was rumored had been accused of rape before joining the Army but was not charged. Grace, it was the fifth man that scared me to my senses. He had been on a hunting trip and came back to find his wife had been raped and murdered. No evidence was found of Indians. Nothing was stolen. She had been choked and beaten to death. It was talked around that his wife had been seen more than once with a black eye or bruises on her face and neck. It was also rumored that he had done it and then hightailed into the woods. Nothing was ever pursued past the initial round up and search in the near area for some tracks leading away from the cabin. None were found but his so it was told. I think I might know what happened."

Grace just sat across from Alex listening and saying nothing. She had not even taken a sip of her coffee. She sat not moving and listened to every word he spoke.

Alex continued, "As we rode into the night my mind took me through my military time and my drinking. When I first joined the Army I did not drink much except on social occasions. Then I remembered my first battle. I wanted to drink after that and did the first chance I got. Every time I would remember seeing my best friend dead without his scalp I wanted to drink. I didn't drink a lot then, but I did drink to ease the mind.

"As time went on I saw some really horrible things happening. However, I still maintained control of the alcohol. As I went through each battle in my mind and all the unspeakable things that I had seen happening to men, women and children on both sides, I finally came to the thing that I realized had turned me from a social drinker to an outright dangerous drunk. It was the thing that sort of culminated with all the rest and there was no more room to shove it back.

"We had gone to a very small post a three day ride from here. There were reports of restlessness among the Indians and a dispatch of thirty of us had been sent to check it out. It was a small village there with about eight cabins and a few families scattered nearby that had all gathered at the Post when we arrived. The outlying families had brought and placed their wagons in a semi-circle in front of the Post. Some of the women were preparing food on open camp fires for their supper. Others were making beds for their children to sleep inside the Post on the floor. The men were busy cleaning their weapons and getting ammunition ready for what might come.

"There was a deep feeling of camaraderie amongst everyone even though all were aware we were in a very dangerous situation if the Indians decided to attack. Everything seemed to be quiet and we all bedded down for the night.

"The next morning was a blue sky day, very much unlike the night before which was cloudy and a bit chilly. All the soldiers were awakened before dawn and had eaten breakfast, but the settlers were just getting their breakfasts when the hellish yelling started. The Indians were coming out of the woods at a dead run.

"We barely had enough time to get our weapons up and in hand before they were in shooting range. Some of the settlers were still scrambling to do the same. The women were trying to get the children back into the Post when the first volley of arrows hit. It seems that the advancing party which looked like it was about fifteen or so Indians was a decoy.

"Another larger group had sneaked up from behind the Post on both sides and had already killed several with arrows before we fired our first shot. I turned around and saw a few of them on horses breaching the wagons. I was able to shoot one and the rest were killed shortly thereafter but not before they had killed two women, one child and fatally injured a soldier.

"The women and children were screaming and the Indians just seemed to keep coming. We were finally able to see them begin to withdraw back into the woods where the original fifteen or so had come from. But I could hear firing from the back of the Post. I ran around the corner of the building. I did not get very far and collided with an Indian and his horse. I guess the horse must have kicked me in the scuffle because I don't remember anything else.

"When I came to as I was raising my head off the ground I saw a little girl who looked to be about three or four years old with long blond hair who was standing between me and the woods crying hysterically. I saw the Indian coming for her. I aimed and fired, but he kept coming. My pistol had jammed.

"As I stood and watched he leaned down and snatched the little girl by her dress but somehow lost his hold and wound up holding onto her by her hair. He rode a few yards with her screaming and being bounced against the side of the fast moving horse as she was trying to grasp her hair. I still hear her screams at night." Alex took a deep breath and continued. "It was all happening so fast and the thought flashed across my mind that he had taken her captive and at least she would survive this carnage. Grace, what that savage did next, and he truly is a savage, I still see every day. He took that little girl still holding her by her hair with her screaming to the top of her little lungs and swung her in a circle and then released her. She went flying through the air and landed hard against a huge stone. I heard her skull crack as she hit the rock. She was silent instantly. I knew she was dead.

"I had no weapon, but I started running for him. I meant to kill him no matter what. He was screaming madly and disappeared in the woods, but before he did he looked back at me and grinned. I was looking at pure evil and I knew it. I stood there motionless for a few seconds filled with rage. I walked over to this little girl. She had the prettiest blue eyes. I tried not to focus on her face. It was frozen in sheer terror for such a little one. I just kept staring into her lifeless eyes and saying over and over how sorry I was that I couldn't save her. I kept asking her to forgive me. I have often wondered why he didn't kill me too. I think whatever part of him that feels emotion wanted me to keep reliving the horror of what he had done. He did not know it, but he was successful in releasing more evil."

"Oh Alex", she said, "I did not know". She then got up from the table, walked over to him and sat in his lap. She put her arms around him, cradled his head and cried with him as she comforted him as best she could. They talked on into the night and early morning hours. Grace asked him to share with her all that he possibly could. Alex told her about every battle and every memory that haunted him especially when he was a child.

He said he would never hold anything inside again. He also told Grace once more that he was done with drinking in his life whether Grace did leave for good or not and he would certainly understand if she did. He was done with the bottle.

When it seemed that there were no more words to be said, Grace stood up took the hair pins out of her hair and let it fall. She then slowly lifted the skirt of her long dress up and at the same time positioned herself in his lap facing him. Grace ever so slowly pulled his head down to her for a long and deep kiss. Alex whispered her name and stood up as she wrapped her legs tightly around him and he carried her to their bed. They made breakfast as the sun was coming up and then he left her to report back to the Post for duty.

Alex had stayed true to his word and had not drank since that night. They had never been happier. There were times during this period that he would tell Grace about things he remembered from his childhood. Other times he would return from a mission and be a little withdrawn.

She could tell immediately when something was bothering him and would not let much time go by before she would say, "Alex, my love we must talk."

As the weeks progressed into months it became easier for him to tell her what needed to be told. There were nights after having one of these talks that too many times included children, whether it be settlers or Indian children being massacred, they would lay in bed holding each other and let the tears fall freely. They called these times "the washing away of madness".

CHAPTER 6

The rain had not stopped for two days. It was windy and cold. Grace had not left the cabin since it had started. Alex had stacked wood for the fireplace and stove on the back porch and the only time she even opened the door was to grab more firewood. He had been called to the Post because of the rapidly rising Missouri and the danger flood waters would pose for the village if the Missouri overflowed its banks. It had flooded a few years earlier and most were aware of the danger. The previous owners of this cabin had originally built closer to the banks of the river. The Missouri waters had taken their frame house and a portion of their land.

Alex was concerned that the cold winter which had brought copious amounts of snow in the Rocky Mountains as reported by some of the trappers and the snow melt now draining into the rivers which fed the Missouri could be a real hazard for them. There was much talk at the post about the earlier flood a few years ago and the damage it had done to St. Louis. The town was in a very precarious situation because of its location being just a few miles below where the two great rivers met.

Not only was Grace worried about the Deveruex family in St. Louis, but she could not help but worry about her parents being downriver on the Mississippi at New Madrid. The Ohio River joined the Mississippi from the east just a few miles north of New Madrid, Missouri. She tried to keep her imagination from running wild with her as she knew the Missouri was only inches away from overflowing its banks. She kept busy with various chores. The cabin was warm and cozy inside. Grace had decided to utilize the time by doing some extra baking. Alex had gone to the hen house to collect the eggs for her earlier when he was able to come home for a quick bite of dinner. He kept telling her to stay inside and keep warm. This was pneumonia weather. He didn't have to worry. She was perfectly content being in the cabin and out of the cold and damp weather.

The rain finally stopped late that afternoon. Alex came home and had supper. He told her he would be staying at the Post tonight.

"It appears that the river has crested," he told Grace, "but caution requires that we continue to monitor it closely for the next few days. We just don't know how much territory this rain has covered." Grace packed him food to take with him and Alex went back out into the cold damp night.

The river did not rise anymore that night or in the days that followed. Spring came singing in with birds happy and jabbering away as they made their nests. Soon they would hold the eggs that would be cracked open when the baby birds pecked themselves out into the world. Grace felt like she could hear the trees talking as they made new leaves. She loved walking in the woods behind the house this time of year to see all the new growth. Spring always smelled so good and she breathed deeply of the fragrant air.

The next day was on the edge of being hot. Grace had decided to pack a picnic lunch and go to her favorite "spot away from home" as she called it. She liked to go there and see what was going past on the river if anything. Alex was going to be away for a few days and she needed to get out of the cabin. Grace grabbed her lunch and a canteen of water and headed out.

She walked down the main street toward the dock. Just a little way before reaching it there was a piece of property on the river that was not cleared. Grace had found the place accidentally one day when she thought she might find some blackberries. As she had wandered into the stand of trees and underbrush she worked her way toward the water. Grace noticed there was a slight incline as she walked. Suddenly there was a cleared opening situated on a bluff which extended out and into the river. Not a high one, but nonetheless a bluff which afforded a fabulous view of the Missouri all the way to the bend in the river to her left or east and the dock to her right.

There was always some shade where she could put her lightweight blanket down that she had made just for this spot. She and Alex would sometimes come here for a picnic. The first thing she noticed was a galiot moored to the dock. She had seen these flat bottom boats on occasion with their cannon and one and only sail up. Still the twenty plus soldiers would be plying the water with their oars to make progress up the Mississippi and Missouri a little faster. These had been used by the Spanish and the French who had patrolled the waters of the Missouri to protect their interests in the fur trade.

Grace lay on her blanket with her eyes closed. She was remembering the visit she and Alex had made to the Boone home a week ago. The Boone family was so large, loud and loving. There were children everywhere and Grace loved it. Daniel Boone's son, Daniel Morgan Boone had moved to the area a few miles east of St. Charles. He had built a two story home on 850 acres that the previous governor had granted to him. The same grant had been offered to his father. Daniel Boone accepted the grant and had moved his family on to the land in 1799. Several families who were friends of theirs also came to the St. Charles area with them.

The Boones had been welcomed in the village and attended any and all social events when possible. Grace especially liked Daniel Morgan's wife, but their family was a large one and with so many children it was not always so easy to make the almost twenty mile trip into the village. Alex and Grace had traveled out to the Boone home a few times when there was a birthday or some other special family celebration. They always stayed at least one or two nights before returning to St. Charles.

As Grace sat looking over the river she watched as a keel boat slowly worked its way toward the dock. She wondered what supplies they were bringing on this load. It was about fifty feet long. There was a man, woman, three children and a dog standing outside the covered area of the boat in the sunshine. Grace could see a wagon in a penned area along with some mules and a cow. She wondered if they were going to settle here or keep going farther into the west. They would probably unload here and take the Boone's Lick Trail forged by Daniel Boone's sons.

There were a lot of crates on board. She hoped there would be some new fabric for the Watkins General Mercantile. Mrs. Watkins kept telling her they had ordered some and it should be arriving any day now. She needed to make a couple of new dresses especially for social events as St. Charles was growing and there were at least one or two invitations a month now to some special occasion. She had worn the same three dresses over and over again that she had brought with her from St. Louis almost seven years ago. She would give those to Hannah at the Inn for the woman who had just started working there.

Grace was mentally designing her dresses, when she heard Agatha singing.

Agatha stepped into the clearing.

"There you are" she said. "I have been to your house, the mercantile and thought you must be here. I hope I am not disturbing you."

Grace was happy to see her. The truth was that she really was not in the mood to be alone today. She rearranged some of her things on the blanket and made a place for her.

"Alright, out with it Agatha Edwards. You have that funny little impish look on your face and that twinkle in your eyes when you are trying to hold something in."

Agatha reached out and took one of Grace's hands.

"Grace the most wonderful thing has happened. I am pregnant. Now Grace, you mustn't worry". Agatha had seen the look of fear pass across Grace's face before she could conceal it. It was not without cause.

Agatha had given birth twice in the last four years and both babies were still born. The last time Agatha came near death's door. The labor had lasted all night and through the next day. Edmond had fetched one of their new neighbors who had nine children and had helped deliver countless other babies. She was the most experienced in the area with child birth at that time as there was no doctor then.

She had later told Grace it was the worst bleeding she had seen. They were able to get it stopped, but not before they were afraid Agatha really was not going to make it and they would be burying her with the baby. Grace had stayed with Agatha several days afterwards. She had been afraid to leave her. Agatha had been so pale and weak. Watching her grieve for her baby was almost more than Grace could endure.

Agatha continued, "The pain of losing my babies almost put me in the grave even after I had gained some of my strength back. It felt like the empty place where they should be was just too big for me to keep being able to breathe. For a while I didn't want to, but finally I did come out of it and wanted to live again. You know all this Grace, because you helped me get through it.

"I am talking about this again because I don't know how, but this time it is going to be alright. This baby is going to be fine and so will I. Please Grace, you are not to worry. Just be happy for us." Grace reached out and took her hand.

"Well, it looks like I am going to be a godmother soon." They hugged each other and started planning a special supper to announce the good news to the family and close friends.

Agatha said, "Grace, do you remember that time when I took some of our apples to that superstitious Millie Watkins. She and I were both pregnant at the time and when I told her I was going to use the rocking cradle that Edmond had built for the first baby she started throwing all that salt over her left shoulder just like I was a bad luck piece she was having to ward off. She even took one of her shoes off and put it on the table to ward off the bad luck. You know she always dresses starting with the left arm and foot. I am telling you Agatha something is not right with that woman."

Then Agatha started doing her imitation of Millie. First she puckered her mouth up like she had just tasted a green persimmon. Then she started blinking her eyes like something was in them. Next she started pretending she was getting a pinch of salt and throwing it over her left shoulder. Agatha started talking imitating Millie in an exaggerated version of her whining high pitched nasal voice.

"Now Agatha, you know you can't use that cradle. It's terrible bad luck. The best thing is to just get Edmond to chop it up and use it for kindling." While Agatha was talking she continued steadily blinking her eyes, pinching and then tossing imaginary salt over her shoulder.

Agatha continued, "Also take those baby clothes and use them for smudge pots to keep the mosquitoes off of you and Edmond when you are night fishing down at the river for catfish. By the time she got done telling me what I needed to do and not do the whole kitchen looked like somebody had been in a salt fight."

Agatha said, "It took all I could do to keep from slapping her silly. Instead I just crunched myself across all that salt on the kitchen floor and headed out the door.

"I shan't repeat what words I called her. Suffice it to say that Millie Watkins had been cussed up one side and down the other by the time I got back home.

"But still I can laugh about it now. Poor Millie and her endless supply of salt. You know Grace, some people are just so stupid or ignorant you just can't stay mad at them. It is a good thing Millie married into the Watkins family. She will always have access to an endless supply of salt. It's a doubly good thing too, because Millie keeps little piles of it in the corner of each room and under all the window sills. She also has horse shoes nailed over every door in that house." Agatha could sound and act just like her. As always when she did her Millie imitations Grace was in peals of laughter.

Grace and Agatha spent the afternoon enjoying each other's company. It was rare that they got to spend this much time together without work or family members being involved. They had finally talked themselves out and were watching as another keelboat was passing. There was a woman sitting on the front with long black hair. Grace and Agatha both commented about how pretty her hair was.

"Look there's Frantz at the dock. He is probably looking for something he had Mr. Watkins order for his new place," Agatha said. "Since he built his little cabin across the creek, he talks of nothing else. His latest project is finishing his porches across the front and back."

CHAPTER 7

Frantz stood on the dock and watched the keelboat work its way in. All the keelboats had a four inch square piece of wood for the keel and derived their name from it. It was made this way to act as a shock absorber. This one looked to be about sixty feet in length and nine feet or so in width. It had a sail, mast and rigging. There was a good sized cabin constructed of boards with windows on each side and a shingled roof. It also had a swivel gun mounted on the front deck which was called a small cannon by some. It was used in the event of an attack from Indians.

Frantz figured this one would be heading up the Missouri to one of the forts to trade their goods for furs. He counted twenty two men on board. There were nine men on each side of the boat with the long poles they were using to walk the boat forward.

What was really holding his attention was the woman sitting on a barrel on the front of the boat. As the boat reached the dock and was tying off Frantz managed to get a good look at her face. She was stunning in her beauty.

He felt certain she was a slave. It was in her eyes and he recognized and knew well the look of desolation and despair that came with being the property of another human being. He had a hard time keeping from out and out staring at her. The eyes were a light brown and her skin a deep olive. Her hair was black, long and straight. She was wearing it loose and kept having to pull it out of her face, because of the breeze that seemed to have no particular direction in mind. Her cheekbones were high and with the straight hair it made him think she might be part Indian. It was the mouth that could not be mistaken for anything but Negro blood that coursed through her veins, just as it did through his. Her lips were full and prominent as if in a constant pout. Knowing that she was a part of the same race as he sent a pulse of energy through his body that he was not able to explain.

Frantz sensed that for her sake he had to avert his eyes elsewhere, but it was not an easy thing to do. However, it had become absolutely necessary not only for her but the physical reaction he was starting to have from just looking at her. He quickly removed his hat, propped up one leg on a stump, placed his hat in front of his crotch and wiped his sweaty forehead with his shirt sleeve.

His reasoning for the hat removal would fool most people if any were paying attention, but it had not fooled her. When he looked up again she was looking straight at him with wide eyes and the slightest rise in one eyebrow. He immediately looked away embarrassed at being caught. He could not ever remember being affected so within just a few seconds of looking at a strange woman out in public.

Rosa was her name. She dared not look at Frantz standing on the dock in his condition too long or she knew she would have to giggle. If her owner heard that he would immediately perceive something was amiss. A beating would ensue or at the very least he would back hand her. She looked away.

She really wanted to stare at this handsome man indefinitely. She felt some strangeness about him that made her feel a commonality to him, but did not know what it was. Anyway, she knew better than to do little more than a few casual glances his way. Her owner was crazy and would punish her for her show of interest in another man, whether true or imagined. He seemed to miss nothing she said or did.

One of the crew had mistakenly shown her some kindnesses when they first left out of New Orleans. As soon as the owner had discovered this, he had taken her away from the camp site that evening, tied her to a tree and beat her with a leather strop. When they landed in Natchez he had fired the man and found a replacement. He had made it clear from the start that she was his property in all ways and was not to be approached from any of the crew. From that day of the beating on Rosa had kept her sanity by daydreaming about a life of freedom.

She made herself ignore the handsome man with the blue eyes, black hair and light olive skin. It was not an easy task. She got up and went inside the boat and sat by the window where she would not be so easily seen and could look out with abandon.

She overheard the pilot making plans to go to the Inn for a night of drinking. He was talking to another man that had been talking earlier with the handsome stranger. Francois was watching as his stable hand along with a couple of the crew were busy unloading some whiskey. He was giving the pilot money. He had been in St. Louis a few days earlier and happened to encounter the pilot at an Inn where they were both drinking. Francois asked if he would be interested in delivering his load of whiskey. The pilot had said he had a pretty full load, but he would do it since St. Charles was so close.

In the meantime Frantz collected his supplies from the other keelboat that had arrived earlier and loaded them on the wagon. He could not help but glance back to the front of the boat where the woman had been sitting, but she was gone. He did not know that she had moved inside and sat just out of his view. She was watching him intently through a window.

He headed back to the farm to drop off supplies and on to his new cabin. It had taken him almost two years to get it built in his one day a week of off time. Edmond had helped him some, but his time away from the post was spent mostly helping on the farm.

Frantz had picked out a spot that overlooked the river and was close enough that he could hear the water rushing over the rocks in the creek. On the creek was a water fall a few hundred feet inland and he went there to bathe and cool off in the summertime.

At the point where the creek ran into the river was a rock bluff that was about fifteen feet high. From the top of the bluff the land rose in a gracefully sloping hill both from the creek and the river. At the crest of the hill he had built his home. It was a perfect spot.

He had not been staying in his cabin but a few weeks. His plan was to complete it totally and then gradually add suitable accommodations for the pigs, cows, chickens, another horse and a couple of mules he planned to purchase. He wanted to make his place as self-sustaining as possible without depending on Agatha and her Dad. He had figured that with the land they had sold him from the creek to their western property line and to the back property line on the south, he would be able to make it profitable, whether it be in crops, animals or both. He just had to arrange his life, so he had the time to do it.

Frantz had planted a garden in front of the cabin which was beginning to bloom. He would be having fresh vegetables soon and would most likely give most of them to Agatha for now. Even though he was not preparing his breakfast and dinner here yet, he planned to. Frantz thought he was going to have a hard time adjusting to living without Agatha's cooking at every meal. However, he wanted the solitude of his own home enough to let his stomach suffer the consequences of his cooking. Agatha had promised to keep him supplied in bread and butter until he could learn to improve his practically non-existent cooking skills.

Since they were realizing the need for more help, Frantz had decided to talk to Agatha and Matthew about hiring someone else on permanently. There were more and more families moving in now with young men who were looking for work. Frantz was anxious to start working his own land.

For the first time in his life Frantz realized the benefits of being free of slavery. The property that had been sold to him was his land in every way. Friends and connections of the family had helped to make sure all the necessary paperwork was recorded properly. There would never be any issue of true ownership of his land. In this part of the country there was a problem with freed slaves attempting to be owners of property. Only Agatha knew that he had once been a slave and was given his freedom. She promised Frantz it would be a secret taken to her grave. Because of it, she had made doubly sure there would never be any questions to arise from the transfer of title to the land over to Frantz.

The knowledge of being a property owner and having his own home sometimes overwhelmed him. It was not because of the work involved but because of life's uncertainties. He had reached a goal he had dreamed about for most of his life. Good fortune had sent him to the door of Matthew and Anise looking for work the day he had arrived here. It now seemed a life time ago.

The only thing missing that would make his life complete now was the love of and for a woman. He had now started to dream about a wife and children. There had been a young Indian woman he had been interested in, but only a few days after meeting her she was gone from the area. She had been with a small band of Osage that was traveling through and had stopped for a short while to hunt in the area. He went to bed early and dreamed of the beautiful woman on the boat.

Rosa had made her bed on the bow of the boat and watched the stars until she had dozed off. She was sleeping soundly when the drunken pilot and some of the crew returning from their revelry at the Inn awakened her. She listened as they relieved themselves overboard of some of the beer and whiskey they had drank. One by one they crawled in their beds and it was quiet for a minute or two. She kept hoping the pilot would pass out, but when she heard his footsteps heading for the bow she knew it was not to be.

From the first day with him in New Orleans he had told her to call him Master. His name was Claude Bonaparte. The kindest thing he had ever called her was Woman. There was never any conversation between them and he had not bothered to ask her name. One of the crew had. He and some of the others started addressing her by her name, but the pilot quickly stopped that. He felt it was too personal and told them they would call her Woman as he did. Not only had her life been taken from her by this horrible man, but her name also. He reached down and pushed roughly on her shoulder.

"What is it Master?" Rosa said.

"Come on you little whore." He said as he jerked her to her feet. He headed toward the stern of the boat and dragged her on to shore and over to some bushes near the dock. He knew they wouldn't be seen from the street in case there was anyone passing by.

He slapped her across the face so hard it knocked her to the ground. Before she could begin to get up he kicked her.

"You worthless whore. I saw you watching the men on that other boat today".

"No Master, you are wrong. Please don't hit me. Please no more." That was all she could get out before he pounced on her. He was always rough with her, but tonight he seemed to be excited by the obvious pain he had caused. As he was forcing himself into her he

77

continued to strike and curse her. After he had finished he staggered back to the boat.

Rosa lay there with her face throbbing from the repeated strikes he had made with his hand. She thought he would have permanently injured her if he had not been busy elsewhere abusing her body. At least it had kept him from using his hand full force on her face. She knew she would be black and blue. One eye was already starting to shut. She checked to see if any teeth were loose or missing.

Rosa did not move for a long time. She wished she could just drift away into a peaceful darkness and not wake up. Her life had been one nightmare to the next since the day she was taken captive from her home to be sold into slavery. That was almost five years ago. At least no one had beat on her at the plantation. Even though she was a slave there she was taught English and some basic arithmetic. Now in these last few months with this cruel man her life had become almost impossible to tolerate.

As she lay there she kept thinking that she should have taken the chance and run in St. Louis. There seemed to be more people there and her chances of getting work or help might have been better. She spoke English well enough to get by. The Spanish she had learned from her father who was held captive by the Spanish slave runners and worked on their boats for years. Her mother was full bloodied Comanche and had taught her basic sign language that she could use with the different Indian tribes. She also had picked up a good bit of French from some of the crew after leaving New Orleans five months earlier. Languages seemed to come naturally to her.

She had hesitated attempting an escape here in St. Charles, because she had no money and knew no one here. Lying there on the river bank she vowed that she would get away from this crazy man somehow. She knew she could not stay here in St Charles. It was too small. She would have to return to the boat. Rosa limped back and went to her pallet she had made. She promised herself there would be a way to escape and she intended to find it.

The solution needed to come soon, because the further they went west into the wilds of the Missouri River wilderness the more difficult it would be. St. Charles was the last town. She had heard the crew talking about a couple of military posts and Indian villages on up the river. Rosa did not know what she was going to do. She only knew she could not bear to live this way much longer.

The boat left early the next morning before day break. The men did not always use their long poles to navigate the Missouri River. When they did use them there were nine men on each side of the keelboat. They would plunge the poles to the bottom of the river and walk from bow to stern then rapidly return again and repeat the process. In this way the boat moved forward. Today they were bushwhacking because the water was high. They did this by grabbing tree limbs and branches along the bank then pulling the boat forward. When there was a steady breeze they could move out away from the bank and use their sail, but there was none today.

It had been about two weeks since they had left St. Charles. Rosa was sitting on top of the cabin in the front of the boat. This way she could detect the slight breaks or riffles on the surface of the river caused by snags or sawyers lying under the water. She had learned this is what the river men called the trees that had fallen over in the river caused by the bank caving in during high water. Some or all of the sawyers would be submerged. The snags that were so dangerous were on trees or logs that were stuck to the bottom of the river. The river had dropped and the current slowed quite a bit in the last few days. The men were relieved since it was not quite as hard to move the boat forward, but still a grueling and arduous task. From the drop in the water level it was making

Rosa's job a little easier as more and more riffles were appearing.

Rosa also had to keep an eye out for floating logs and tree limbs. These were more abundant in high water times, but had become less frequent. She was glad that two other crew members were also helping look today. She was having a hard time keeping her mind on the task at hand. With each tree limb or log that floated past them, she would visualize herself perched or hanging on it some way and riding the river away from this boat and back towards St. Louis. She knew this was not a good option. Most of the wood sunk lower under the surface as it absorbed the river water and would eventually sink to the bottom.

Rosa made up her mind that she would wait until they came back through St. Louis, she would escape this boat then and the man she called Master. She let her imagination run away with her after having settled on where and when she would leave the boat.

CHAPTER 8

The pilot and crew had been closely watching a storm brewing up the river. It was not certain yet if it would reach them. The wind was blowing slightly but was not holding to one direction or the other. The crew was on the verge of collapse due to the exhausting battle with the swollen river for almost two weeks now. Even though the levels were dropping and the current slowing the pilot decided to find a camp site and let the men rest for a couple of days. He knew from experience that a crew that was too tired was prone to mistakes resulting in accidents which endangered the lives of everyone and the safety of the boat. They were low on meat and needed to replenish their supply anyway. It was a perfect time to stop.

Shortly after rounding a bend they passed a small creek entering the river from the north bank. Just beyond the creek was a low rising bank with no sign of sawyers or snags. Claude decided to make camp there. The boat was poled to the spot adjacent to the bank. Two crew members with rope in hand, one on the front and another on the back jumped overboard and secured the boat to some trees. A wide board used as a gangplank was positioned between the bank and the boat and the crew began to unload. All the men were excited about the break and anticipated a little drinking in the evening.

After the boat was tied off Claude bounded to the top of the cabin where everyone could easily see and hear him.

"All you men who want a washing in the creek, do it now before the possibility of that lightning storm arriving here. By the time everyone is bathed and the evening meal is cooked we should have an idea of whether some can sleep on land or will have to sleep in the boat tonight. Tomorrow morning the hunting parties will go out. Tonight we drink."

Rosa knew he was making the crew bathe first, so there would be no excuse for one of them coming up on her accidentally when she was bathing later. The crew knew it too. None of them were willing to take any chances with antagonizing the pilot after what had happened on the Mississippi. No one wanted to be left on the bank alone in this wilderness. Half of the crew went to the creek first while the other stayed with the boat for security. After all of the crew had taken advantage of the creek with a good amount of time used for scrubbing and frolicking, they returned to the camp site refreshed and in good spirits.

While the crew had been in the creek Rosa had peeled potatoes and scraped the last of the carrots for the evening meal. She had also gathered some wood for the cook fire. She told the cook she was going to take a look around and see if she could find any greens, roots and maybe some berries or wild plums before she came back from her bath. Rosa knew she would not be bothered by the pilot, because he was busy getting the crew and equipment ready for the hunting expedition tomorrow.

Rosa followed the path the men had made to the creek. She placed her clean clothes on a rock. It was so peaceful here after days of the constant struggle to move up the Missouri. The men were constantly grunting, groaning and cussing with the straining on the poles, oars or rope. The pilot was continually hollering orders and the men who watched for the logs, snags and sawyers were constantly shouting their finds. The water was clear and cool as she waded and listened to the beauty of this quiet place. She could hear an occasional crew member, but very faintly. She shut the boat and its noise out and listened to the sounds of the birds who were returning after being scared off from the rowdy crew earlier. Rosa decided she would go up the creek bank a little ways and see if she could find some berries or fruit before she bathed. She had already spotted some greens and would pick and clean them when she was ready to return to camp.

She had walked up the creek a short distance when she decided to take advantage of some rocks in the stream and cross to the other side. Rosa was working her way back toward the river when she spotted a small dewberry patch. She quickly filled one of her leather shoulder pouches she had brought with her and decided to look around for some more dewberry vines.

She was back at the creek bank and near the river again. Rosa was intently searching for another dewberry patch when she saw through some bushes some vague coloring that she knew was out of place. Rosa walked over to the overhanging bushes and pulled them back. She could not believe her eyes. It was a small canoe that had been almost completely hidden by the underbrush. Someone had painted a sun on the side and the faint yellow color was what she saw. It was pure luck that she had seen it. From the looks of things it had been there for a while. There was a paddle in the bottom along with several inches of water and a lot of leaves and twigs. She felt certain that whoever had left it had intended to return way before now. They had carried it to this spot for hiding it temporarily. Because it was left upright she felt they had not intended to be away from it a long time.

In a flash she knew this was her means of escape. Because it was small she managed to get it tilted against a tree enough to empty out the water. She quickly grabbed some leafy green vine and made a temporary basket to hold the berries and left them under the canoe. She found some dead brush and concealed the canoe even more. Rosa eased into the creek and looked back to see if it was visible. It was not. She was so excited it took all of her energy to focus on collecting the greens, getting her bath and dressing to return to camp. She wanted to get in the canoe and head out now, but knew she had to wait and format a plan. She needed a little time to calm herself, so she could think clearly.

Before going back to camp Rosa took a stick and on the sandy bank she wrote down some numbers. She had heard the crew talking and figured they were somewhere around two hundred miles upriver from St. Louis. If the flow of the river was back to its regular speed or close that would mean it was moving about three miles an hour. She divided twenty into two hundred and realized it would take her between three and four days to make it back to St. Louis if she did not stop except when absolutely necessary. She rubbed out her figures in the sand and wrote her name. With this time frame in mind, she gathered up her greens and went back to camp.

For the first time since being in Claude's captivity Rosa was happy. She had to really mentally work to keep it from showing. She wanted to dance and sing now that she had a way to escape. She walked into camp and put the greens in the stew pot. The cook sent her to the meal barrel. This time she collected a little extra for the fried bread.

Rosa usually cooked the bread and today was no different. She was able to cook a few extra pieces and stuff them into her pockets without being seen. Her clothes were so grease stained it would not be noticed. She had managed to remove a few pieces of dried meat from a barrel stored on board and hide them in one of her pouches on the boat along with the bread in another.

She dared not take much for she knew it would be missed as their meat supply was so low. Now her hours of boredom she had filled with making pouches from small animal skins would pay off. She had several and she knew no one would bother to have counted them, therefore a couple would not be missed.

As they sat around the fire that evening, Rosa tried to figure out how she could get off the boat without rousing any suspicion. She need not have been worried. Claude had allowed the men to drink far more than their normal nightly ration of whiskey. They would sleep soundly. Claude was a fast drinker and had quickly taken his fill. He had decided to go to bed early and was already asleep and snoring loudly when she went back to the boat. It had started to rain and some of the crew came on the boat and bedded down. There were a few that had made covers out of some old canvas they draped over strung rope and placed around the camp site. They crawled under those for the night.

Rosa did not really want to start out in the dark and the rain too. The rain had started coming down heavier and there was now a lot of thunder and lightning. The more she thought about it the more it made sense to go during the storm. She would be able to find her way back to the creek in the lightning flashes. Since she would be wet anyway, she would just swim the few feet needed to cross the creek to where the canoe was hidden. That would save her from having to go back up and across the creek, then down again to the canoe. With this rain there would be no tracks left of anything. She could just launch the canoe and be on her way.

She eased out of her bedding and went to get her chamber pot. Claude had fashioned a curtained area in one corner for privacy. It was just large enough for her to get inside and squat over the pot. She picked it up and walked out on deck. She was going to try to make it look like she had slipped and fallen overboard half asleep while trying to rinse it out. It was not unusual for her to rinse the pot at least once during the night. She did not like the odor.

There was a short rope tied to the stern of the boat. Rosa always used it to clean the pot. She would tie the pot to the rope and lower it in the river and back up again rinsing it with the collected water. She pulled the rope up, tied it to the handle and threw it overboard. Rosa could see the current tugging on it. She knew it would fill up, but she had tied the knot extra tight to make sure it did not come loose. Rosa wanted them to find it still tied and in the water.

She took the buffalo skin she used for cover and folded it with the two pouches of food inside. It was not unusual for her to wrap herself with it at night before going out of the cabin if it was cool or raining. She figured if they thought she fell overboard they would think the buffalo skin went with her. None of the crew had any idea she could swim.

Rosa carefully crossed the gangplank to the bank. She could barely make out where the tents were scattered. She carefully headed in the direction of the trail they had followed to the creek. Just as she was near lightning flashed and she could see the trail just in front of her. She began to carefully work her way through the woods.

The rain was steady and she could barely see five feet in front of her, but the flashes of lightning helped her find her way. When she got to the creek she stood only long enough to make sure she was headed straight for a spot where she could easily climb the bank and was not too far from the canoe.

When she was satisfied she had selected the best spot she waded in the water with the buffalo skin on top of her head. She was balancing it with one hand. She was just a few feet from the bank on the other side when the water came up to her chest. She easily swam a few feet with one hand balancing the fur and the other treading water. She was not afraid of storms but did not like to be out in them. She quickly climbed the bank, turned to the right and waited for the next flash. She knew she was only about twenty feet from the canoe. She reached it and was able to get it turned back over.

The bank here was a steep little sand bank, so she decided to push it over the edge and slide down the bank with it while holding on to the side. Rosa was afraid if she just slid it in the water she might not be able to see it before the current had a chance to take it on into the river. She could not take that chance. She threw her buffalo skin in along with her pouches safely folded inside and the berries she had picked. She pushed the canoe to the very edge of the bank where it was ready to tip over and down the bank. She sat beside it with her legs hanging over the edge of the bank and holding the canoe with both hands they both slid down the bank. She let go of her hold just before she landed in the creek with a big splash. She did not want to turn the canoe over. She immediately got her head back above water and grabbed the side of the canoe while treading the few feet to the shallower water. When she could stand and get in the canoe without tipping it over she hopped in. Lightning flashed and she grabbed the paddle and headed the little canoe toward the river.

Rosa knew it was dangerous to be on the river now. Not only was there danger from the storm, but there was no way she would be able to see all the trees and snags at night with no moon light. She had to take the chance. She knew the storm would wash away all traces of her and the canoe back at the camp site.

She felt certain that once they realized she had probably fallen overboard, Claude would have some of the men searching the bank for a long distance back down stream to see if they could find her somewhere possibly clinging to a tree in the water or at the very least her body. She regarded the storm as a gift and she was thankful for it. Rosa kept her eyes focused in front of her even though she could see little in the water as the storm raged on.

She decided not to cover with the buffalo hide as she would not have a dry spot to keep her food. There was enough to get her to St. Louis if she had no problems and only ate a few small bites twice a day. She was not going to be sleeping this night anyway. She wanted to get as much distance as she could between her and the boat. She did not think the pilot would head back down stream in the boat to look for her, but she did not want to take any chances. He was crazy, but she felt his lust for money would win out over his lust for her.

Rosa did not know how long she rode the river in the storm, but it was a few hours. The heavy rain let up a little while after she left but there was a light and steady rain most of the night. The canoe had taken in several inches of water by the time day break arrived. Rosa put into shore as soon as she found a safe place. She tilted the canoe and emptied the water out. She had checked her food and it was dry. She wished she had something to start a fire with, but she didn't. Finding flint and something dry would take entirely too much time. She rinsed the berries and ate a few along with some bread and a few bites of meat. She was tired, but did not want to stay on shore and sleep. She only wanted to keep moving down river.

She knew they would have discovered her missing by now and would be searching for her or her body. Rosa felt she now had a safe distance between herself and Claude but did not want to take any chances. She pushed the canoe back out in the river. She wrapped herself in her buffalo skin and rowed the canoe into the main channel of the river. She had begun to warm a little when the sun came shining through the clouds. It was not long before she was completely dry from the warmth of the sun.

Rosa had seen a few dangerous spots where the sawyers had fallen in the river and were protruding. There was always a chance of hitting a snag where a tree had wedged itself in the muddy bottom. She also had to keep an eye out for the drifting trees and logs that were submerged. Once that day she had rowed up to one that was submerged a few inches before she realized it, but luckily was able to push her canoe with the paddle safely away from it before any damage was done. There were no limbs to snag her canoe that she could see. She still gave the floating log a wide berth.

CHAPTER 9

As she drifted and paddled Rosa's thoughts took her back to the days when she was with her family and lived among her people, the Comanche and how she had been taken from her home and family. It was in the winter time and Rosa had told her mother she was going to search for clams in a spot on the bay she had seen earlier. It was not where the tribe usually searched, but a good distance further from camp. Her mother had told her to be careful and not stay in the cold water too long.

Rosa had been intent upon her search along the shore and was about knee deep in the water in a slough when she had heard men's voices. When she had turned and looked behind her she had seen two men advancing toward her in a canoe. She had seen immediately that they were not Indians but Spanish soldiers. She had not been afraid as the soldiers had visited her people a few times and had always been friendly, unlike the ones who had captured her father off the coast of Africa. What she did not know was that these two were from a pirate ship. The uniform jackets they had worn were taken from a Spanish ship they had ransacked, burned and sunk. They had seen her when they rounded a small island near where she was searching for the clams. They had decided to take her then. Rosa had stood calmly in the water holding her raking tool her father had made for her. She had watched as they approached.

She had called out a greeting in Spanish which totally took them by surprise. They had pulled the canoe up on the bank then turned and asked her what she was fishing for. She had told them it was clams and lifted her rake up out of the water where they could see the prongs. One of them had asked if he could see what she had gathered in her pouch. Still unafraid Rosa had walked out of the water, laid her rake down and opened her shoulder pouch for them to see. The two men had approached her with one standing in front and to the side of her. The other walked behind her as though going around to the other side of her to look in the pouch. He grabbed her from behind in a bear hug. Rosa had not been able to get loose. She had started screaming and asked what they were doing in Spanish.

"Let me go." Rosa had shouted. The other man had stepped in front of her. Rosa still had not been able to move her arms, but was kicking at him with all her might. The last thing she saw was a fist coming toward her face from the man who stood in front of her.

Rosa had slowly sat up in the canoe as they were approaching a ship. They had tied her hands behind her in case she decided to jump overboard. She had been placed in a contraption of ropes they lowered to the canoe and then pulled up the side of the ship and onto the deck. She had looked back at the shore line of her homeland one last time. Rosa knew her parents would be heartbroken when they discovered her gone. She wondered if she would ever see them again. She had a strong feeling she would not.

Just like her father had been, she was now a slave. And just like her father Rosa was captured and put on a ship. Her father was such a big strong man that instead of being sold he had been kept to work on Spanish ships. He had worked on different ships until they were attacked by the Comanche when on land west of the Mississippi. Like the Spanish, the Comanche had also been impressed with his strength and especially his bravery during the Comanche's attack. They too had decided not to sell him. They could have sold or traded him to the Mexicans or back to the Spaniards, but instead they accepted him as one of them. He had soon taken Rosa's mother as his woman. They had been deeply in love.

She knew her father would not have stopped looking until he had found some sign of her. Rosa did not know that he had found her rake and partially spilled pouch of clams which had started to smell. He also found evidence of where a beached canoe had been and the footprints of what looked like Spanish soldiers along with Rosas'. He had known in his heart that his daughter had been captured just as he had so many years before.

Rosa had been led to an opening in the floor of the boat. Her hands had been untied and the pirate had indicated with his hands that she was to go in and down. As Rosa had very slowly started her descent down the ladder she had heard murmuring. The opening above her had been abruptly closed. It had been dark except for the light that came through the grated opening she had entered. The odor that immediately had hit her was so foul she had felt sick. It seemed to have penetrated her entire body. She wondered how she would be able to keep breathing in this wretched, stinking air. When she had reached the bottom of the ladder she turned and placed the back of her hand over her mouth. Her eyes had adjusted a little to the darkness and she had been able to make out the outlines of men, women and children.

Rosa had not stopped the tears that poured from her eyes. As she had stood there making no sound with the tears sliding down her cheeks and chin, one of the women had stepped up to her. She had reached out and put her hand gently on Rosa's chest before she had whispered some words that Rosa did not understand. She had been as dark skinned as Rosa's father. Even though she had not understand all the words the woman spoke she caught a touch of Spanish. She had completely understood the look in the woman's eyes. It had been filled with compassion and encouragement. Even though the woman was filthy Rosa had not hesitated. She reached out to her and the woman had held her while she cried.

The woman had taken her to an unoccupied spot on the floor and they had sat down. During the rest of the day Rosa had discovered that there were only two buckets used for bodily functions. Once a day they were raised on a rope to the deck and emptied then lowered back down. Afterwards they had been fed with buckets of gruel that were lowered. They had to dip and eat with their hands. Often times the children received nothing unless an adult intervened and gave them food. Once these buckets were pulled back up one bucket with a dipper was lowered with water. At night there was enough room to lay down for sleep as long as they were touching one another. At first Rosa could not sleep because of the stench and heat. Soon fatigue overtook her and she had slept out of sheer exhaustion.

Rosa had been on the ship close to two weeks. Three times she had been ordered on deck in Spanish and was taken to the Captain's quarters. After he had brutally raped her she was then used by two other members of the crew. Each time it had been the same three men. The first time she had fought desperately. After that when she was selected two of the men would hold her while the third one raped her. She was not the only woman who had suffered this fate. Knowing this somehow made it gradually easier to push out of her mind. She had replaced those memories with thoughts of her family and their life together.

A storm had forced the ship to anchor in a protected cove for a few days. Even though the constant rocking of the ship was bothersome many had taken advantage of the rain that drained and fell through a corner of the closed hatch and were able to clean their hands and faces a little. The fresh air that blew down when the hatch was opened was received with much gratitude. Rosa later learned from some of the slaves on the plantation she had been taken to that she and the others on her ship were very lucky to have been treated so well. She had trouble believing this until she had heard it from several more of the slaves.

When the ship arrived in New Orleans the captives had been immediately sent to the auction block, after some of the crew had thrown buckets of salt water over them to remove some of the filth and stench.

She had translated for some of her Comanche people who had also been taken. Rosa understood what was being said in Spanish so she knew what was happening. She always spoke Spanish with her father when they were alone or with her mother. He was the one who had given her the name of Rosa.

There had been about fifteen men and three women of the group who had been chained together and led to the raised platform called the auction block. Rosa had looked out and had seen quite a crowd gathered for the sale of human beings. She had only understood the Spanish, but French, Creole and English languages had been spoken in the crowd.

She had seen that several of the men had been studying her. As the bidding had begun those men were the ones who had spoken for her. Finally it was obvious that she had been sold to a fairly young looking man in fancy clothes. It turned out that he was a rich Englishman who had recently purchased a sugar cane plantation for his family's holdings. When he had learned Rosa spoke Spanish he was able to communicate with her in his broken Spanish.

The Englishman had been quite taken with Rosa and her strange beauty when he saw her. He had not planned to purchase any slaves that day, but was simply curious about the process. But when he had first seen her he knew he had to have her. She brought the highest bid on the block that night. She was beautiful even though she and her clothing were still filthy. As soon as he had paid for her he led Rosa through the streets to the back entrance of his hotel and to his quarters. He had ordered his personal maid to bathe her and throw away the filthy animal skins she was wearing. While this was being done he had gone out and with the aid of a shopkeeper purchased new clothing for her.

Rosa had never seen such strange contraptions and then understood why the few women she had managed to look at on the street had looked the way they did. The maid had put long pants made of a light material over her legs with a ruffle at the bottom. She then had placed a garment around her chest and waist with sticks scattered through it that ran from the top to bottom and tied it up behind her so tightly Rosa was barely able to breathe. It pressed hard against her breasts and was terribly uncomfortable. It made them appear almost flat. She was used to wearing her tunics which were comfortable and not confining in any way unless she tied it at the waist. Even then she never tied it tightly.

The strangest thing of all was what was shaped sort of like a teepee frame which the maid had put over her head. It had been tied at her waist. Finally she put a beautiful garment the color of the sky over the framed garment. Rosa did not know that her owner had instructed the maid to leave Rosa's hair loose. The maid had loosely tied a shining blue ribbon in her hair that matched the dress. After she was finished she guided Rosa to the mirror. Rosa's mouth dropped open. She wondered how in the world she would get enough air sucked into her lungs to live. Even more she worried about walking around without hurting herself. She thought she must look like a woman rising out of the top of a strange looking blue teepee instead of the smoke that should be there.

She had not had to stay so very uncomfortable for very long. Her master had returned to the room and dismissed the maid. He had poured some sort of drink for them. Rosa had not liked it, but was afraid not to drink it. She had immediately begun to feel strange and had an urge to giggle. She found herself smiling as she was led toward the bed. He had methodically undressed her kissing her as he went about removing each garment. He called her beautiful in Spanish.

Rosa had experienced wave after wave of energy in her body she was not familiar with. She wanted him to continue kissing and touching her. She had laid down on the bed and watched him undress and come to her. He was different in that he was not cruel to her. He actually had been very gentle and had done things to her body that had aroused a need in her she did not know she had. Without any thought she had given in to the sensations and responded to his love making. The next morning she was dressed again by the maid.

After a hearty breakfast they had visited the shop where he had purchased her outfit. He had the woman take her measurements. He had ordered a complete wardrobe for Rosa and directed that it be delivered by a keelboat to his plantation up the Mississippi River about fifty miles out of New Orleans.

Rosa had stayed with him for almost five years. He had realized for some time that the wilds and isolation of plantation ownership were not to his liking. He had started missing England terribly. He had discovered that he was not suited to the heat in the summer and had not tried to adjust. He had become bored and depressed. He had been a kind man, but not a strongly driven one as his father and brother were. Just like the plantation with time he had grown tired of Rosa too. He had taken her to New Orleans with him where he found a temporary administrator to oversee and manage his property until he could return to England and hire a more suitable manager to be sent back to the plantation.

Rosa was with him when he had wound up in a card game and was losing heavily. At the card table was a fur trader who was also a keel boat pilot. Everyone had folded except him and the pilot. There was a lot of money on the table. The Englishman had not had enough money left to stay in the game. The hand he had held would make up for the money he had lost and then some.

The Englishman had noticed how the pilot could hardly focus on the game because of his little concealed lust for Rosa. The Englishman who was by then very inebriated offered Rosa as his ante.

The keelboat pilot had looked at her and the Englishman and said, "I'll take the winch."

Rosa had known her life would not be a good one with this man.

She had leaned forward and whispered in the Englishman's ear, "Please, Sir don't."

The Englishman had felt a tiny pang of guilt, but all he said was, "Quiet woman. I will take one card, please."

By the toss of that one card Rosa became the property of another man. That had been the beginning of a new life and a long nightmare for Rosa.

The pilot had raked up his money, grabbed her by the arm and said, "You are mine now, Winch."

He had taken her to an Inn that was located near the wharf. All Rosa remembered was the filth of the place and his repeated rape of her during the night.

CHAPTER 10

Rosa took a deep breath and sighed. It had now been about seven months ago, but really seemed much longer. Strange how quickly life changed. Here she was in a strange land on a strange river and alone. She was an escaped slave headed for yet another strange place. Nonetheless, she had no regrets of her decision to leave.

It was now about mid-afternoon and Rosa smelled smoke before she actually saw any. She realized she must be near an Indian village, as the smoke was too strong for just one camp fire. She remembered they had slipped past one on the boat in the wee hours of the morning about four or five days ago. Claude had heard reports from other traders that this group was not open for trading and were not friendly.

She did not know the other tribes in this strange land and did not want to take a chance of becoming a victim of this one either as a captive or even being killed. She knew this canoe was probably her last chance to make a life for herself as a free person. Without hesitation she steered the canoe toward the bank of the River. It looked like there was a slight bend up ahead and she definitely did not want to go around it in the daylight.

The bank was not sandy like the last place she had stopped earlier, but she managed to get the canoe up and out of the water. She then took the time to conceal it from sight of anyone who might pass by on the river. She found a fairly dry spot in some high weeds where she took her buffalo skin and rolled up in it. Rosa was exhausted and immediately fell asleep.

Something woke her. It took her a moment to remember where she was. The noise was coming from her canoe. She eased off the ground and was just in time to see a raccoon climbing in the canoe. Rosa knew it was after her food. She rose up slowly and stood. There was a small limb lying on the ground and was just long enough to reach the raccoon. She picked it up and used it as a big switch and swatted the raccoon while making a noise that was somewhat similar to a dog bark and growl at the same time. She could not shout for fear of being heard by the people around the bend. It worked and scared the raccoon. It made a hasty retreat from her canoe.

The moon had come out and Rosa could see very well having been asleep and not having to wait for her eyes to adjust to the dark. Luckily she had heard the animal before he had a chance to get her food. Rosa was extremely hungry and decided to eat a few bites before getting back on the river.

The moon was about half full. She knew there was enough light that someone might see her from shore. She studied a small tree that had fallen over just a few feet from her where the bank had washed away. Its roots were barely in the clutches of the muddy bank. She was not familiar with this type of tree, but it had a lot of leaves on it. With just a little tugging and twisting Rosa was able to get it loose.

She took it and very carefully eased the roots into the front of the canoe. The top of the tree actually stuck out over the other end of the canoe a few feet. Rosa broke about two feet down from the top so there was no apparent point visible there anymore. She stuck the top piece upside down at an angle leaning toward the front of the canoe with the point in the roots for support. The bottom sticking up helped conceal the inside curve of the canoe in front. She did not want anyone to notice the familiar front and back curves of the canoe. She removed all the branches on one side of the tree from the bottom up about three feet. These she put in the front and very back of the canoe.

Rosa put the canoe in the water, raised up the trunk, slid in underneath and let the trunk rest on her shoulder as the cleared portion was facing toward her lap. She wanted enough room to be able to steer with her paddle. It would be very awkward managing the canoe, but she hoped that she, the canoe, her little tree and the shadows would look like a part of a big downed tree drifting down river. Since the moon was not full, there was a good chance that no one would even notice her disguise going by. A dog might get a whiff of her and bark, but before it could get too riled up she would be down river far enough it wouldn't matter.

She took her paddle and headed for the middle of the river. It only took a few minutes to get around the bend. She could see the burning of several fires scattered through the camp. She guessed it must be a little earlier than she had thought, because she could hear the laughter of children playing. As Rosa got closer she could see about twelve fires burning in front of the teepees. When the breeze drifted toward her she caught the whiff of some kind of stew. She could not help but salivate. The little bit of food she had eaten was sustaining her, but by no means satisfying her hunger. She consoled herself with the fact that the raccoon had not taken what she had left and it would suffice for a couple more days.

Just as she had suspected a couple of the dogs had picked up on her scent and started barking which caused several others to join in. She could see a couple of men walking toward the bank appearing to be looking out over the river. She hoped she would be far enough away from them by the time they reached the water that they would not bother to get in their canoes and investigate further. Finally, one of the men shouted and the dogs immediately stopped barking. The men turned and walked away from the water and back toward their camp. Rosa breathed a sigh of relief and only then realized how it seemed every muscle in her body had been tensed. She let the canoe drift while she let her racing heart slow down to its normal speed.

Hardly any time had passed before the river had taken her out of site of the camp. It seemed like a long time to Rosa for she barely let herself breathe while she glided past only having to adjust the direction of the canoe with the oar a few times. She was terribly glad, because of the strain of not seeing ahead of her well through the leaves and the weight of the tree on her shoulder she was beginning to feel really tired already. She waited until she was a safe distance further down from the camp and then guided her canoe toward a sandy bank. As soon as it hit the sand and was not in danger of tipping over with her she moved the tree on her shoulder to one side and got out.

She quickly removed the loose limbs and the top of the tree. Just as carefully as she had put it in she removed the tree from the canoe. The last thing she wanted was to tear a hole in her canoe from being careless and in a hurry. Once that was done, she relieved herself. After smelling the food she was really hungry, but forced herself to ignore it and hopped in the canoe and headed back toward the middle of the river.

Rosa had made it through the first full day and night of being on the river. With the second dawn just as it had with the first came a surge of renewed energy. Right then she felt as though she could ride this river forever. It felt so good to be alone and away from Claude. She felt sorry for the crew, because she knew they would somehow pay for her absence. Rosa forced herself to not think about it.

The sunrise had brought with it the singing of the birds she looked forward to every morning. She even saw a brown bear fishing in one of the pools left by the high water on a sandy bank. There were also cranes taking advantage of the small fish that had been trapped in the pool. Had it not been for the bear she might have stopped to fish some herself. The raw fish would not be so good, but would have definitely eased the hunger for a while.

Rosa was tired, but she felt an energy she had not known since she was at home and living with her mother and father. She knew there was a very real chance she might make it to St. Louis only to be placed in captivity again, but she had to try. Claude had certainly spent enough time telling her she would be caught if she tried to escape.

The sun was very warm today and Rosa had begun to sweat. It was nearing midday when she came to a wide place in the river. She realized there was another river flowing in from the south side. She remembered this one from the trip up. She knew the one she had passed earlier was called the Osage River named after the people that lived in this area. She did not remember the name of this one or if it had a name. There was a huge sand bank in the middle of the Missouri where the two rivers met. .

Rosa decided to stay to the left of it or closer to the north bank. She also decided to stop and rest for a while. It was a good piece of luck that she did. Just as she was getting her canoe pulled up and covered, she heard voices coming across the water just ahead. She quickly ducked behind a tree. As she peeked out she saw another keelboat working its way up the river. They were working their poles. It was not quite as large as the one she had been on. The men were mostly speaking English. She was happy they were using the poles. She thought she would surely have been discovered if they had been using the line.

Rosa really did want to take a nap, but now she was uneasy about doing so. What if they decided to stop close by? It was very unlikely this time of the day, but she could not take a chance. She ate the last few bites of her food and waited until they went around the next bend. Then it was back in the river. She was really beginning to feel the lack of insufficient sleep. Rosa decided she would not stop anymore today, but keep going if she could.

Late in the afternoon she knew she had to get some rest. She felt as though she could not lift the paddle another time. It would not be long before dark. She was also having trouble keeping her eyes open and was afraid she might drift off and drop the paddle. She went into shore where there was a little stream coming into the river. She drank from the stream and made a bed with some dry leaves. She was chilled and took her buffalo robe and rolled up in it. Immediately she was asleep.

Rosa awoke suddenly and opened her eyes. It was dark. Something had awakened her. What was it? Then she heard the grunting and realized it was a wild hog. She couldn't tell exactly where it was, but it sounded like it was not between her and the water. She knew it was close by. Rosa eased up to a squatting position from her bed of leaves with her robe around her. She waited a few seconds until she could get her night sight and bearings then started running toward her canoe. She was glad she had not pulled it too far inland this time. There was a tree that had fallen at an angle partially in the water and she had used it to conceal it from the river. She could hear rustling and a squealing grunt in the underbrush behind her and was certain that the hog was chasing her. Rosa ran as fast as she dared in the woods at night. The moon was almost full and the light was good. She reached the canoe and shoved it in the river. She just barely had time to hop in and grab the oar before the hog ran out of the woods and reached the sandy bank. She was just then dipping her oar in the water. Her heart was racing but she knew he would not come in the river after her.

From the position of the moon Rosa determined she had not slept more than three hours. It had helped, but she was feeling the need for more rest, some warm food and a bath. She couldn't seem to get warm even though the rowing usually warmed her up. Rosa tried to concentrate on what she might do when she got to St. Louis. There had to be something she could do to survive. She was getting really cold so she took her buffalo skin and covered herself while she rowed. She thought the chill must be from so little sleep and food. The robe did help to warm her a little, but she was having trouble keeping her eyes open. She was so tired, but she kept fighting to stay awake.

Rosa had been rowing for hours. She knew it had to be after midnight and nearing the early hours of morning. She let herself imagine sitting by a campfire with a stew on the fire simmering after just returning from a refreshing bath. She closed her eyes and could smell the stew cooking. She drifted into a hazy sleep, but roused when her head starting falling toward her chest.

All at once Rosa felt the canoe slow down abruptly and heard a sort of muffled pop. Water began to fill the canoe and she knew she had hit a snag. The canoe was filling with water fast. She could do nothing but throw the robe off and plunge in the cold muddy water and start swimming. She would utilize the flow of the river and swim at a sharp angle toward shore. It would be difficult but not as hard as trying to swim straight in. She really had no choice if she wanted to make it. Rosa was a good swimmer, but had never needed to swim a long distance and never at night. Now she would have to do both.

She was so tired from too little rest and not enough food. She only hoped she would make it. She had heard the men talking when they were not too far out of St. Louis and they had said the river was close to half a mile wide in many places and a mile or more in others. She just knew it was a big muddy river. Rosa allowed herself to look up toward the shore and could tell she was getting closer, but she was also getting very tired. She thought about just floating to rest for a while. She was afraid she might wind up back out in the middle of the river if she did that. It was getting harder and harder to raise her arms, but she would not give up. When she thought she could not make one more stroke and stopped to get her bearings her foot touched bottom. She was almost to the bank. She forced herself to make a few more strokes. Her hands hit bottom and she started crawling through the water up and on the bank where she lay until her breathing slowed. She remembered thinking she should get out of the wet clothes and try to make a fire before she passed out.

CHAPTER 11

Frantz awoke, dressed and made his way to the back porch where he had built a shelf between two of the support posts. He kept a bucket of water there so he could wash up every morning. He dipped some water in the large clay bowl he used as a wash basin. He splashed the cold water across his face. Grabbed his towel off the nail where it hung on a support post and dried his face. The moon was getting ready to set so he did not light a lantern yet. He was excited about getting started today but he stood there a few moments just listening to the quiet of the forest in the minutes before sun rise. He could hear his beloved creek. He looked up at the sky and marveled at the brightness of the stars and thought how good life had turned out for him.

Today would be his first morning to have coffee on his new front porch. It was also Sunday, so he would not be going to the farm. He went back in the cabin and lit the lantern. He got his iron kettle and went back out and filled it from his bucket. While the coffee was making he sliced off enough salt pork to last for the day and cooked it. He wasn't quite ready for breakfast yet, so he put it aside. He had chicken eggs where Agatha insisted he bring some home with him every few days after work along with a loaf of bread she had made yesterday.

Frantz poured himself a cup of coffee and went out to the front porch. He sat on the edge with his legs hanging off and sipped his coffee. By this time some of the birds were waking up and welcoming the day. He went back in and got his second cup. He sat and watched the sky as it slowly begin to lighten up. He decided to walk down to the river and watch the sun come up. Once he reached the river he knew it would come straight up over the water this time of year. He never tired of watching it.

As he came closer to the river he noticed a significant drop in the water level from yesterday morning. There was more of the exposed muddy bank with lots of drift wood and logs scattered about. As he glanced to his right upriver he saw a piece of driftwood that caught his eye. It almost looked like a person lying in the mud. He knew his imagination was being over active again, but he was drawn to it because of the unusual shape. He stayed further up the bank and out of the slushy mud but walked toward the odd shaped piece of wood. The light was changing fast now and as he came within a few feet he realized it was a human. He could see that it was a woman from the clothing and shape of the body.

Frantz approached slowly as he felt he was encountering a dead person. The woman was lying on her stomach with her arms out in front of her. He could tell from the marks in the mud she had crawled from the river and collapsed where she lay. Her hair was black, long and straight. He could not see her face. He squatted down and searched for a pulse at her neck. To his surprise he found one, but her neck felt very hot. He was certain she had a fever. It was still cool outside and she was very warm to his touch. Her clothes were still soaked from the river. He reached down and turned her over and picked her up in two fluid motions. As he straightened himself up and hefted her to a better position for carrying, her hair fell back and out of her face.

Frantz almost dropped her he was so shocked. It was the beautiful woman he had seen on the boat about two weeks ago. All kinds of thoughts raced through his mind as he hurried toward the cabin with her. It did not take but a few seconds to know she was burning up with fever. He had to get her out of these wet clothes as quickly as possible and in something dry. His mind was racing. Should he wrap her and go get Agatha first or try to get her dry first?

He decided for her sake it was best to get her out of the soppy muddy clothes and into something dry and warm. He took her in the house and laid her on the bear skin rug he had in front of the fireplace. He ran over by his bed and grabbed a blanket. Rapidly he removed the wet clothing and wrapped her in the blanket. He built the fire up, pulled the bear skin rug far enough away that the blanket would not catch fire from any embers that might pop and fly out of the fireplace. He grabbed his pillow and stuffed it under her head and rolled her on her side. Rosa did not make a sound.

Frantz ran to his stable and grabbed his bridle and put it on his horse. He did not take the time to put on the saddle. He raced toward Agatha's house and found her in the kitchen cleaning the breakfast dishes.

"Agatha", he said, "you have to come with me quickly. I don't have time to explain. Please grab whatever you might use to treat pneumonia and say nothing to anyone. I will saddle your horse for you."

She stood there with her hands over her pan dripping dish water for only a couple of seconds as Frantz went back out the door and toward the stable. She knew Frantz well enough to know she needed to do exactly as he had asked. She kept her mind clear as she grabbed a case and put the strap over her head and across her chest. She went to her supply of medicines and salves and began to select bottles of liquid, dried herbs and poultices. She made herself focus on her task and not let her mind wander as to what was going on. At the last minute she grabbed an empty bottle and filled it with honey. She had just sealed it when she heard Frantz coming with her horse.

Agatha ran out the door and Frantz helped her mount then jumped on his horse. They rode hard toward the creek. When they got to his cabin he hopped off of his horse at a run and tied it up to a post at the porch and grabbed her reins and did the same. She had dismounted and they both ran in the house. Agatha saw Rosa lying on the floor, the pile of muddy clothes, the rug pulled out and the roaring fire. She had the strangest sensation that she knew this woman.

She told Frantz, "Go get me some water, soap and clean rags." As he hurried to fetch these, Agatha checked her forehead. It was hot. She put her ear to her chest and listened. She could hear wheezing and thought she heard a rattle also, but was not sure. She would listen again when she turned her over on her stomach.

Frantz came back with a bowl of water, rags and soap. He placed them beside Agatha on the floor. The woman still lay motionless.

"Frantz, we have to get her clean of the mud. There are too many germs that can be in that river mud to leave it on her. Her body does not need to try and fight another thing. This pneumonia is going to take nearly all of her reserves she has left to battle it. We have to bathe her quickly. I want you to wet and then squeeze as much water as you can out of all the rags except one. I am going to use it to soap her and you come right behind me and rinse her with the other ones. Before we start go grab another blanket and one of your clean shirts."

Frantz was all too happy to let Agatha give him instructions. She had nursed her Pa through a bad case of pneumonia last winter. Everyone had been afraid he might not make it, but he did. They bathed Rosa and washed her hair. Agatha said they should leave her by the fire to let it finish drying. She hoped the bathing would help cool her fever a little. She took a salve and rubbed it in on her chest and on her upper back. She then mixed some sort of poultice and did the same. They wrapped some clean rags around her chest then dressed her in Frantz's shirt. Rosa had stirred very little and when she did she was mumbling in a language neither understood but thought it was an Indian dialect.

"Frantz, I am going to go back home and make some chicken soup. While I am gone I want you to keep a cool compress on her forehead. I think it is more important she rest right now than waking her to force anything down her throat. There is no telling how long she had been in that cold water. When I come back if she has not stirred we will wake her."

Frantz realized he had not eaten anything and decided he would have a piece of bread and some salt meat. As he sat at the table watching Rosa sleep he tried to figure out why she was in the river. He wondered if the boat he had seen her on sank upriver and she had somehow managed to make it this far back downriver. If that was the case what had happened to the crew. The reappearance of this beautiful creature in his life was a very puzzling mystery. He silently prayed that he had found her soon enough and that Agatha would be able to save her.

Agatha returned with a crock of soup. She put it in a pot and hung it high over the fire to keep warm. She checked Rosa's forehead and thought she was a bit cooler. She decided to let her rest a while longer.

"Now," Agatha said, "tell me why there is such a big secret tied to this woman being here."

"Agatha, I believe she is a runaway slave."

"Why would you think that?"

"A couple of weeks ago I was at the wharf to get our supplies and she was on one of two keelboats that came in. It was the larger one and was headed up the Missouri to do some fur trading. The pilot had brought in some whiskey for Francois. I stopped by the Inn later and asked him about the pilot and this woman. He did not really know a lot. Only that he met the man in St. Louis and arranged to have him deliver his liquor. Anyway, she was sitting on the front of the boat as it came in. I got a good look at her as the boat was docking. I recognized the look of despair in her eyes that I and the other slaves on the plantation had."

"That's why I felt I knew her when I came in," Agatha said. "Grace and I were at our spot on the river and saw you at the dock. We saw the other boat arrive and then the second one with the woman on the front. I remember it vividly and her stunning hair loose and being blown around in the wind. It glimmered in the sun. Don't worry we will keep this between the two of us for now.

"I will think of something to tell Pa and the help." She sipped on her tea for a little while seeming to be deep in thought. "I have an idea. Since we need to keep everyone away from here I am going to tell them you have contracted something that is contagious. What yet, I don't know. You just keep yourself on the property and watch her. I will be back this afternoon. This is a perfect opportunity to bring the other young man in that is wanting work. It will free you up. I have got a feeling this young lady is not going to be trying to go anywhere for a while. She is going to need you."

"Thank you, Agatha."

Agatha got Frantz to hold Rosa up and she managed to get a little water down her throat followed by some tonic. "If she wakes up give her some broth from the soup even if it is only one spoonful. I will be back before dark. Keep her covered well. She might try to throw it off."

Frantz was not used to sitting and doing nothing for hours, but he did not want to leave his patient for long. He did go back to the river and check to see if there might be anyone else who had made it to shore and needed help. He did not see any signs of anyone else.

Agatha came back with a plate of food for him. Again they managed to get some water and medicine in Rosa. They moved her into the bedroom. Agatha left right afterwards, because it would be dark soon.

Frantz ate and made a bed on the floor using the bear rug again. He brought some fire wood in. He intended to keep some hot coals going to keep a chill off the cabin and the soup warm. He left the lantern on low, so he would be able to check on his patient during the night. He was worried about being able to sleep. He did seem extremely tired and supposed it was the strain of the day and no real physical activity. He lay down, closed his eyes and went to sleep almost immediately.

Frantz was awakened by a wheezing cough. He remembered the circumstances of his being on the floor and the room partially lit. He went to the bed and Rosa was having a coughing spasm. He reached behind her and lifted her up to a sitting position. He put a small wooden bowl in front of her and mimicked coughing and spitting in it, so she would know what it was for. She tried to say something, but could not. The coughing was too intense. Finally a bit of phlegm dislodged and she stopped coughing. He laid her back down. He motioned to her that he wanted her to stay in the bed. He then walked over to the kitchen table and came back and gave her a spoonful of liquid medicine and a drink of water.

She was wide awake and did not take her eyes off of him. Rosa could not believe it. She was looking at the handsome man who stood on the dock in St. Charles. Maybe she was dreaming, but when another fit of coughing started she knew she was not. This one was not so bad. The man came back to the bed with about a half bowl of soup.

Frantz was nervous about trying to get her to eat, but he didn't need to be. As sick as Rosa was she was hungry. The broth was the most delicious thing she had ever tasted. She let him feed her most of the bowl before she turned her head away.

Frantz wrapped his arms around himself and shivered acting as if he were cold. He then pointed at her. She shook her head to indicate no. Frantz took her bowl over to the kitchen and came back with some water. He mimicked taking a drink and pointed at her again. She was enjoying watching this man using his communication skills without actually speaking.

Before she thought Rosa said, "Si, gracias."

She took the water. Frantz's eyes grew large.

He said in English, "You speak Spanish?"

Rosa answered back in English, "Yes, I do." In spite of how she felt, she could not help but smile at the look of surprise on his face. "Please, can you tell me where I am? Is it close to St. Louis? I must go there."

"No, you are in a place called St. Charles. St. Louis is a long day's ride from here in a wagon." Frantz said, "Don't worry about trying to get anywhere now. I found you on the riverbank. You were soaking wet and passed out. I think you have pneumonia and you must rest. You are safe here."

Rosa wished she could believe that. She was so tired. She knew it was only a matter of time when this man like all the rest would want to use her body for payment of his kindness. After all, she had already seen how she affected him that day on the dock. Rosa could not trust anyone. She would stay here until she was better. She could not stay long. It was a small place and word of her being here would travel fast. She would leave for St. Louis as soon as she had her strength back.

Frantz lay down on his rug once she was sleeping again. He was intrigued by this woman who spoke three languages. He wanted to ask her a lot of questions, but knew he had to wait. He finally drifted off to sleep too.

Agatha woke them the next morning. She brought fresh baked bread and butter. She set about making coffee. Frantz reported over his cup that their patient had eaten a little soup and awakened several times with coughing spells. Agatha asked if she was coughing anything up. Frantz told her she was.

"Agatha, our patient not only speaks an Indian language but she also speaks Spanish and English." Like Frantz, her eyes opened wide in surprise.

"That is wonderful." Agatha walked over to the bed to check on her. Rosa was awake.

"Hello, I am Agatha. I must say you look a sight better than when we found you yesterday. Do you feel like eating something this morning?"

"My name is Rosa. Do you have any more soup?" Agatha smiled as she looked over at Frantz.

"Our patient is going to be just fine with some bed rest and continued treatment. Frantz, why don't you go on out back and clean up some. I am going to put some more salve and poultice on Rosa's chest and back. I will call you when I am done."

As Agatha was reapplying the salve and poultice she said, "Rosa, when I first saw you last night I had the feeling that I knew you. After Frantz told me you were on a boat that came through here a couple of weeks ago, I remembered. My friend Grace and I were having a picnic down by the river a little ways from the dock. We saw you coming in on the boat. I noticed your shining black hair blowing in the wind and thought how pretty it was. I hope you don't mind. I brought you one of my sleeping gowns. You really do need to stay in bed and rest."

Rosa would have no trouble staying in bed. She felt as though she could sleep for a week. She watched this woman as she worked to make her well. She decided she liked her very much. Rosa felt Agatha was one to speak what she was thinking most times. She liked that. She had not had anyone to talk with or to her in months. What she heard from Claude other than a few orders was cussing and filthy words. It was not talking. It was refreshing just to hear Agatha's voice and smell her cleanness. Being confined on a boat with sweaty stinking men for months on end, she had forgotten what it was like to just be in a clean environment. When Agatha was done dressing her and straightening the covers she checked Rosa's forehead for fever again.

"You are still running a fever, but not as high as last night. I think it best that we keep you on a light diet of soup today. When you are ready for more just let us know. I must get back to my place and fix dinner for three hungry men."

"Thank you, Agatha."

"You are most welcome, Rosa. Listen, I want you to know that no one else knows you are here. Your reason for landing on Frantz's river bank is yours to keep as long as you want. Neither Frantz nor I will question you. When or if you want to talk is up to you. Rosa, you have nothing to fear from Frantz. I have known him for years. He is a good man and will protect and take care of you. He will not expect you to repay him in any way. Now you rest. I must get back home."

Rosa thought a lot about what Agatha had said. She felt that it was true and hoped with all her heart that it was. Frantz had given her medicine and food throughout the day. Agatha had been back in the late afternoon with smoked ham and vegetables for supper. She knew Frantz could manage frying up some ham and cooking a pot of vegetables which he did. When Rosa smelled the ham cooking her mouth watered. She ate a little piece along with her soup for supper.

Agatha took her time walking back home. She was really curious about Frantz's mystery guest, but would keep it to herself for now. She had a strong feeling that Rosa would be around for quite a while. When Agatha reached the house, Matthew had not questioned her about Frantz other than to ask how he was doing.

After four days of bed rest, Agatha's medicines and Frantz's nursing Rosa was not running any fever and was now out of bed. Frantz had cooked a pot of chicken stew and served it up with Agatha's bread and butter.

After they ate supper, Rosa insisted that she help with the dishes.

They stood at the kitchen work table side by side. Frantz washed and she dried and stacked the dishes.

Rosa said, "This makes me think of the plantation I lived on. Sometimes I would help out in the kitchen."

Frantz only asked, "Did you like living on a plantation?"

Rosa laid her drying rag down for a second, took a deep breath and said, "It was not so bad."

Frantz did not dare ask any more questions. He wanted to badly, but knew it was a lot for her to reveal what she had in these few sentences. He knew there was much more, but would wait for her to tell him. He made them a cup of tea and they drank it in silence.

Rosa got up from the table and said, "Frantz I am feeling much better now. Why don't I sleep on the floor and you take your bed back."

"That is not going to happen Rosa." They went to their beds and both slept well.

Agatha brought her a couple of dresses that she had held on to thinking she might be able to wear them again if she made some adjustments to where they were a tad larger. They fit Rosa perfectly.

Frantz had put a blanket over the bedroom door so she would have some privacy. He had moved his sleeping area into the main room. He was glad he had made an enclosed bedroom now. He had decided not to, but at the last minute changed his mind. His cabin was not large, but it was big enough.

Rosa was now well and filled with energy. Not once had she left the property. She spent a lot of time in the garden. She loved fishing and would catch trout out of the creek. Agatha had taught her how to make bread. Frantz loved it when he came home from working and there was hot food waiting to be put on the table. Frantz had gone back and was helping Agatha a few days a week until the new hand had a grasp on how things were done. He had told Agatha he wanted to concentrate on finishing his place. He was anxious to get his animals bought and settled on the property.

Frantz had completed fencing a portion of the property and had purchased a milk cow, so they had fresh milk and butter now. He and Rosa together had built a covered area for the cow. With Agatha's guidance Rosa and Frantz both were becoming quite adapt in the kitchen.

Nothing else of a personal nature had been said by either of them except Rosa had talked a little about her mother and father and their life in the Comanche tribe. She had not mentioned the boat at all. One late afternoon Rosa had told Frantz she was going to go down to the river before dark and watch the sunset. He was wrapped up in his plans for all his out buildings and fencing for his animals. He was working on an estimated cost for the materials. He got up after a few minutes and walked to the front door. He saw Rosa coming up the hill at a full run. She had a look on her face of sheer terror.

"Rosa what is it?" Frantz asked. She had darted passed him into the cabin. She had turned and was looking out the open door way and pointing toward the river as she backed away. Frantz turned and saw nothing.

Again he asked, "Rosa tell me what is wrong."

"A keelboat is coming down the river. It might be Master. He can't find me. I won't go back with him, I hate him." She had started to cry. Frantz went to her and took her by the upper arms and made her look him in the face.

"Rosa, it is alright now. I will not let him or anyone harm you. Please, don't cry. Are you sure it is the boat you were on?"

"I don't know. It was still a ways up the river. It looked like it, but I am not sure."

Frantz said, "I have an idea. There is a spot we can go to where we can look and not be seen from the river. It's over by the creek. Let's go there now, so we can find out if it is your boat."

They went to the spot on the little creek bluff. There were a lot of trees and bushes in this area. Frantz pointed to a spot and told Rosa they needed to sit down there. They would be able to see the boat, but it would not see them. They sat and waited. It was not long before they had a good side view.

Rosa grabbed Frantz's arm and said, "It is not them. Oh, Frantz, it is not them." She put her head on his chest and clung to him crying tears of relief.

Without any thought at all he held her close and whispered.

"Hush now. Don't cry." He gently eased her away from his chest. While lifting her chin he said, "Rosa, look at me. I don't know what you experienced on that boat or even before then. All I know is that I love you and have since the first day I saw you at the dock. No one and I mean no one will hurt you or take you away as long as you are with me."

Rosa did not say anything. She just looked in his eyes and waited for the kiss she knew was coming. Their need for each other was great as they lay down in the grass together. Afterwards, they just lay in each other's arms not talking. Neither wanted to take a chance of breaking the spell they had just made. They fell asleep.

Frantz opened his eyes to the sound of a small animal crying. Rosa sat up.

"What is that, Frantz?"

"It's a small animal crying and it is very close." Frantz said. They quickly dressed and followed the crying sound to the creek. They found a baby wolf dog near the creek bank in what appeared to be a den made in some exposed roots of a fallen tree. Frantz had crawled under an overhanging rock ledge and pulled it out. He handed a little puff ball to Rosa. She took her apron and pulled it up and around the puppy. She cradled it in her arms as though it were a tiny baby.

She looked up at Frantz and said, "It must be the weak one in the litter and has been left by its mother. We have to try to save it."

"Alright, Rosa. We will try, but do not get your hopes up. This little half dog and half wolf is mighty young. We have no way of knowing how many days it has gone without its mother's milk."

They carried him to the cabin and with much attention from both of them after a few days he began to grow. Frantz had arranged with Agatha to collect a little milk from one of her cows who was nursing. They diluted the milk with water and fed him a few drops at a time. Baby is what they decided to call him. Because he was so little they made a bed for him inside. Still, Frantz caught Rosa quite often with him snuggled up to her while she slept. They both agreed it was very much like having a newborn baby around that had to be fed every few hours. And like a baby the feeding times eventually were farther and farther apart. Soon all were sleeping most of the night.

Rosa and Frantz would sit out on the porch and talk after supper, if the mosquitoes weren't too bad. It was one of those evenings. Rosa had now been with Frantz for about three months. They had been inseparable since the day at the river.

Rosa told him all about when she was taken from her home, the inhumane treatment from the pirates she experienced on the trip to New Orleans and the cruel existence she had lived on the boat with Claude. Frantz could not hide entirely his anger for these men that had hurt her. It showed in his facial expressions and the way he unconsciously squeezed her hand at times as she talked. She also started telling him about the Englishman who had bought her.

Rosa moved her chair over beside Frantz and took his hand.

"Frantz, I was his slave. That was made clear from the first day. My job was only to please him. He told me I did it well."

Frantz interrupted her and said, "Rosa you do not have to tell me this."

"Yes I do. I want you to know all there is to know about me. My love is all yours, Frantz. There will never be another man for me. There is and will always be only you.

"There was no love with the Englishman. He would talk to me about how he felt being away from his home in England. I would tell him the same about me being taken from mine. I was given free rein to the library after very quickly being taught to read and write. He suggested books for me on subjects that interested him. We would sometimes discuss them for hours. He had hired a tutor who taught me the basics of math and a little geography. I would spend my days reading and studying. I wanted to learn all I could. Already I knew my life could change in a moment and I felt knowledge would give me some power.

"At the end of each day I was expected to be dressed and wait for his summons to dinner unless there were guests. If I was not to eat with him a servant would notify me and I would be served in my room except for the times I decided to go down to the kitchen. All of the help would have had supper already, but I always had something to read with me. That was permitted, but I would have to take off my gown and put on clothing worn by the servants. This was in case I was seen by one of the guests that had arrived and no one had thought to notify me.

"I was not happy, but I was not unhappy either. I was just there. I never called him anything but, Sir. He asked me to call him by name, but I wouldn't. He did not force it. I really didn't care to know him too well. I just wanted to stay busy to keep from thinking about being nothing more than a piece of property.

"I told you what happened in New Orleans with that monster Claude. I knew the Englishman was tired of me, because he had almost completely stopped coming to my room. He was spending more time away from the plantation. I didn't care. It gave me free time to spend in the library reading everything I wanted to read that he had not suggested. I am thankful for this man who gave me the gift of reading.

"I really did not think that he would do what he did in New Orleans. I thought before he left he might just put me to work in the house and I would be there always or until I found a way to get back to my people. Truly way down deep I did not see that as an option. But I never dreamed he would rid himself of me in such a callous manner. I have to believe it was because he was drunk."

Rosa told him of the days and nights spent with Claude on the trip up the Mississippi River. She explained how she survived by constantly thinking of ways to escape and the panic she started to feel when they left St. Louis on the Missouri River and she still had not found a way to get away from him.

"I saw you that day you were on the dock. I thought what a beautiful interesting man you seemed to be. I could not do anything but glance at you. Once we were docked I went inside and pretended to be busy. I sat in a place by the window where I could look out and see you clearly. Claude and the crew were busy unloading and I was not disturbed. I remember that my heart jumped when you left. I did not understand why then, but I do now. I dreamed of you almost every night after we left St. Charles. And now the river has brought me to you."

"Frantz, I have told you all about Claude, the Master. He is a snake in the grass. If he finds out I am alive he will stop at nothing to get me back. I know that it won't be too long before he comes back through here. I am afraid when he stops here and goes to the Inn someone might say something and he will know I am here. I am afraid for you Frantz."

Frantz leaned over and kissed her lightly. "Hush, Rosa. I told you not to worry. Can we go to bed now?

Rosa stood up and with a smile on her face pulled him to follow her.

"Come along, my handsome strong man. Come and lie with me. Tell me about the babies we are going to make."

They went to bed.

CHAPTER 12

The next morning Frantz finished his chores and came in the cabin to find Rosa busy in the kitchen.

He poured a cup of coffee and said, "Rosa, can you sit down at the table with me? There's some things I need to tell you."

She poured her a cup and sat down.

"This is going to sound almost too good to be true in some ways, but we are more alike than you realize. I lived on a plantation not too far upriver from New Orleans on the Mississippi. I was born there. Only I was born out of wedlock. My father was the owner of the plantation. My Grandparents were from Africa. They had come from the same village and had been in love when they were captured. They managed to live through the horrors of the trip across the ocean and like you were sold in New Orleans. They were lucky that they went to the same plantation. My mother was born a little over a year after they arrived. My mother's skin was very dark like your father's. She was very beautiful and caught the eye of the young master. He took her when she was still very young. I was born when she was fifteen. I have my father's light eyes and light skin. He loved my mother and his wife knew it. She was cruel to my mother every chance she got.

"When I was eight my father took us to a modest but comfortable house in New Orleans that he owned. He told everyone that I was his orphaned nephew and my mother was disguised as my nanny. He said that he wanted us there in order that I may be properly educated. Of course, the staff knew differently. No one dared say anything, because my father, unlike so many other masters was a kind man.

"Anyway, he had granted my mother and me both our freedom shortly after my birth. She would always ask him where she was supposed to go without him. My father spent a lot of time with us in New Orleans. We were all happy when we were together. I grew up calling my real parents, Mama and Papa. I became an educated young man. Like you I loved learning, but deep down I wanted my own place. Before he died he had arranged with his lawyer to have the house put in my name and have it recorded showing me as his son and heir, not his slave. My mother was heartbroken after he died and did not live but a couple of years afterwards.

"I sold the house immediately and caught a boat to St. Louis. From there I came to St. Charles and found work with the Stone farm. I wanted to learn firsthand about taking care of the land. Because Agatha's parents took me in and treated me like family, I did not get in a hurry to leave them. You know the rest. Only Agatha knows the truth about me. You see I was born a slave too. Even though I am not anyone's property now and was not when I came here it is not a situation one talks about.

"I wanted you to know everything about me as well. Now as to women, I had infatuations with a couple of young ladies in New Orleans, but lost interest within a very short period of time. After coming here there was no one who interested me except for a young Osage woman who left shortly after we met. I think that might have been partly Agatha's fault. She was and will always be like a sister to me, but when I looked around here there was no one to compare to her. Maybe deep down I felt more for her than I would for a sister. I am not sure about that. Whatever it was it was not and would never have been anything close to what I feel for you. Every day I say a thank you to whatever force let you come to my river bank."

He got up from the table and told Rosa he was going into town. He asked her to go with him.

He said, "Rosa, if they don't already it won't be long before everyone is going to know you are here. If nothing else nosey Mrs. Watkins at the General Mercantile will have figured out I have a woman living with me just from the purchases I have made lately. Her wagging tongue has been flapping a plenty, I am sure. I won't you to meet some folks and know where they live. These are my friends. They like us all have their imperfections. But they are my friends and people you can trust if anything should happen to me."

"Frantz, I want to change my dress. It won't take me long." Rosa said.

Frantz replied, "I will get the horses hitched to the wagon. We may as well stop by the Mercantile and let Mrs. Watkins get a good look at what she has been gossiping about."

When Rosa came outside and pulled the front door closed. Frantz looked up. His heart skipped a beat at how beautiful she was. His face mirrored what he was feeling. Rosa walked to him and kissed him.

He took her in his arms. "Rosa I want you as my wife." Frantz said. "I can't ask the preacher to marry us as long as you are the legal property of another man."

"Frantz, if we were with my people the Comanche we would already be husband and wife. In my heart it has been so since that day on the river. I might have asked you to bring my father a horse for my hand at least." she teased him. "It is not required that you give a gift for your wife, but I am worth a horse don't you think? Besides, I am not sure who I legally belong to since Claude paid money for me and the Englishman never gave him a bill of sale. They were both drunk. Claude could think of nothing except getting me bedded."

Frantz pushed her away from him enough that he could see her face and still holding her he said, "Rosa are you sure no bill of sale was given to Claude?"

"Yes, I am certain of it."

"Well, this might change things a little. Rosa, how would you feel if I introduced you as my fiancé?"

"Nothing would make me happier."

"Well, until I can get all this figured out that is what we will tell everyone. Until then, we will keep what we do know to ourselves. Let's go, my wife to be and introduce you to St. Charles."

Neither Rosa nor Frantz had a way of knowing that the Englishman had tried to find the pilot the next morning at the docks and give him a bill of sale he had made and signed. He had asked around for Claude and had been told he had left on his boat hours ago. He had then walked to the edge of the dock, taken the bill of sale out of his pocket, torn it into pieces and tossed it in the river. He had stood there for a few moments watching the torn pieces of paper floating on the water and had whispered, "Goodbye, Rosa." With a deep sigh he had turned and walked away.

They stopped at the Stone place first. Agatha and Matthew had finished milking early. They were now sitting on the front porch enjoying another cup of coffee after just finishing breakfast. While Frantz was telling them the good news, Edmond came home. Agatha introduced them.

Rosa smiled and said, "I am so happy to meet you, Edmond. I have been wondering about the lucky man that captured Agatha's heart." To Agatha's Papa she said, "I have heard so much about you from Frantz. It is so good to meet you at last." Both men could not help being affected by Rosa's beauty. They stood there grinning from ear to ear.

Matthew stepped up to her and said, "Rosa, it does our hearts good to meet the cause of Frantz's recent happiness. Welcome to our family, young lady." He then gave her a big hug. "You know I have been dying to find out what the big secret was at Frantz's place. From the happiness that has been beaming from his face I already knew it had to be a woman. It's a good thing that I am a patient man and knew he or my daughter would tell me in good time or I would have already been over to solve this little mystery." They all had a good laugh.

They did not stay long as he was anxious to get on to the village. Agatha invited them to supper that night. She instructed Frantz to let Grace know she would be expecting her and Alex too.

Next they went to the General Mercantile. Mrs. Watkins greeted them as they came in the door. Frantz had prepared Rosa for her, so after he introduced her as his future wife, Mrs. Watkins mouth puckered up into an ugly frown as her eyebrows shot up to almost her hairline.

Rosa could not help herself. She took Frantz by the hand and led him over to where the fabrics and lace were displayed.

She picked up a piece of red lace and said gaily, "Darling, how do you think this will look with that piece of black shiny material you bought for me in St. Louis? You know that material I showed you that I am making my new sleeping gown out of?" Frantz had told Rosa that Mrs. Wilkins had the hearing of ten dogs and never missed anything anyone said with those ears of hers. It was kind of comical to watch her pretend to be busy and not listening to every single word that was spoken. Frantz knew exactly what Rosa was up to. It took all he could do to keep from laughing.

He cleared his throat and said with this huge grin on his face and in a high volume, "I don't know, Sweetheart but I can hardly wait to see."

Just as Frantz had expected, Mrs. Wilkins piped in right on cue with a big, "Humph!"

Her face puckered up even more if possible and her lips went into what looked like an upside down smile. She turned around like a soldier in formation with both arms stiffly swinging and her nose stuck up in the air.

She marched over to the curtained door leading to the back of the store shouting as she disappeared, "Mr. Wilkins, you need to come up here and take care of these folks. I've got to check on my beans in case they need more water."

Frantz and Rosa burst out into laughter. Mr. Wilkins did come out. Following introductions with a big genuine smile and handshake from him, he wished them much happiness in their new life together. He didn't say anything, but he had been listening and enjoying the conversations. He heard Mrs. Wilkins in that "mad stomp" of hers he called it and quickly moved away from the curtain to avoid a tongue lashing from his wife. It didn't happen too often that she was run to the back of the store. She was too afraid she might miss something. Of course he would hear all about it for a week and pretend each time he didn't know what had happened until something else to gossip about came along.

Their next stop was in front of the Do Duck Inn as the locals fondly called the Canard Inn.

"Wait here just a minute, please Rosa."

Frantz was gone for only a couple of minutes and came out with Francois and Hannah. He helped Rosa down from the wagon.

He folded her arm through his and said, "I would like for you to meet, Rosa. We will be having a wedding ceremony in the very near future at the church."

Francois and Hannah both congratulated them and commented on how well he had kept Rosa a secret.

Frantz admitted that he could not have done it without Agatha's help. He then went on to tell them how they actually met. They chatted on for a few minutes.

Hannah said, "You are a lucky man to find such a treasure on the river, Frantz. Young lady you have picked yourself a fine man to marry. I could not be happier for you, Rosa."

Frantz asked, "Francois, do either of you remember the man that delivered you some whiskey about three months ago? He brought it in on a keelboat. He was the pilot of the boat and went by the name of Claude."

Francois remembered Claude. Hannah thought she did. Frantz explained the situation and asked if he came back through St. Charles would they get word to him somehow. They both agreed to do so.

From there they went to see Grace. She insisted that they stay for dinner. Alex would be home shortly and she was anxious for them to meet. Rosa was amazed at how much Grace reminded her of Agatha even though they looked nothing alike. Rosa would have thought they were sisters, if she had not known differently. When they left shortly after eating, Rosa knew that she had made two new friends. What a wonderful life she had now she thought to herself. She snuggled even closer to Frantz, wrapped her arm through his and sighed deeply.

On the ride home, Rosa was quiet. She wondered why she had been so anxious about meeting these people. Of course, she knew she had been terrified that Claude would find her. But that was not the only reason. Some people did not take kindly to an Indian woman marrying a white man and she knew it. Mrs. Wilkins was proof of that, but other than her everyone else was genuinely happy for them. She knew there would be others that thought the same way Mrs. Wilkins did, but she didn't think there would be that many. If there were, most of them would keep it amongst themselves. That was because of Frantz. He was educated and a land owner with his own working farm and had gained respect among the people who knew him.

Rosa knew he would keep their respect as long as they thought Frantz was all white. She could imagine what they would think if they knew both were slaves. They would try to take the land and could do so, according to the Missouri slave laws Frantz had told her about. It did not matter that he had been legally given his freedom long before he purchased the land. There would be some who would turn against him immediately.

Why couldn't people just take the time to look at each other in the eye, no matter the color of the skin and know that we are all human beings trying to find our way? What drove people to be so cruel to one another? She knew the ship that captured her was obviously after the money that would come with the selling of the captured people on board. But what about the raping of the women while they were being transported to New Orleans and the inhuman conditions they were forced to endure while on the ship. Were there truly evil spirits that lived in some people and they had no way to choose goodness? She felt strongly that was the case with Claude. You could see it in his eyes. The few times she had looked at him eye to eye her skin had crawled and she had to look away quickly. She understood mean spirited people. She had seen a couple of them growing up amongst her tribe.

Rosa did not think Mrs. Wilkins was mean spirited in all her ways. Frantz had told her how she would sometimes put extra food in the bags of a few of the extremely poor customers that came in the mercantile. If any of them came back to let her know she had made a mistake, she would just tell them quite firmly that she did not make mistakes and walk to the back of the mercantile leaving the customer standing there scratching their head. Something or someone had taught her along her way to look at others with disdain if their skin was not white.

That evening they returned to Agatha's for supper.

As they were all seated Frantz said, "Rosa and I have decided that it is best to share with you her history. Agatha already knows most of it."

After he had told them about finding her on the river bank near death, he explained her captivity and the sale of her to the Englishman. He told of how this man had then used her as an ante in a poker game and lost the hand, the lack of any record of this transfer of ownership to the pilot and that he had gone back to England with plans to never return to the plantation.

Frantz said, "The cruelty that Rosa experienced from this river pilot, Claude will not happen again. I do intend to marry Rosa through the church even though we are already man and wife in the eyes or our Creator and the Comanche way. We believe Claude will be stopping here on his return trip from the upper Missouri. That could be any day now. It is very likely that he will discover Rosa is here. At that time, I will deal with him. We just ask that all of you keep an eye out. If you see or hear that he is back, let us know if you can."

The next day Frantz left early for some business in town. Baby had followed Rosa out to the garden and was watching her pick some beans when his ears perked up.

"What is it Baby?" she asked. Rosa looked toward the path from the creek and saw Frantz riding back with another saddled horse following. He came up to the edge of the garden.

Rosa walked up to the horse and rubbed his neck. She said, "What a beautiful animal. Where did you find him? Where is his rider?"

"I didn't find him, Rosa. I bought him. He is yours. I cannot give your father a horse as a gift for you, but I can give a horse to you as a promise of my love."

Rosa mounted the horse. When she looked down at Frantz there were tears in her eyes.

She said, "I will call this horse, Promise. Now come and ride with me, my husband."

It had been a couple of weeks since their trip to town to introduce Rosa to everyone. Frantz wanted to go hunting for some fresh meat. The next morning he fed the animals and milked the cow while Rosa made breakfast and gathered what they needed from the house for their overnight stay.

Rosa had made herself a tunic along with some leggings from the deer skins Frantz had killed in the weeks passed. She also had made some new moccasins. She had dressed in them today and had braided her hair. Frantz had told her time and again how much he loved seeing her in her native dress. Rosa wore it when they worked outside together or when they were going to be in the woods for a while.

She helped Frantz pack the horses and they headed them toward the forest. Baby started to follow them with her tail wagging while running and jumping along in excitement, but was learning she could not go all the time. Rosa told her to go back home several times. Rosa and Frantz both stopped and waited for her to start back to the cabin. She finally turned and went back toward the barn with a pouty look on her face and her head and tail hanging down. They could not help but laugh at her when she stopped, looked back at them and barked once, as if making sure they understood how displeased she was with their decision to leave her.

They rode their horses up to the north end of the property and crossed into the unclaimed land. Frantz had made arrangements with one of Agatha's hands to milk and feed the animals the next morning. They set up camp by a small stream. Rosa busied herself unpacking the items needed for cooking while Frantz put up a tent. They had a bite to eat and then went to see what they might find.

They found a spot where the animals came to water at the stream and the trail through the brush that they took to get to it. They eased back away from it and waited in a spot down wind. It wasn't long before they spotted a buck headed for a drink of water. Rosa motioned to Frantz that she wanted this shot. She took an arrow from her quiver, loaded her bow and released. It found its target and the buck fell instantly dead. She had been taught by her father how to make bows and arrows. He had also taught her how to hunt with them beginning when she was young.

As they both worked to skin, clean and cut the meat up they noticed storm clouds were starting to gather. Both agreed that they were probably going to get wet and decided rather than take a chance of being cramped in their tent for several hours while it rained, they would rather pack up and go back home. They had just finished loading the last of their camping gear and the meat when the lightning and thunder started. They were no more than three hours from the cabin.

The rain started a few minutes into their ride. They did not try to talk through it, but concentrated on getting back home as quickly as possible. When they were close to the cabin, they could hear Baby barking through the rain. Both of them pulled in their horses and listened.

"Something is wrong Frantz. She is upset."

"I know. Let's tie our horses here. I am going to go and see what's going on. I want you to stay here until I come back." He grabbed his gun and disappeared in the woods.

Frantz eased up behind the barn. He peered through a knot hole and could not see anything. He eased inside and worked his way to the front of the barn. He could see the back and one side of the cabin now as he peeked around the side of the partially opened barn door. He had left it shut. Baby was at the corner of the house steadily barking. Suddenly a man stepped off the side of the front porch carrying a gun and started walking toward the back of the cabin. Frantz knew it was Claude from the description Rosa had given him. He watched as

Claude went to the back door of the cabin and started to enter. The rain had almost stopped completely.

Frantz stepped out of the barn and started walking toward the cabin with his gun aimed at Claude.

"Hold it right there, Mister. I would advise you not to go through that door. Get your hands in the air after you have very slowly laid that gun down on the porch. Hush Baby, it's all right now."

Baby hushed.

Claude put the gun down and slowly turned around.

"I have come for my property. I understand that you have been keeping a woman called Rosa who belongs to me. Where is she?"

Frantz did not lower his gun. "Let me see your document showing ownership."

Claude said, "I don't have to show you anything. You have my property and I want it back."

Neither one had seen Rosa coming up toward the back of the cabin.

"You are a cruel and mean spirited man, Claude. I will never go with you anywhere again. Never. This is my home now." She had her bow pulled taught and an arrow aimed at Claude. He knew she wouldn't miss.

"Well, hello Winch." Claude sneered. "I didn't think you had drowned. We searched for you along the river bank for two whole days. It was no surprise at all to me when I heard you were playing house with this here feller. I even heard talk that you two were getting married. Well that's not going to be happening. You are mine. Play time is over and it's time to get back to the boat. You are my property and you know it."

"Like the man said, show me the papers. You and I know the Englishman never returned with a bill of sale before we left the dock in New Orleans. As far as I am concerned you are just a man who had some good luck at the poker table that turned bad when you lost some of your winnings."

Frantz said, "I suggest you leave now and if you know what is good for you, you won't be back. This is private property and if I see you on it again, I will kill you. I will leave your gun at the Inn in the morning for Francois to hold until you are ready to leave St. Charles." Claude started walking in the direction of the creek.

He walked past Frantz and said, "You keep the winch. She is nothing but a filthy Indian squaw anyway. He stopped and was slowly turning as he said, "I would like to know how she got here."

Frantz had glanced over at Rosa and did not see the slight change in Claude's stride as he was reaching for the knife he had hidden under his shirtsleeve and beginning to turn. Rosa did.

She shouted, "Frantz, look out." She released the arrow and Claude released the knife.

Frantz fired while diving sideways to the ground a second after Claude released the knife. He had managed to move his body just enough. The knife hit him in his arm during the fall. Claude was not so fortunate. Frantz had hit him in the face.

Rosa ran to Frantz who was pulling the knife out. He was bleeding profusely. She told him to hold it tightly and ran in the cabin and grabbed some rags she had for bandages. She came back out and tied a strip of leather above the wound for a tourniquet. She then put the rest over the wound and told Frantz to press. She helped him inside and cleaned it as best she could. Rosa stitched it up, applied some salve and bandaged it. She watched Frantz and checked his arm to make sure the bleeding had almost stopped. When she was satisfied with her work, she made him get in the bed with instructions not to move until she returned with help.

Rosa went and retrieved their horses. She tied Frantz's in the barn with the deer meat still packed on its back. She took the camping gear off of Promise and rode to Agatha's as fast as she dared. Agatha sent the farm hand to the fort and rode back on Promise with Rosa.

Edmond and Alex appeared with three other soldiers shortly after Rosa returned to the cabin. They told them not to worry. It was obvious what had happened and they would relay the events to the proper authority. They took Claude's body with them and left. It was dark when they headed back to the Post.

Rosa went out to the barn and unloaded the meat. She took it to the back yard and with a couple of lanterns worked into the night cutting it into strips and placing it over the smoking fire she had made. She was constantly going to check on Frantz who had fallen into a deep sleep after she had made him a strong drink of herbs, roots and tree bark. As she worked she realized that she was truly free now. They would no longer have to fear anyone or anything coming between them again. She knew if by some weird chance she and the Englishman were ever to meet again he would not create any problems for her. Rosa began to sing a song her mother had taught her as a child.

A few days later Francois came riding up to the cabin. Frantz was sitting on the porch watching Rosa work in the garden.

While he was tying his horse to the railing he said, "Morning Rosa. Good to see you are up and about, Frantz. Heard you had a bleeding good time of it."

"Well, what a pleasant surprise," Frantz said. "This is the first time you have been out to the place." Francois walked up on the porch and took a chair.

"It looks to me like you have found yourself a little piece of heaven in more ways than one, my friend. I am mighty happy for you and Rosa, Frantz. I have wanted to come out since I first heard what happened, but wanted to wait until you were out of danger from that bleeding to start back up. I feel like this whole mess is partly my fault. If I had been at the Inn instead of in St. Louis you two would not have been caught by surprise. Hannah was so busy when his boat came in she didn't know which end was up. There were four or five trappers drinking along with Claude's crew and another flat boat crew that had delivered a family with their wagon, animals and belongings from Ohio. Once they had them safely unloaded they advanced on Hannah. It was just too busy for her to pick up on or hear that Claude's boat was one of them that had come in. She feels mighty poorly about it. She had to pull the stable boy in to help serve drinks and food."

"Well, Francois you tell Hannah not to fret. Truth is having to kill a man is never a good thing. But when it comes to protecting your family and loved ones it can happen. Claude was a real cruel and evil man. The demons living in him had been there a long time I'm thinking. He would never have left Rosa here with me whether you had been there to recognize him or not. Even if you or Hannah had stopped him from coming out that day, he would probably have appeared to leave and only tied his boat up downstream a short distance and come back in the night.

The situation we found ourselves in could not have ended without someone dying. Claude saw to that even though we tried to avoid it. I am just grateful Rosa was not hurt and I am going to be around to take care of her. It could have ended a lot worse. When you put it in perspective, I guess it could not have ended in a better way even though there should have been one."

The two men set there in silence for a while. Each one deep in their own thoughts.

Francois spoke up and said, "I guess you two will be calling on the preacher soon. I hope we can plan a big shindig for you afterwards. You know we would close the Inn down. Hannah would get a real thrill out of decorating and feeding everyone. On a purely selfish note, it would help her feel like she was making up for not getting a warning to you. She has been downright cantankerous and hard to be around since this happened. You would be doing me a great big favor."

Frantz smiled and said, "Well I will talk to Rosa and see if we can't get Hannah's mind on something else and give you some relief."

Rosa walked up on the porch with a basket of vegetables she had picked from the garden. "Hello, Francois."

"Hello, Rosa. I just came to explain that I was out of town and why no one came to warn you. I can't tell you how sorry I am about what happened."

"Now that I know Frantz will be alright I'm not sorry, but thank you."

Francois left shortly afterwards. On the ride back to town he thought about how lucky Frantz and Rosa were. He wished with all his heart that he could get Hannah to marry him, but so far she had refused. She kept saying she did not want to be put in the position she was in when he met her. It had taken a year or longer after they met before she told him all of what had happened to her.

He would never forget that night over ten years ago when he first met Hannah. He had just completed a verbal agreement to purchase an Inn in Philadelphia that morning. It was close to nine o'clock in the evening when he had finished dinner and rode over to the Inn. He had planned to arrive around this time. He wanted to see what type of customers were around and how many. He had been told that there were a lot of businessmen among others, but he wanted to see for himself. Supposedly the owner had been getting up in years and was ready to rest some.

When he arrived he did not tie his horse to the hitching rail out front, but decided to take him to the stable and see how it was situated. The stable was a part of the business also and located in the back of the Inn. Francois walked toward the back between the Inn and the building next door. It was dark and he thought one of the first things he would do was light it up. The alley was about fifteen feet across. He figured that was more than enough space to get horses, wagons and carriages between the two buildings and to the stables.

He could hear the piano playing and some of the more inebriated customers loudly vocalizing their thoughts above the general den of the crowd. As he neared the back of the building he could barely hear the noise. He had cleared the alleyway and could see a light coming from the stable located ahead and off to the right. To his left he heard the voice of a woman nearby. It sounded like she might be crying, because there was an awful lot of sniffling going on in between the words. As he drew nearer he focused on what she was saying until he could hear her clearly speaking with what he thought must be a Scotch or Irish accent.

"You stupid, stupid, stupid idiot. What's wrong with you? Did you honestly think you were going to hop up on that bed and spread your legs for that greasy, stinking no account varmint and then grin at him while he bounced up and down on top of you? All that just so he would give you a silver dollar. You should have shot him. No, what you should have done was gone back to the plantation. At least it would have been the same stinking, uninvited and unwanted varmint crawling in your bed at night. You wouldn't get rich, but there was food to eat. So what if you worked your fingers to the bone. So what!!!! Now what are you going to do? You have spent the last of your money on this ridiculous dress, shoes, fan and hair pins so you could look pretty, attract men and sell yourself until you figured out what to do next. You can't do it and now you have gone and got yourself fired from even serving drinks. This is a fine kettle of fish you got yourself into Hannah Morgan."

Francois could not hear who she was talking to, because the woman had started sobbing hysterically. When his eyes finally adjusted to the dark corner where she was sitting on the ground he did not see anyone else. She did not see him, because she had her head bent down and her hands over her face while she wept uncontrollably. He took his handkerchief out and holding his arm straight out with the handkerchief held and hanging from his thumb and index finger he advanced toward her.

"Mam," he said, "Mam, please don't shoot me." He said in case she really did have a gun. Here's my clean handkerchief I would like to offer you. I didn't mean to interrupt your conversation. I was just on the way to the stable to board my horse."

The woman stopped crying, looked up at Francois and said, "What conversation?"

He really didn't know what to say to her as he continued to stand there with his arm still sticking stiffly out and the handkerchief hanging, but he said, "Well, I couldn't help hearing you talking to another person after I came down the alley."

"I was not talking to another person," she said sniffling and somewhat haughtily. "I was talking to myself. I always do that, especially when I am upset." She reached out, snatched the handkerchief out of his two fingers and loudly blew her nose.

"Well, Ms. Hannah Morgan, if you don't mind my saying so, it sounds like you have found yourself in a bad situation." Francois found a lantern hanging on a nail and lit it.

"How do you know my name?" she suspiciously asked looking at him with some trepidation showing on her face. Before he could answer she added, "Don't you be getting any funny ideas running around in that big head of yours, Mister."

Francois could not help but grin a little bit at this attractive and vivacious woman as he replied, "I overheard your name when you were chastising yourself."

"Oh," Hannah said as she handed him his handkerchief back after another loud blow. Francois carefully stuffed it back in his pocket.

"My name is Francois and I have just purchased this place. Well, I will officially be in ownership tomorrow that is. Since it appears that you are in need of a job, what about working for me?" Hannah's mouth opened wide, but before she could flare up he held out his hand, palm up and said, "Before you say no, just hear me out. I need someone that is willing to work and help me get this place in shape. I won't know exactly what you will be doing, but I do know what you won't be doing and that is having some fellow bouncing up and down on top of you including me.

"Don't misunderstand me, please. You are a very attractive woman, but tying myself to one right now is not a part of my plan. This place is going to need a lot of work to bring in the type of clientele I intend to have. Ladies of the night will need to seek employment elsewhere. I will expect you to work and work hard. If you get to know me, you will learn early on that I am a businessman and a gentleman. I will pay you a fare wage and if you or I are not satisfied after a month has passed we can part company." Hannah sat there with her mouth still hanging open.

"What do you say to me escorting you back to my hotel and getting you a separate room to stay in as a part of your wages until you can find quarters more to your liking? Shall we shake on it?"

Francois stuck out his hand. Hannah closed her mouth reached up and barely touched his hand looking as though she could not believe what was happening.

After he settled her into a room, he left the hotel and returned to the Inn. He stayed until the owner had quickly shown him what few things about the place that would not be apparent to a new owner all the while explaining that any other questions he might have could easily be handled by the help.

The next morning Francois took Hannah to breakfast. He placed some money on the table by her plate.

"Ms. Morgan, I would like for you to spend your first morning shopping for some appropriate clothing to work in. Please purchase dresses that are similar to what most women call their 'Sunday best'. The lady of the night attire you are wearing now certainly will not be needed."

As soon as he saw the look on her face that said she would like to kill him, he regretted saying the lady of the night part. Afterwards, they both sat in silence while Francois was finishing his coffee and while Hannah ate. She did not make any indications that she would take the money. It continued to lie on the table where he had placed it.

Francois said, "Look Ms. Morgan, you are going to earn every bit of that money. Your position will be to assist me where and when you are needed most. For example, I may send you to the bank, to the market or to pay a vendor. You will be overseeing the cook, maid, buying and selling of household supplies and Lord only knows what else I will need you to help me with. We can announce your position as my personal assistant. Now I know some eyebrows will be lifted, but your position will demand respect from the other employees. As far as what the other fellow is really thinking I have always felt it is really his business as long as he keeps it there and doesn't interfere in mine. You can read, write and do arithmetic, can't you?"

"Yes, I most certainly can!" Hannah said.

"That's good. That will be a tremendous help. It is important to me for the business to promote an air of professionalism at all times. This will be a place where gentlemen can come and have some drinks and food without worrying about some drunk bloke starting a fight night after night. I am not saying there won't be an occasional fracas, but I aim to keep them at a minimum. This money for clothing you can consider as an advanced bonus at the end of the month, if things work out. If after a month you decide not to stay and work for me, keep the money. Consider it a loan if your pride prevents you from taking a gift."

Hannah's eyebrows rose a little, but she picked up the money and put it in her purse pulling the draw string handle tight. She still had not said more than a dozen words since last night. Francois knew she was trying to determine if she could really trust him. He had purposefully given her a lot more money than she would need to purchase several dresses, hats, shoes and under garments. He had done this just in case she decided to take the money and run. He knew the woman needed a break even if she did not stay and work for him. He hoped she would. Francois thought she would be a valuable asset if she stayed. He didn't really know why. There was just something about her.

Francois finished his breakfast and got up from the table.

"Come to the Inn after you have shopped and had some lunch. We will get you started. Oh, make sure you get some big aprons. We might both be starting out cleaning and cooking if all the help left with the previous owner. Don't worry. Cleaning will not be your job as long as we have help."

Hannah looked up at him and said, "Thank you."

Francois didn't know whether she was thanking him for the job, the money or both. He left Hannah sitting at the table with a look of uncertainty on her face still.

Francois went by his attorney's office, the bank and from there straight toward the Inn to formalize the purchase with the remainder of the money he owed. When he arrived to his consternation he saw nothing had been cleaned from the night before. The place was a disaster. There were tables filled with dirty glasses and empty bottles. Some had been so cluttered they had slid off the table and still lay on the floor. A few glasses were broken. There were even dirty plates where food had been served on some of the tables. The seller told him the help had celebrated the selling of the business with him and would be slow arriving today. The ones that should have arrived by now were the cook, cleaning lady and the stable boy.

After the seller had completed the signing of the papers, he shook Francois' hand, wished him success and walked out the door with a pouch full of money whistling a lively tune.

Now as Francois stood looking around at the mess he saw in every direction, he wished he had not told Hannah to spend the whole morning shopping. He was standing behind the bar with a broom in one hand and scratching his head with the other while he silently cussed the workers he had never met. He had not had the nerve to check out the condition of the kitchen yet, but decided he may as well get it over with. He was headed in that direction with the broom still in his hand when he heard footsteps. Francois turned around and there stood Hannah a few steps inside the door holding several packages wearing what was obviously some old very ragged, but clean clothes.

"I hope you don't mind my dropping by here before starting on my way to do the clothes shopping. Instead I decided to take the liberty of picking up some food from the market. I thought I might just check to see if there were some things that needed doing before we could open the doors for customers." Hannah stopped and looked around at all the mess.

"Oh, dear me." She said. "Looks to me like I made the right decision. You appear to be a man who likes things clean, neat and tidy. Well, I do too. Why don't we start with me in the kitchen and you out here in case we have some morning drinkers come in? You might want to think about hiring new people. Seems to me like workers who drink so much they can't or won't show up for work the next morning can hardly be considered an asset to the business. There surely are some people out there who would be glad to have a job and appreciate it. I will fix up a sign and put it in the window as soon as I have some food going. That should bring us some kind of help for tomorrow if not before." By this time she had made it across the room and was standing in front of him. She stuck the packages in his arms and walked back to one of the tables with the dirty plates and started back to the kitchen with a stack.

"Sir," she said as she stepped around him and walked into the kitchen, "please don't just stand there. Put those on that cook table and try to see if you can find something you can use to bring more this way while I get some clean glasses washed up. The sooner you get the tables cleaned the sooner you can start pushing that broom you was holding while I get some food cooked." She then turned, looked at him and added, "Sir."

Francois had followed her and was standing in front of her. He said, "Hannah, thank you for having the good sense to come here first."

She reached out, grabbed his hand and gave it a firm shake.

"You've got you month, Sir. From now on you will call me Hannah."

Without waiting for a response she grabbed a water bucket and headed out back in search of a well or spring. This time Francois was the one left with his mouth hanging open. He walked out of the kitchen and picked up the broom again, forgetting what she had said about finding something to put dirty dishes in and started sweeping. It wasn't long before he heard dishes begin to rattle and pots and pans banging. This big grin slowly spread across his face. He started whistling a tune as he began sweeping up broken glass off the floor. It wasn't any time before he was heading toward the noise in the kitchen with a load of dirty dishes.

Francois and Hannah made an excellent team and within a year the hard work was paying off. Both were making more money than ever before. Francois was so pleased with Hannah that he offered her ownership in a portion of the business. They agreed on an amount and made an arrangement where she would pay for it in installments deducted from her share of the earnings. Hannah could not believe how much her life had changed since she had left the plantation barely over a year earlier. She shuddered to think what might have happened to her, if Francois had not found her.

After one particularly busy night when the customers and help were all gone, Hannah asked, "Would you like to buy your partner a drink?" It was a rare occasion when either of them drank.

He poured them both a drink and brought a bottle that was half full over to the table. They each finished their drink pretty much in silence. Without asking if Hannah wanted another Francois poured them both another. He knew her well enough to know there was something on her mind she wanted to talk to him about, but had no idea what it was about.

He had not acted upon it, but Francois had fallen hopelessly in love with Hannah and had known from the beginning that she would withdraw from him if he pursued her. It had been more difficult than he thought, but he had kept his feelings hidden and enjoyed the friendship that had developed between them. After exchanging small talk for a few minutes Hannah quit slowly turning her glass around in her hands and looked at Francois.

"You know, I never have told you how much it means to me that you took me out of that alley that night. That was the second time that I have been totally without money and nowhere to go. Would you like to hear about the first time?"

"Yes, Hannah. I would like that very much.

"Well, Francois, as you already know I was born in Scotland. My family was considered to be poor. There were seven kids. I was the fourth born or middle child. We would all have been without a home most likely if it had not been for my three older brothers leaving our village and going to work in one of the linen mills. They managed to get money back to us every few weeks.

"Our village had a school which I was able to attend. I wanted to go on to university, but there was just no way. So, when I accepted that it was not going to happen, I left and joined my three brothers in Aberdeen and started working in the linen mill. I hated it from the first day.

"The mill owner was having trouble keeping workers. In order to do so he built some of the better workers with family housing. He had built a house for my oldest brother and his family to keep him and the two younger brothers working. An additional room was added for the two younger ones. As there was nowhere for me to sleep in the main part of the house, my brothers partitioned off a tiny area with a small bed in one corner for me. We were used to being crowded, so after their meager furnishings had been rearranged it worked.

"Try as I might, but there was no liking to be found anywhere in me for this work. After two years of it I just couldn't force myself to keep doing it. I hugged all three of my brothers, kissed them goodbye and turned my sites on London.

"I had heard one of the girls talking about her brother who was there. He had mailed her to join him saying he felt certain she could find work with one of the rich London families. That was all I needed to hear. I knew I could clean and scrub anything if that was what it took to get me out of the noise, dust and drudgery of that mill. My plans were to do just that until I found something else.

"Well, as it turned out I was just one of hundreds of women who were looking for the same work. I was out of money and about ready to head back to Aberdeen when I was able to secure a position. I thought how fortunate I was and eagerly scrubbed, rubbed and polished my way through the first couple of weeks. The work was exhausting, but it was better than the mill. The food was good and I did have a tiny private room on the third floor. At least I thought it was private until the owner used a key while I was sleeping and came in. I don't have to tell you the details of what followed I am sure. I know the woman who was in charge of the staff along with some of the other women who worked there had heard my screams during the night. Yet, no one came to my aid. The hopelessness and helplessness I felt afterwards was so great it felt as though I was forcing myself through mud the next day just to get through it. As awful as it was, I still did not want to go back to the mills. I made myself function day after day, but found no enjoyment of life in anything. It seemed that life was sucking itself right out of me and I was beginning to give up finding a way to live in the world.

"Again I had heard other workers talking about how critical the situation for locating work had become. They said we were fortunate to have any kind of position and better do everything necessary to hang on to it. They did not look at me when they said this, but might as well have.

"On my Sunday afternoons off I would usually go to the park just to get out of that house. A couple of times I heard some of the women talking about how many people had managed to secure passage to Canada, Australia and the United States. I even heard that some of them were making arrangements to travel on a ship and pay after they arrived by working it off. Leaving the continent for another frightened me.

"Once more I was working in a place I literally hated. I had stopped fighting the man. He was too strong for me. Each night I dreaded going to my bed and even more going to sleep. I never knew when he was coming. Because I was so tired all the time it was becoming more and more difficult to get through the days. I began to lose weight. I ate to keep going, because I had not given up hope entirely. One day I realized I had to find a way to be one of those people who left. I would find a ship.

"I was only given Sunday afternoons off. When my next one came, I spent the whole afternoon at the docks. It was risky I knew, but I had to find a ship that would take me to America. It was a new land and there just had to be a place for me. I went to the docks five Sundays in a row searching for someone who would take me. I finally found one that would take me as a single woman and with no portion of the fare collected before departure. It was going to Boston and the captain told me there was a family that was looking for a single educated woman and would pay my fare when we arrived. I didn't volunteer the information that I had never gone to university. I suppose it was my proper English that convinced him to take me. In return for my fare I would agree to work for this family for four years as their indentured servant. At the end of that time I would be released to go and do as I wished. The captain said the ship would be leaving in three days which would be Wednesday morning. I made arrangements with him to board the night before. The timing could not have been better for me. We were getting our monthly wages on Tuesday morning.

"It took all I could do to keep from running through the rooms of that house shouting for joy those two days. I managed with much concentration to keep my sad and despondent look about me, but it wasn't easy. I sent a post off to my family telling them of my plans on Monday. I packed my valise on Tuesday and hid it near the back door. I planned to leave that night after dinner.

"One of my duties was to serve supper at night. After everyone had finished their pumpkin soup, salad and then the main course I was dipping the desserts to be served. No one was talking. In the silence came a low rumbling and growling sound from the head of the table. The rapist owner had a look on his face of confusion and then disbelief. He knocked over his chair as he quickly stood up with his face all scrunched up, his eyes bulging and his cheeks puffed like that was going to help him somehow. He turned toward the dining room door and started walking. He was trying to run really and moving in

149

a most peculiar way. His body was tilted backwards, with his knees bent more than necessary. He would lift his knee up high as though he were stepping over something and take two or three quick steps and then pause with one or the other foot hanging rather high in the air before continuing on. His butte cheeks appeared to be squeezed together so tight that they might disappear entirely. For the first time in weeks I smiled. No one saw me as they were all watching him in absolute amazement wondering what on earth was going on. I knew the excessive amount of turmeric and the two spoons full of castor oil I had managed to get into his soup was already working and would be for the entire night. It was funny really how he had babbled on about how good the soup was that evening and all the while me worried that he might detect a strange flavor and not eat it."

Francois could not help it. He had just taken a sip of his drink and spewed it all across the table as he bellowed out in laughter. They both wound up laughing and crying tears of hysteria. This time they shared his handkerchief.

As Hannah dried her face she said, "After he was out of the room we could hear him as he made a stomping mad dash for the chamber pot upstairs. It sounded like a herd of horses had entered the house."

They both started laughing again. "I finished serving dessert and walked to the kitchen when I really wanted to run. I did not stop but kept going and retrieved my valise. When I stepped out the front door of that house, I did run and didn't stop for two blocks until I reached the waiting coach I had hired to take me to the dock. I wanted to take no chances of not arriving safely to the ship. The driver must have assumed I was in a hurry, because he put the horses at a fast pace as we raced toward my freedom. I didn't care how fast he went. I looked down as I grasped the edge of the seat for balance and realized I still had my apron on. I untied it and threw it flying out the window. I won't ever forget that feeling as

I looked out and saw it hit the street. It seemed as though I had taken a noose from around my neck and had thrown it out instead. I changed into my one of my two dresses and stuffed the uniform in my valise.

"On the trip across the Atlantic I realized that I was still not completely free in that I could not pick nor choose who I worked for. I was legally bound to this plantation owner until our agreement had ended and my debt was paid in full or at least that is what I thought. I found out later that was not entirely true.

"It turns out Indenture Contracts could be bought and sold or exchanged for goods. In other words, I could be sold to someone else or simply used as a trade. My contract terms however, would not change.

"There were rules that could affect the contract length of time if broken. As a female indentured servant, if I became pregnant additional years could have been added to my service time. Man nor woman was allowed to vote, marry, leave or travel without permission. In addition we could not buy or sell anything.

"Once we landed in Philadelphia and I left the ship there was a man waiting for me. He had been hired to escort me to my new home. I and my belongings were loaded in his carriage and we were on our way. It seemed as though we would never get to the end of the trip as we rode for hours through dense forests. Occasionally we would pass through a small settlement. Finally at long last we made a turn off the road through a field. The driver told me we were on the plantation. We rode mile after mile through tobacco fields, past swampy areas and then more fields as far as one could see. It still took a good portion of the afternoon to cross the plantation land before we reached the main house.

"I was actually content on the plantation. The owners were kind to me. I knew what was expected of me each day. I was hired to assist the governess with the care of the children. That I knew how to do well. The owner was quite a bit older than his wife. He had remarried when his first wife had died. The governess told me he had an older son who was away studying at a university in England.

"After two years had passed I met Mark who lived on a small farm by the plantation. It turns out that he had been an indentured servant for this same family. When his contract had been completed he was given a few acres of land. You see, some of the contracts had what was called "freedom dues" that were paid at the end. They could be paid in land, a gun, money, food or clothes. He had received land. He stayed and worked a couple more years for wages and soon had enough to get the basic necessities needed to live on his own land. Because he was a man of many skills he was often called to the plantation for various little jobs. We became fast friends and before knowing what was happening we were in love. He had managed to build a little one room cabin on his land. All I could think about was the day I would have my freedom and could live out the rest of my life with him.

"I was finally in the last year of the contract and had started counting the days. One morning when I awoke and went downstairs for breakfast as I neared the kitchen I could tell something had happed from all the unusual chatter I was hearing. It turns out that the son had returned from England.

"That very day I met him in an upstairs hall way. He grabbed me by the wrist and said, 'Well, just look at the welcoming home present dearest old Papa has bought for me to play with.' I jerked my arm free of his grasp. He just laughed a cruel laugh and I knew my release from him was temporary. My days of total happiness were to leave me sooner than I thought. He was in my room that very night. I did not dare say anything. He told me if I did he would swear that he caught me off the plantation going to meet Mark. Obviously he had been asking the staff about me. I never left the plantation except with explicit permission. I did not want to do anything that might extend my time. I kept my mouth shut and tolerated it.

"Mark knew something was wrong immediately. When he found out the son was back he knew what had happened. It took all I could do to keep him from confronting him. I convince him that we could get through. There was less than a month to go now and I would be free. Mark said he was evil through and through. Before he left for England he would use the slave girls and then beat them and threaten to do more if they told his Papa or the Mistress. Everyone was afraid of him. His Papa seemed to have a blind eye when it came to this son of his.

"One day when Mark came to do some repairs I tried desperately to avoid him. I had a black eye and did not want him to see it. He found me and when he saw it he knew where it came from even though I made up an excuse. He went looking for him. He found him and was punched in the face. Mark screamed at him that he better not lay another hand on me. The son came at him and Mark didn't hit him, but sidestepped him and pushed really hard. He lost his balance and his head landed on the corner of a stone step. He was killed instantly. There were witnesses, but the chance of the truth not being accepted was too great.

"Mark fled to Philadelphia. He gave me the name and location of a person to contact there when I arrived who would know where he was. It was his friend who had come over on the boat with him. The day my contract ended I left for Philadelphia. When I arrived his friend told me he had not seen Mark since they were at the plantation together. I searched for him for weeks and had very little of the money left. Finally one day I found out he had been the victim of a yellow fever outbreak in a nearby town. I was devastated. I laid in bed for a week before I finally got up. The ugliness in my life had finally won. Something had broken inside of me and it wasn't just my heart.

"I took the last of the money and bought those horrid clothes you found me in. I know you gave me too much money for just a wardrobe that morning. I thought long and hard about taking it and disappearing, but something wouldn't let me do it. Once I decided to take your offer, there was no turning back and thank God I took it! I have known that you have had feelings for me for a long time. I have had them for you too, but I made a decision that morning when I decided to work for you. I would never let another man use or abuse me again.

"Francois, I want you to use me. I want to use you, but I can only promise you faithfulness if you want it, but not love."

The cigar that he had been chewing on slipped from his mouth when once again it fell open in shock as Hannah stood up and said, "Shall we go to bed?"

Francois had ridden past Matthew and Agatha's farm without a glance he had been so deep in thought. Before he knew it he was jerked into the present when he found himself back at the Inn. He barely had time to dismount and hand the reins to the stable hand when Hannah came flying out the back door looking like she had been wrestling with a sack of flour and lost.

"Francois where in the devil have you been?" she said smearing more flour across her face as she tried to get her hair out of it. "The cook is sick and I had to send her to bed. I have been up to my ears in flour literally trying to get fresh bread made, after knocking over and breaking a bowl full of it. The place is filled with early morning and some hung over drinkers who are wanting food now. There is no one here to do the shopping for the hungry folks that will be coming in tonight."

Francois thought to himself, 'Well, that explains the flour fight. Lord, I sure do love this woman and if you can, please get Rosa to agree to have the wedding celebration here before I turn to the bottle for relief.'

"Now, now Hannah," he said. "You knew I was riding out to see Frantz. I told you before I left where I was going and that I intended to visit for a spell."

"Humph! Well maybe you did, but I never heard you." She said and turned practically running back inside as though her dress tail was on fire. He knew as soon as she calmed down a little she would remember him telling her his plans. She would then be asking all about his visit and how Frantz and Rosa were doing. In the meantime he would check out the bar, help her clean up the mess in the kitchen if need be and send her on an errand, before she could get started on another tirade for who knows what reason.

CHAPTER 13

It was a warm late spring day in May of 1804. As always happens after a cold lingering winter has finally left, the earth's creatures seem to be in concert performing their own celebration of life. There was a huge oak tree that three men could not reach around which stood near the horse stables at the St. Charles Post. The birds that lived there were busily and loudly tending their nests. There were two squirrels appearing to chase each other in play and having a grand old "racket making" time. Not to be outdone was a blue jay staying in character by being ornery and loud with a mocking bird whose nest was in the tree. The mocking bird was having none of the blue jays' antics near her nest and let him know by running him away from the tree in what sounded like angry blue jay talk.

Alex and Edmond came out of the fort, mounted their horses and headed toward town. They had been given orders to meet William Clark and his boats at the dock. He was Co-commander of the Corps of Discovery. He and Meriwether Lewis were co-commanders of the expedition which was beginning to be known as the Lewis and Clark Expedition. Now that the Louisiana Territory belonged to the United States government,

Thomas Jefferson was anxious to learn all he could about the newly purchased land that extended to the Rockies in the west. He also wanted to know about the land west of the Rocky Mountains that ran all the way to the Pacific Ocean. When Napoleon had finally sold the port of New Orleans and all other lands that made up the Louisiana Territory, the president wasted no time in appropriating funds from Congress to explore these lands west of the Mississippi. He placed Meriwether Lewis in charge.

While their horses slowly ambled along Alex said, "Edmond, life can be downright interesting sometimes. I mean, who would have thought we would be riding out to meet William Clark here in St. Charles. I understand Meriwether Lewis is still in St. Louis waiting for last minute supplies. We haven't seen or heard anything of either since we all fought together in the Northwest Indian War in Ohio.

"What do you think about going on a trip like this one? Everybody is calling it the Lewis and Clark expedition even though it is officially known as the Corps of Discovery. President Jefferson is sending them to find the North West water route through the Rocky Mountains and then on to the Pacific Ocean. Do you know how far that is? I have heard that it is estimated they will be traveling might near four thousand miles just to get there. Not only that, but they will be seeing land no white man has ever seen, encountering Indians who may not be friendly and who knows what else. Lewis is probably the best pick to get along with the Indians. You remember how we used to sit and listen to him talk about the time he lived in Georgia as a young lad? He spent a lot of time with the Indians there."

"Yeah, I do remember." Edmond replied. "I also remember him talking about hunting at an early age and camping with the Cherokee. It seems that these people were not taking kindly to the whites coming onto their lands. Somehow Lewis established a friendship with them. It used to be right upsetting to his mother with him sneaking out before daylight to go hunting. After she realized he was most likely in the company of the Cherokee she began to rest a little easier. She knew Lewis just like her loved the woods and was most comfortable there.

"I don't reckon it much matters what I think about this venture. There is no way I could join the expedition. The truth is with our baby only a few weeks old, Agatha doesn't seem to want me no farther away than shouting distance. I am sure it has something to do with the loss of our other babies. Besides I heard the Commander talking and he said that with their crew of about forty five men they had already doubled the amount they had originally planned to take. It doesn't sound to me like they will be looking for any more volunteers at this point. Clark is stopping here to wait for Lewis who is still in St. Louis. He is having to buy additional supplies to support the larger number of crew than what he had originally planned for.

"Listen Alex, I was really looking forward to meeting and maybe talking with Clark after the dinner tonight at the Ducettes. If I know Agatha, she is going to want to head home with the baby right after we eat. I am counting on you to keep me informed on anything of interest I might miss."

They made it to the dock just in time to see three boats that had just come around the bend. The big boat was leading. Along with it were two smaller boats called pirogues. One was red. It was an impressive sight with all three boats having their sails up.

Alex said, "Looks like we didn't leave a minute too soon. They must have left way before daylight."

William Clark stood near the bow of the big boat as they were approaching St. Charles. He could hardly contain his excitement. At long last they were on the verge of beginning their mission. As soon as Lewis finished his last minute business in St. Louis and joined them they could really begin their journey.

It seemed like it was only yesterday and not a year since he had been sitting in his brother's house back in the Indiana Territory. He had agreed to manage the family estate after leaving the military. Clark thought about the day he had been working in the library when he had heard a rider approaching. A minute later his personal servant York had come in and handed him a letter. It was from Meriwether Lewis. He had been a little surprised since he had received a letter from Lewis a few weeks ago. He had been even more surprised when he had read it.

Lewis had asked him to join as co-commander of the expedition to explore the recently attained Louisiana Territory. The mission was to seek commercial opportunities, establish a presence there, to collect information about the flora and fauna, about the people of the land, where the northwest water way was through the Rocky Mountains and to reach the Pacific Ocean.

Clark loved his family dearly and was glad to help them, but he had been more than ready to be out and about in the newly obtained lands west of the Mississippi River. He had not hesitated in accepting the offer. Clark posted a letter immediately, however it was lost. Lewis assumed Clark wasn't interested since he had not heard from him and asked another man to join him. When the acceptance letter had finally reached Lewis he informed the other man that Clark would be sharing with him the command of the expedition.

He knew Jefferson had asked Lewis to be his Secretary-Aide and he had accepted. Clark also knew Lewis was a childhood friend and neighbor of President Jefferson and was not surprised that he had selected him to carry out this mission. Clark had much respect for Meriwether Lewis as a man, friend and now fellow soldier again. They both had been given the rank of Captain.

There was a good crowd gathered at the dock anticipating their arrival. Several had brought food and made a picnic out of the occasion, since no one knew what time William Clark and his men would be arriving. Along with Grace, Rosa, Frantz, Matthew, Francois, Hannah and the Watkins family were some Indians, French trappers, a German family, a Spanish couple, more neighbors and anyone else who could manage to get away. The Ducette family who was hosting the dinner party that evening was also standing at the dock. Several children were running about, laughing and having a good time in general.

Anyone who didn't make it today would most certainly be at the public celebration planned at the grounds of the Methodist Church Saturday afternoon. There would be lots of good food, music, dancing and merriment aided no doubt by a few swigs from some jugs that would be shared behind the church house.

Clark stepped off the boat and walked toward the two officers that were approaching. A huge smile crossed his face as he recognized Alex and Edmond. They stopped, came to attention and saluted Clark. He returned the salute.

"Well in all tarnation, I never expected to see you two here. The last I heard you were done with the military shortly after we left the Ohio Territory. It is good to see that is not the case. Our country and these recently attained lands need good capable men such as yourselves."

Alex and Edmond both could not help but smile under his genuine praise. They had developed much admiration for this officer during their time of service under him.

Alex said, "Welcome to St. Charles, Sir."

"Thank you, Sir." said Edmond as he shook hands. "Arrangements have been made for your supper this evening with the Ducette family." Introductions were made to many in the crowd that had gathered around.

Clark excused himself and went back on board the boat before dismissing a small portion of his crew until midnight. He was very specific about the time they were to be back on the boat. He also stressed the importance of maintaining a behavior befitting of their station on a mission of utmost importance. He then gave a few orders for the remaining crew before they started setting up camp.

After he had left the boat the second time, Grace walked over, took his arm and said, "Now Captain Clark, I insist that you come home with us for a spot of tea before dinner."

They climbed in the carriage and with Alex and Edmond riding along beside they headed for the Monet house.

When they stopped in front, Clark said, "Mrs. Monet, I do like your rose arbor over the gate. In fact the place is a wonderful display of color. I never took much notice of earth's vibrant array of colors until I met and started spending time with my fiancé. At least I hope to make her my wife after this trip." Grace's face lit up just as it always did when anyone commented on her flowers.

"I insist that you call me Grace, Captain Clark. Now you men make yourselves comfortable on the porch while I get the tea ready."

Alex said, "That is quite an impressive boat. It looks to be about sixty feet. I heard it came all the way down the Ohio River from Pennsylvania."

Clark said, "That's right. Lewis made the plans for it and hired a man in Pittsburgh to build it. He was somewhat in a tither with the boat builder. Seems that his time spent with the bottle instead of spent working on the boat delayed departure for almost two months. As a consequence of the builder's habit, instead of leaving in early July, he did not depart until the end of August.

"By this time Lewis was experiencing quite a bit of consternation. It was because of the lateness of the season for one thing when the river is normally low. In addition to that many were saying they had never before seen the water levels in the river so low. This aggravated an already cumbersome situation. After finally getting the boat in the water and loaded it then had to be partially unloaded. The water level was too low to support the load. The remainder of the supplies were carried by wagons quite a distance overland until a place was reached where the depth of the Ohio River kept the bottom of the boat at a safe distance from the bottom of the river."

Grace came out and served them their tea. She settled in one of the chairs and listened for a while as the men talked. Edmond left saying he would see them at dinner. Captain Clark left shortly afterwards for the boat.

Clark and his men spent about a week at St. Charles waiting for Captain Lewis to join them. During that time there were disciplinary issues with some of the crew. It seems that a couple of them had been reported absent without leave and another one for drunken and disorderly conduct. They were punished swiftly. Clark knew that it was imperative for the success of the expedition that everyone follow orders. Even though these men had volunteered as civilians they had spent several weeks at River Dubois being trained as a military unit. After this period of indoctrination and training, the crew was chosen and the men had been enlisted into the Army.

Lewis had arrived from St. Louis and that afternoon the Corps of Discovery started their journey up the Missouri River. Practically all of St. Charles who knew they were leaving had turned out to bid them farewell. Most everyone had been introduced to the vibrant red headed William Clark at the church social the past Saturday. There was quite a bit of cheering from the crowd as the three boats began their ascent up the Missouri River through the new lands of the United States.

CHAPTER 14

Frantz and Rosa had been working in their field preparing a space for a corn crop. When they decided to quit early and go to the house together Rosa asked him to walk to the river with her. They leisurely walked toward their spot by the creek on the river bank holding hands.

When they were situated Frantz said, "Rosa I don't want to wait any longer to be married in the church. I know you don't care what everyone thinks, just as I don't. But by going through a church ceremony it will let the whole town know how we feel about each other. I want everyone to see how proud I am to be loved by you and how honored I am to have you as my wife. We can talk to the........"

Rosa reached out and put her fingers over his lips. "Hush Frantz, say no more."

"But, Rosa."

"Frantz, please hush and listen to me. The reason I asked you to take a break from work and come and sit with me here is this. You will be a Papa this year. I will marry you. The baby and I will carry your name. We are a family. She smiled at him then and said, "Now, close your mouth and breathe. Oh look, there are the boats." They sat contentedly holding hands and watching the boats pass ever so slowly up the river.

Frantz did not waste any time talking with Francois and Hannah about reserving the Inn for a wedding celebration. Hannah was excited, just as Francois said she would be and set about planning a menu even before Frantz left.

In the meantime, Rosa had gone to tell Grace and Agatha the good news. She found them at Grace's house. She asked if she could join them when they were meeting again to sew. They both spoke up and said she could. They were excited about helping her with the making of her wedding dress. Rosa noticed that several times when Rosa had visited Grace and occasionally at Agatha's she had found them together sewing. Sometimes Hannah would be with them. A lot of times they would be at the table drinking tea or coffee each with a Bible beside them and their sewing project pushed to the side. Rosa didn't think too much of this, because she had spent so much time with her Englishman reading and discussing this holy book of the white people. She explained that she wanted to learn to work with the fabric and make the delicate stitches that they used. They all planned to meet at the mercantile the next day to select fabric, thread and lace for Rosa's dress.

Grace and Agatha had kept their informal sewing circle only between themselves and Hannah when she could join them. They had done this on purpose. They didn't always do a lot of sewing, but always they did a lot of talking. Especially when they met at Grace's house. At Agatha's with her Papa, Matthew and the two work hands there were usually a lot of distractions. Also, they wanted to keep most of their conversations private. So they met at Grace's most of the time.

After they had met at the mercantile they decided to get together in a couple of days to start Rosa's dress. Agatha had discreetly told Rosa to bring her Bible. Rosa had spent a lot of time reading Frantz's Bible until he came in one day and gave her one he had ordered for her. She read it almost every evening and found the stories fascinating.

They met at the appointed time at Grace's house. When Hannah arrived Grace and Agatha explained to Rosa that they did not want their gatherings to be talked about outside of their circle.

They told her they talked about whatever came to mind between friends and some things would be frowned on by the community. Grace said it might even be considered talk from witches. This did not seem odd to Rosa at all. She had been used to hiding in ear shot of her mother and a couple of her friends while they talked about things in secret. She had learned at an early age it could be dangerous to have a free spirit along with a free tongue.

Because of the limited amount of time before the wedding that was just three weeks away the women set to measuring Rosa for her dress. The material they had selected was a soft yellow cream satin. They had all agreed to make her dress with a lace over bodice attached at the round neck and loosely gathered. It would hang just over the waist line which would actually be above the waist and just below the bodice. Here where the skirt was attached would be a minimal number of gathers. The sleeves would be long and of lace also. They had to work with the amount of material available. Their design was original and unique in this part of the country. They did not know it had been introduced in Europe just a few years earlier and was called the empire waist. They all loved their idea and began to work on their creation.

Rosa asked, "Why did you want me to bring my Bible today?"

Hannah spoke up and said, "Many days we have a discussion about things we find questionable or of interest in the Bible. We have found that anyone who reads this book with an open mind has questions. However, you never hear these questions mentioned by the so called men of God that come to preach. If someone is brave enough to question anything they are quickly warned of the dangers of hell and the consequences of being blasphemous. We all attend the church meetings when possible to socialize mostly. However, we always have the hope that someone will be on that pulpit one day speaking of some of the things the book says that are never talked about. But it never seems to be anything but more of some man reciting an assortment of memorized verses or consistently selected readings, warnings of hell fire and damnation and an occasional reminder to love one another thrown in."

Hannah went over to her Bible and opened it up. She brought it over and stood by Rosa as she held it up for her to see.

"For example, have you noticed in the very first chapter of Genesis here." she pointed to a verse. Rosa followed her finger and read out loud the following.

"Gen 1:26   *And God said, Let us make man in our image, after our likeness: ......*"

"Pray tell us who he was talking to?" said Hannah. I can't tell you how many times I have read that verse and never saw it before. Obviously God was not alone or he would never have said this. So just from these few words we know He is not alone and we look like him and whoever he was talking to. Anyway, there you have it. If you have any ideas about this please share them with us when we get together again. Right now we have to keep our minds on cutting this dress of yours correctly. We might be in a really bad situation if we make a mistake and needed more of the same material."

Grace spoke up and said, "I guess you can see why we don't discuss or talk about our sewing circle. If you stop and think about it, we four are somewhat unique in our backgrounds and way of thinking about things. We don't fit into what we call the church pattern. It would not do for one of the women living here that does not allow themselves to have a free mind or free spirit to ask to join our sewing circle or Bible study. We could not allow them in and continue to have the freedom of discussion we now enjoy. It is too dangerous to take a chance of being accused of God only knows what. There are a few sad, angry and lonely people about who would thrive on knowing that we even have the audacity to ask questions that don't blindly follow what is being preached by a few."

Rosa replied, "I thank you for letting me join your group. Your secret is now my secret. I too have passed many hours reading this book and have many questions. I am happy to learn."

It was quite a hectic time getting everything ready for the wedding, but the women managed. They spent their time focused on making Rosa's wedding gown.

The day of the wedding came. Frantz had purposely tried to invite everyone in or near St. Charles. When he and Rosa were approaching the church it appeared that a good many had come. The church had filled already and a crowd was standing around outside. No one wanted to miss a shindig when possible, but most of the women were just plain curious about the Indian woman Frantz was marrying..

Frantz stopped the wagon, walked around, put his hands around Rosa's waist and stood her on the ground. When she turned around all eyes were on her. Most of the men were openly ogling Rosa. Several of them received a sharp elbow in the ribs from their significant other. She was beautiful.

The Watkins family were among those that did not arrive early and get a seat. Mrs. Watkins puckered up her mouth and said in a low tone, "Would you look at that dress. You might know that woman would have to wear something totally out of style."

Millie replied, "Why Mama, I think you may be mistaken. I just saw a drawing in a paper from New

Orleans this week saying this was the latest fashion out of Europe."

The only reply Mrs. Watkins gave was her usual loud and resounding, "Humph!"

Rosa took Frantz's arm and they walked together into the church. As soon as the service was over everyone was invited to the Inn for food, music and drink. Hannah had outdone herself with the food. There was a roasted pig, deer steaks, beef roasts and fried chicken along with a variety of fresh vegetables, cakes, puddings and pies. She had even had the cooks to prepare a tender beef stew for little ones and older ones that might have trouble chewing.

There were a couple of trappers staying at the Inn. They had confined themselves to sitting in the shade underneath an oak tree in back of the Inn. Hannah had told them about the Inn being reserved for the wedding party. She made sure they would be provided with drinks. When Frantz and Rosa realized what was going on both insisted they join the festivities.

The trappers were mighty glad to be a part of the celebration.

Alex went over to where the two were and asked, "Have you seen or heard any news of the Lewis and Clark Expedition?"

One of them spoke up and said, "Yes, as a matter of fact we do have news. It was less than a year ago when we saw these three boats tied up. We headed straight in and banked our canoe alongside their boats.

"They were setting up camp. We were mighty glad to see some faces that didn't want our skins and scalps. Their hunting party came in shortly after we landed. They had killed a couple of deer and we were happy they asked us to eat with them. We had been eating pemmican and were about out of it. The fresh meat was mighty tasty. We shared with them what we could about what lay ahead upriver. We had not been long past two sand bars they would be approaching in the next few days and told them the best side of the river to take to avoid the sawyers that are just below the surface. Also we warned them that they were approaching an area where they needed to keep a sharp watch. The Indians around this part of the river and for several miles upstream did not want white men on their land and would not hesitate before attacking."

The other trapper piped in and said, "That fella Lewis is without a doubt an educated man. We listened as he and Clark talked about the different groups of Indians they had seen and visited with that were living on and near the rivers. It was quite a bit they had learned about these people after traveling the country for such a short time. We asked how much trouble they had encountered with the natives. The red headed one, Clark stood up and called a young squaw over. He introduced her as Sacajawea. She carried a baby in her arms. She hardly looked much past a little girl herself. But I tell you, there was a spirit about this young Indian woman of pure strength and knowing. He explained that they weren't sure about taking the interpreter they had hired and his family with them, but they knew the woman and her child traveling with them should let the people know they came not intending to harm anyone. So far, they had encountered trouble only one time on their whole trip.

"You could tell William Clark was quite fond of her. He told us how this young woman had been invaluable as they worked their way into the country and met with tribe after tribe. Clark said they discovered early on that this young woman knew much more about the people and was able to communicate with them better. She had been able to sit in with them at some very important meetings held with the different indigenous tribes they visited. This was something that women were never allowed to do."

The other trapper said, "Mr. Clark had his servant, a fellow named York to fetch some papers for him. It turned out that Clark was the map maker on the expedition. He asked our opinion of the ones he had made. In all honesty there wasn't much we could offer, except for the name of a place or stream in a spot or two. Again we were down right impressed with these two men. Those fellas will be bringing a lot of useful information back with them if they make it. We certainly believe if any large group can it would be them."

In spite of a few snide remarks made by a few of the jealous women everyone seemed to be having a good time. Frantz and Rosa left in mid-afternoon. The families that had to travel a distance out of town also left before dark. Others stayed into the evening long after Frantz and Rosa had gone home.

All in all it had been a fun time for everyone. The only altercation was between two young men who both fancied they had claims on the same young lady. She had danced with both of them throughout a good portion of the afternoon. When Hannah saw the men in a "nose to nose" heated conversation, she found Francois and steered him quickly toward them. He interceded and sent them both outside for a cooling off period. However, the cooling off did not happen and their discussion advanced into a fist fight. After both were having trouble standing up with hardly sufficient strength to make another jab or swing and wearing bloody noses and split lips they decided it was time to call an unspoken truce. Arm in arm they staggered over to the water trough and cleaned their faces before rejoining the festivities. Unfortunately these two longtime friends did not know the young woman was not really interested in either one of them. She was only taking advantage of their doting attentions to hopefully catch the eye of a tall lanky fellow whose wife had died a little over a year ago in childbirth. By the time they went back inside the recipient of their affections was dancing with the young widower after boldly grasping his hand and dragging him to the middle of the dancers. The smiles along with their facial expressions as they danced told the two suitors all they needed to know. With looks of total frustration the fellows walked toward the bar shaking their heads and talking about what strange creatures women were.

Shortly afterwards, Francois announced last call and the revelry ended about 10 pm. All the food had been cleared and the musicians had stopped playing. The last of the merry makers staggered out of the Inn. Most had smiles on their faces and a couple of fellows were bellowing out a song as they staggered along supporting each other across the shoulders.

It had been about three weeks since the wedding. Agatha was sitting at Grace's table nursing the baby. Hannah had brought one of her favorite dresses she could no longer fit into. She was going to alter it for one of the women that worked at the Inn. Agatha had brought along a bag of quilting scraps to piece together. She was not really worried about sewing today. She had found something in her Bible reading that she wanted to get the other's thoughts on. The baby had started teething and was really fussy today, so she knew it would be difficult to get much done with her sewing.

Rosa was the last to arrive. The women had a good time teasing the new bride. Rosa's face told them all they needed to know. Even though she did not think the wedding ceremony would make a difference it had somehow and not just with Frantz. She truly felt that she belonged with this amazing group of women.

Grace had taken it upon herself since she had the most time on her hands to keep a journal of their sewing circle questions or what they deemed pertinent thoughts to ponder. Since Hannah had brought up the question at their last meeting of who God was talking to when he used the words us and our, they had made an agreement. It was decided that all four of them would start at the very beginning in Genesis to read and see what else they might find of interest or have questions about. They soon realized that none of them had read Genesis all the way through.

The girls had affectionately and secretly named their little group the sowing circle. It turned out each had the King James Version of the year 1611 which had been translated and written in Early Modern English and reflected the Latin influence in the spelling. They did not bring their Bibles with them as they were a bit heavy and cumbersome.

Today Grace had placed her Bible on the table opened to the first chapter in Genesis. Hannah reached across the table and pulled the Bible toward her. She turned it so she could read it.

She said, "You know, I am so glad we decided to do this. I did not have to read far before I was amazed at what I found. Chapter two of Genesis filled my head with more questions. The first thing that caught my attention are these two trees that are in the Garden of Eden. One is the tree of life and the other is the tree of the knowledge of good and evil. God tells Adam that if he eats of this tree he will surely die."

Agatha pipes in and says, "In the third chapter there is a talking serpent. Isn't that odd? Now really, a talking serpent or snake. He told Eve she wouldn't die if she ate from the tree. He told her they would be as Gods knowing good and evil." Rosa sat down beside Hannah who slid the Bible over to her where she could see it better.

Rosa said, "Well they both ate and their eyes were opened and they knew they were naked. Why didn't they know they were naked before? It goes on to say that they covered themselves with fig leaves and made aprons. When they heard God coming they hid in some trees in the garden. God called them and asked where they were. Anyway, Adam answered and said he was afraid because they were naked. Then God asks who told him they were naked and if he had eaten of the tree. Adam said they had and blamed the woman and the woman blamed the talking serpent."

"This is a very strange story," said Grace. "Why would God not know what they had done or where they were in the garden? He knows everything, right? I thought God knows even our every thought."

"Well, I surely don't understand this," said Agatha. "I just know it sounds like two children admitting they had done wrong and blaming someone else after being caught by a parent who wasn't looking when they were being disobedient."

Rosa continues, "God curses the serpent to go upon his belly and eat dust all the days of its life because of what it had told to Eve? It sounds like this serpent must have been standing up before it was cursed. What kind of serpent stands up, then has to crawl on its belly forever. Adam and Eve are then cursed and clothed in coats of skins. Now here is another verse where God uses us again."

"Genesis 3:22 *And the LORD God said, Behold, the man is become as one of* us, *to know good and evil: and now, lest he put forth his hand, and take also of the tree of life, and eat, and live forever:*"

Grace says, "What is all this about eating knowledge of good and evil from a tree in a garden? God is talking to other beings and appears to be concerned that man will take and eat from the other tree which is the tree of life and live forever. Why did he put the tree there in the garden if he didn't want them to eat from it. Why would God not want man to have this knowledge?

"It seems to me that the God who created the heavens, the earth and every living thing would not have to worry about such things. It almost sounds like there is a different god in this garden from the God that created the earth, sun, moon and stars. Or maybe all the story is not here. Or maybe it is a different story about man's creation altogether. As I said before, this is all very strange when you stop scanning over the words with your eyes and listen to what they are telling you."

Agatha starts gathering her things. "Sorry ladies, but I have to leave early today. Let me know if any ideas come out that we haven't talked about."

Rosa and Hannah cuddled and made baby noises to the little one before they headed out the door. Hannah headed toward the Inn walking. Rosa was riding her beloved Promise. Grace carried the baby and followed Agatha to her wagon.

When she was seated she handed her the baby and said, "Agatha, we have talked about so much today I am not sure I will get it all written down from memory."

"Don't worry, Grace. I am taking some notes myself. This is too interesting to let it just slip away. I am sure between the two of us we will get most of our questions and thoughts down. It is obvious that we have named our circle well for we are definitely sewing little and sowing more questions than fabric."

They laughed and hugged each other while promising to get together again soon.

CHAPTER 15

Grace could not believe herself and what she was doing. If she was caught the consequences would be severe she knew. Breaking the law, especially when it involved runaway slaves was taken very seriously in these parts of the country. She could not help herself. She just could not turn her back on a child that was hungry. It had all started two days ago when she had gone down to the spring to put her with her freshly churned butter.

She especially loved this walk. Once she reached the woods that abutted the back of the property the land began sloping downward a few hundred feet to a tiny branch. Grace sensed the unseen presence of others here almost as soon as she entered the woods. It always felt so familiar to her as though she had been here in an earlier time. A time before she was born. She could not explain that. It was one of those things that just was. Two days ago had been no different as Grace had followed the familiar winding, meandering path through the trees down the hill toward the branch and to the spring box.

She had just stepped into the small clearing and that was when she had seen them. It was a man, woman and child all three down on their knees. They were on the other side of the branch busily scooping water up in their hands. They had not heard Grace coming and when she made a startled cry three dark faces looked up at her with such surprise and naked fear on them it had wrenched Grace's heart. The man started pulling the little girl up in his arms as though he were protecting her from an unstoppable danger headed straight for her body. The woman positioned herself between Grace and the child. Then they all had stood not moving. They had just continued staring at one another saying nothing for it seemed the longest time.

The man turned toward the woman and without speaking they started to walk in the opposite direction away from the cool waters of the branch. Grace had surmised in those few moments that this black family were runaway slaves. The fear alone had told her that much. She could see that they had been running for a while by the condition of their clothing and the obvious lack of sufficient nourishment.

Before she thought about it she called out, "Wait. I will not harm you. I want to help you." They did not stop. "Please, Grace said. At least let me get you some food. Something for your child." The woman stopped, turned around and looked at Grace. She reached back with her hand to touch her husband's back who was also stopped, but had not turned around. The woman said something to the man and he turned also. "Stay here out of sight and wait for me. I will bring you something to eat."

Grace did bring them food back. She encouraged them to stay a couple of days hidden in the woods near the spring until they could rest and let their bodies gather new strength. They told her their supplies had been lost when they were crossing the river in the night on a not too sturdy raft that had broken apart. They had managed to keep their daughter on two of the small logs that had held together while they hung on and kicked toward shore. Alex was away from home and Grace managed to prepare extra food without rousing any suspicion. She did not want to include anyone else in her secret. To keep neighbors away, she made sure she could be heard during the day having her fake coughing spells. Many in the town were sick and the ones that weren't definitely did not want to be a victim because of throwing caution to the wind. If one of the girls came she would have to deal with it then. Because so many were sick, she really did not expect anyone to pay her a visit.

Over the next two days, she fed the family and gave them some old clothing she and the girls had been collecting for quilt scraps. Some pieces were not much better than what the slaves were wearing, but they were a clean changing for them. She managed to get a cook pot, knife, spoon, dried gourds, a small ax, two blankets and some smoked meat and fish together for them. In addition she took an extra buffalo skin that had never been used, a sack of ground corn and some licorice sticks for the little girl. She gave the woman a small leather pouch she could hang around her neck with a needle and some thread in it. To Grace it was not nearly enough, but to the family it was treasures beyond anything they could have hoped for.

They all agreed the less known about them and their destination the better for everyone. All she knew was that they were headed north where there would be help to get them to a safe place. Grace said a silent prayer as she watched them disappear deeper into the woods. The little girl was being carried by her father. She clutched the little corn husk doll Grace had stitched and stuffed for her. Her faint smile and timid wave goodbye made up for all the trepidation Grace had felt during their short stay in the woods by the spring. She could not help feeling that they were not traveling alone, those three. She had not seen anyone else around.

It had been a while since Grace had been down to the branch. She liked to go there as much if not more than the spot on the river near the dock. The branch was the place to be truly alone. In all the time she had lived here, not one soul had she encountered there except for the family she hoped she had helped. The cool fall days had arrived early this year and she had not needed to use the spring box to store her butter. As she walked along she wondered about the family and their journey to a new life. She hoped with all her heart they had found a place to live life freely without fear. How one human thought they had the right to enslave another was just beyond Grace's comprehension. She had learned that the cruelties she had only heard until her friendship with Rosa and what had happened to her. Rosa had been lucky on the plantation, that is if you can call being a slave lucky. She had learned much about the beatings, sexual abuse, not enough food, clothing and shelter. A lot came from them hearing the neighboring plantation owners' talk amongst themselves of their cruelty to their slaves. However, most of it came from the accompanying slaves that traveled with them when they came to the plantation of the Englishman. She always managed to talk to some of them, because she was very curious about the world that was close around her. She wanted to hear what it was really like and knew she would from most of these people. Why would a loving God allow this to happen to his created beings? She had heard it said that it was because people had free will and placed themselves in evil's way. She knew that could not be right. Not all the time at least. What choice or free will did little children have? It was a mystery how evil was allowed to run rampant in this world. Being a victim of it had little to do with free will most of the time. Most certainly never for children.

When Grace reached the branch and situated herself on her favorite stump, she looked up and to her surprise an elderly black man was standing on the other side near the spot where the family had been drinking from the branch. She knew he wasn't there when she came into the little clearing or she would have seen him then. He had certainly moved quietly. He was holding a hat in one of his hands down at his side. He had a smile on his face as he looked at her. She quickly thought that somehow word was out that she would help those running for safety with food and clothing. Grace noticed that this one's clothes was neat, un-tattered and very clean looking. She could not help but feel a tiny bit of fear start to settle around her. She wondered if she would have the courage to help again. This man did not look hungry.

As her mind raced through the possibilities for his being there, the man bent over and placed something that was red on the ground. When he stood back up he nodded slowly at Grace, put on his hat and while still smiling at her promptly vanished. He did not walk away into the trees. He did not move. He vanished. It reminded Grace of the way a lot of swirling dust looked when caught in a ray of sunlight. The only difference would be that the dust would look sort of like tiny flecks of gold outlined within the man's shape while slowly swirling toward an unseen place and disappearing. Grace was totally stunned. She had never seen anything like it. People did not change into tiny swirling gold flecks and disappear into thin air. Did they?

Grace sat very still for quite a while mentally going back over what had just happened. She was really having difficulty believing her own eyes. Finally she decided to go over to the other side of the little branch and see what it was that he had placed on the ground. At this point she really didn't expect to find anything. When she reached the spot where he had been standing just minutes earlier, she looked down at the ground and there lying in the grass was a patch of red cloth about four inches square with tiny yellow and blue flowers. She recognized it immediately as one of the two patches of material she had sent along with the little girl. She reached over and picked it up.

As her fingers gently rubbed the cloth she remembered telling her she could make her doll a shawl or maybe an apron. Grace knew then she was right when she had felt they had not been traveling alone. They had with them what must be a guardian angel maybe like the one the disciple Peter had that was mentioned in the New Testament. She knew this angel wanted Grace to know they had made it to a safe place. What a wonderful gift he had given her. She could not wait to tell Agatha about it. Grace wished she could talk to her mother who might know more about it. She was very open minded and had always encouraged Grace to ask questions about anything she didn't understand.

She had just received a letter from her parents a few days ago. She took it out of her pocket and read it again. It seems that her father had decided to start his own saw mill since he had the experience from his time working in St. Louis. New Madrid was growing rapidly and a mill was needed close by. They were doing well with the boarding house and now the saw mill. Catherine had finally conceded to hiring help in the kitchen.

Her mother had written that the mill was keeping Charles with longer hours, but knew they would decrease once he had some experienced people he could promote to take on more of his responsibility. Catherine again mentioned that Grace and Alex might want to think about moving there if and when he left the Army. The opportunities were many she wrote. The settlers were coming through more and more especially from the east out of Kentucky and Tennessee. The boat traffic had increased greatly since Jefferson had secured the ownership of New Orleans and the port along with the freedom of travel on the Mississippi River. Quite a few folks were coming in on flat boats down the Ohio and settling on or near the Mississippi in the New Madrid and Genevieve area. There were now United States Army military posts in both Genevieve and New Madrid. Alex had even mentioned possibly transferring to one of them. It really never went further than a few comments exchanged. They never actually made any plans to leave St. Charles.

CHAPTER 16

Orders had been given for another peace keeping mission. These Indians lived a few days ride up the Missouri River. Alex and Edmond along with nineteen other soldiers were traveling the wagon trail that had continued well past Daniel Boone's land toward the west and the Pacific coast. More and more people were moving into the new lands and the trail was beginning to show the markings of many wagons' passage. It would later be known as the beginning of the Oregon Trail.

The soldiers had camped the night before, on a crystal clear rocky bottomed creek that flowed right over the trail. They were refilling their canteens and giving their horses a drink before starting on again. Alex rode his horse over beside Edmond's to drink.

"Edmond, how close do you suppose we are to keeping these Indians from making out and out war on the white settlers coming through this land? I keep thinking how difficult it was to finally get the Ohio land settled and safe for new settlers to come onto. You know it took ten years of fighting the British, the Indians and then both together to get that territory secured for people to live in safely. It took a while to get most of the Indians and British out of there still."

Edmond looked up at the trees overhead for a moment then said, "The flow of people now heading west must be making it harder for the Indian chiefs who want to keep peace. It is also difficult for many of their young braves who can see clearly what the future holds for their people. They are trying to stop the invasion of their land the only way they know how, by killing, mutilating and kidnapping the white people. The chiefs that want peace can't keep some of them from joining the renegade bands that have been attacking settlers coming in and the homesteads of those already here. These angry and dangerous groups seem to be increasing in numbers as more tribes are pushed across the Mississippi and further west and south."

"You know, Edmond if I were an Indian living in this beautiful land I am not too sure I wouldn't be one of those renegades myself. After all, it is their land we are taking no matter what papers are signed, peace pipes smoked, beads, whisky and guns handed out, battles fought, lives lost and treaties declared. It is a process that has been happening since God created us. Man for whatever reason goes into another man's land and after much blood shed takes the land as though it had been theirs all along. Before you know it customs and ways of the people living there are slowly lost and mostly forgotten. The new way of doing things has taken over." Alex stopped talking and looked across the creek.

Edmond said, "I wonder what it would be like to just live in peace without worrying about being attacked by another people who live differently. Even some of the Indian tribes make war on others. It seems that there is enough land that people could work together and live in harmony.

The useless slaughter of buffalo for the skins only is enough to send a sane man over the edge. All that food left to rot while some of the tribes are fighting starvation. A hungry man will go to extremes to change that for his family.

"The Indians are no different from most other people in the warring among themselves. Just like the white man there are different groups that fight with one another and other groups that want peace. And sadly in those groups of the peaceful ones some of their minds and hearts are changed and instead of peace they choose war. They are driven toward the money war always brings to a few at any and all costs from the destruction of man and property. It all seems very wrong somehow. Sometimes I feel like we are underneath some kind of power that groups us and maneuvers us like we were all puppets. There must be a better way."

Edmond mounted his horse and said, "Well maybe this mission we are on now will in some way help to make a way to save lives and change man's thinking. All we can do is our small part and keep hoping and praying it's so. Time will tell, but history makes it look mighty grim."

"Let's hope so, because this situation is escalating rapidly and something has to change." Alex replied.

Their horses had finished drinking and they realized the men were doing as they had been ordered and were moving out when they finished watering the animals and filling canteens. They were the only two still at the creek. Edmond took off and caught up with the others. Alex had only traveled a couple hundred feet from the stream when he stopped and stepped behind a tree to relieve himself.

After Alex had mounted his horse and was back on the trail he had ridden only a few feet when he reigned in his horse and sat very still as he listened intently and heard nothing. That is what caught his attention. It was too quiet. He was positioned far enough away from the movement of the troops to notice the quietness. He was opening his mouth to warn the others that they should take cover when he was hit in the back with an arrow. He saw some of his men ahead of him falling from their horses, others scattering and horses bucking and screaming in fright. He could hear his men shouting amidst the terrifying noises coming from the Indians as they attacked. He never would get used to that sound he thought. At the same time that this was happening he had kicked his horse and was riding as hard as he could through the brush to reach a big oak and take cover. The last thing he saw was a barrage of arrows flying through the air and guns being fired creating a smoky haze. He was close to the tree when another arrow hit him and then he was falling from his horse. There was a small ravine right beside him and he landed on the edge of it.

As the Indians were retreating from the gun fire of the remaining fighting soldiers, one of them saw Alex lying there unconscious. He stopped and quickly flipped him over on his stomach. He swiftly broke off the ends of the arrows protruding from his back. This allowed him to rapidly remove his jacket which he promptly put on. Next he took off his boots, along with a leather pouch that contained Alex's hunting knife. He intended to use it to scalp Alex, but heard a horse coming from the direction of the battle site. Instead of taking Alex's scalp he pushed him over the edge of the ravine. The Indian jumped up, grabbed the boots and ran for a thicket of trees back in the direction of the creek. Just as he reached cover of the trees he came upon Alex's horse. He mounted him in a run barely managing to hang onto the boots and disappeared deeper in the trees and out of sight.

Where Alex had gone over the edge of the ravine a tree was growing up the side of the bank and broke his fall. He landed in a heap and lay unconscious on the tiny ledge. The earth had eroded inward just enough underneath a huge rock that he was hidden out of view from above and by the tree from below. The tree and the ledge had saved him from falling another thirty feet to the bottom. During the tumble his head had hit the protruding rock. He had a big gash on his forehead just at the edge of his hairline.

Alex laid unmoving the rest of that day and all of the night. In the late morning he finally regained consciousness. He had no way of knowing that Edmond and two other soldiers had come back to search for him. He opened his eyes but could see very little. He had bled profusely from his head wound. His face and eyes were swollen and covered in dried blood. He was trying to sit up. He did not remember what had happened and did not know where he was.

He got to his knees in a crawling position and tried to raise up, but the two arrows still protruding a few inches from his back scraped against the big granite rock above him and he screamed in agony. At the same time the little space he had been lying in was not large enough for him to extend his legs. Because Alex was in such a mental fog from the pain caused by his head wound and the two arrows still in his body he did not really have the capability to realize what was happening. In moving around his feet had slipped out of the little indented spot and the tree's limbs could no longer hold him. He tumbled the remaining thirty feet screaming in agony as the arrows tugged through the fall and his head slammed against the side of the ravine wall on yet another rock. He promptly passed out when he slammed to the bottom of the ravine feet first. As the bone in his leg broke it sounded almost like a whip being cracked in the air.

Soft Dove and Running Feet, two Indian women who were camped nearby had ridden their horses down to a spot where the creek had widened and had a little depth to it. The spot was very near the trail, but was around a bend and out of sight from the crossing. Some beaver had built a dam across the creek here which had made for a good fishing spot. They were quietly sitting with their baskets in the water waiting for an unsuspecting fish to swim in. They heard the first scream followed almost immediately by a second one. Both women looked at each other wondering who it was and why they had screamed. They knew from the sound of it that someone was in serious trouble. They quickly headed toward the direction of the screams working their way down the rocky creek bank to where the trail crossed. They started walking in the direction the soldiers had taken. They were certain that they were near the place where the screams had come from.

When they reached the site in the road where the soldiers were ambushed there were lots of flies gathered in the area. It was easy to tell where the men and horses had lost blood because of so many black flies that covered the bloody places. The flies scattered and swarmed as the women approached, but went right back as soon as they had passed by a few feet. They knew that someone was nearby and from the sounds of the screams they were hurt badly. But where were they. They signed with each other and agreed that the sound had not been very far from the creek. It was decided they would search the area near the trail from the main battle site and back to the creek. Soft Dove started searching on one side of the trail and Running Feet on the other side.

As Soft Dove reached the ravine she carefully worked her way along its edge. She made sure the ground was stable before she peered over the edge. She had only looked over a couple of times before she saw Alex. One of his legs was folded under him in an unnatural way. Soft Dove knew it was broken. In his tumble the wounds that had stopped bleeding had been torn open and were now bleeding again. Soft Dove could see that his clothing was soaked in blood. She called Running Feet and told her she had found him.

Running Feet came to where she stood. They quickly found a spot where they could easily get down in the ravine to where Alex lay. They checked to see if he was breathing. He was. It was decided that Running Feet would go and retrieve their horses from their fishing spot while Soft Dove figured out how to best try to keep Alex from bleeding to death.

Soft Dove took her knife and cut Alex's shirt in the front from his body. She then cut it into some strips. Tying two of them together she pushed the wound on his forehead together as best she could and then tied the strips tightly around his head. She hoped this would slow the bleeding until they could get him back to camp. She continued to cut his shirt into strips and tied them together. When she cut his pants leg away from the leg that was broken she was relieved to see that the bone had not come through the skin. It appeared that it might be a clean break and would heal nicely if there were no complications.

She would wait until Running Feet got back and could get some bark to make a brace and help her pull the broken bone into place. She left the extra strips she had cut from his pants lying there for the leg brace. She was now ready to turn him over and see what was causing all the blood that was coming from his back. When she turned him as gently as she could and saw the fletching or tail was broken off the two arrows and a small part of the shaft of each arrow was protruding from his back there was no question of the cause. One of them was almost all the way through. It would be a matter of burning her knife, cutting the skin, grabbing the arrow head and pulling it on through. There was always danger in this, but it had to come out. There was no way to be sure how much damage it had done just yet. Hopefully it was as it looked and had missed any vital organs. The other arrow had not penetrated very deeply. Soft Dove knew he was hurt badly, but continued to work in the hopes that they could get him back together enough to reach camp with him still alive. If they could do that she felt she might have a chance with Running Feet's help to save him. They had to try. They could not depend on their man to help them. He was off trapping and would probably be gone for several more days.

By the time Running Feet came back with their horses Soft Dove had managed to pull the arrows out and slow the bleeding by stuffing the wounds and wrapping strips of his clothing around his chest. They quickly took the tree bark Running Feet had cut and set Alex's leg. By the time they were finished both his pants legs had been cut into strips and were used to wrap around the tree bark. He certainly was a strange and pitiful site lying there all bloody with just enough pants left to cover his private parts. The rest of his clothes were in strips tied around his body from head to toe almost.

The women knew it was going to be difficult if not impossible to lift him up and on to the horse with him unconscious. Instead of trying they decided to make a travois with some small branches and vines that should hold together long enough to get him to the camp site. Just having to lift him from the ground to the travois had not been an easy feat because of the dead weight working against them. The climb out of the ravine proved to be a challenge also. It took a little time to find a spot along the walls that would work. The travois almost turned over once but had righted itself just in time. They were both glad that he was not awake. It had made working on his body much easier and would also make the rough ride back to camp more tolerable for the unconscious man.

As they worked their way carefully choosing a path that would avoid hanging the travois on a rock or tree root the women discussed the strange situation they found themselves in. They were not concerned that he was a white man. They both felt life was life and to be cherished at all costs. Besides their man had the white skin. He was a trapper and had left them at their camp while he went off to trap and hunt around the Kansas River. They felt it would please him that they had helped one of his people. The beaver were plentiful in this part of the country and they knew he would be back soon.

They were relieved to get back to their camp without any mishaps. Both of them felt safe in their temporary home. It was a cave and sat back in a granite wall with an entrance that was very difficult to see at any angle. There was a tiny spring that supplied them with plenty of water for their daily needs. The cave had a natural draft that vented the smoke through to the outside. It was easy for them to secure it at night. When their man, Andre had found it there was no sign of it being used by anyone else for many years.

Just as they got Alex inside the cave and the fire built back up a cool rain had started to fall. Running Feet set about warming some water for them to bathe Alex. Soft Dove had much knowledge of the medicinal plants and herbs. She went to a little alcove where several plants were hanging to dry. From some of the baskets on the floor she removed some small leather pouches where she kept assorted dried herbs. She also got a pouch that had a dried leather sealed pouch that contained a poultice. After cleaning the head wound she sewed it up the way Andre had taught her. She cleaned the wounds made by the arrows and applied some of the poultice. She then packed the wounds with cleaned moss. Lastly she wrapped his leg back with clean strips of leather. There was nothing else to do to help heal the leg but wait. She would keep giving him special teas to fight infection when she or Running Feet could get it down him. They bathed him as best they could without moving him too much more. Alex lay unconscious on a buffalo skin sleeping mat near the fire. They covered him well to keep him warm.

Running Feet added more water to their stew just in case Alex woke up and they could get a few sips down him. She took the fish they had caught and covered them with a thick layer of clay. She then put them in some hot coals. When they were finished baking and cooled, she would take a rock and break the clay wrapping. The scales and skin would be stuck to the clay and the remaining fish would be delicious. The rain that had started falling earlier was really coming down heavier. The coziness and warmth of the cave was a real comfort to the women. Neither of them were afraid of being without a man around, but were always much happier and content when Andre was in camp with them.

It had been two days since they had found Alex and brought him back to the cave. It had rained most of that time. It was not cold weather yet, but with the rain the air was chilly. The morning they found Alex their plan had been to bathe at the creek after they had caught what fish they needed. Neither of them wanted to leave the other alone at the camp with their patient long enough to go back to the creek. They weren't really afraid of him, but did not know what to expect once he woke up. That is if he did wake up.

Soft Dove had taken their cooking stones and put them in the coals. She and Running Feet had decided to take a warm bath. They had collected water from the spring and when the stones were heated a little they placed them in the water. Once the bathing was done Soft Dove had gone to her sleeping mat. She had placed it a few feet away from Alex, so she could hear him if he woke up. Running Feet was sitting close to the fire.

Alex opened his eyes. His slightly turned head was facing toward the fire. Running Feet had decided to dry her hair before going to bed. She was sitting naked with her legs bent and her feet together and to her right side. She was between Alex and the fire with her back facing him. Running Feet was braiding her hair and when she turned her head to the side he could see her profile. The fire was emanating very little light and her whole body appeared as a silhouette accented by the soft firelight. There was no other light in the cave. It was quite a compelling and beautiful site. Alex just lay there watching her not sure if he was dreaming or not. He was awake only a couple of minutes before he drifted back to a sleep filled with confusing sounds and images. Running Feet did not know he had been awake.

The next morning Running Feet had caught a rabbit and had him simmering in the stew pot. She also had dug some roots and wild onions she was adding to the stew. Soft Dove was busy checking Alex's head and back injuries. As she was removing the bandage from his head he opened his eyes. Soft Dove told Running Feet to bring him a drink of water.

He took a few sips and faintly asked in French, "Who are you?"

Soft Dove had been with her man for several years and understood some basic French.
Running Feet had only been with them a little over a year and knew only a few words.

Soft Dove put her palm flat on her chest and said in French, "My name Soft Dove. She then pointed at Running Feet and said, "She Running Feet. You rest."

Alex managed to swallow a little bit more of the stew broth and dozed through yet another restless night. The next morning he heard a man's voice. When he opened his eyes he was looking into the face of a bearded white man who was squatted down and leaning over him. The trapper had returned in the night and the women had told him all that had happened.

Alex asked this time in English, "Who are you?"

The man replied with a heavy French accent, "My name is Andre. Looks like you have been in an Indian fight. I am not sure why they did not scalp you or take you as a captive. Either way you are a lucky man. If my squaws had not been fishing near where you were found and heard your screams, who knows what might have happened. I think you might have wound up being a meal for hungry wolves. You have not told me who you are."

Alex just stared at Andre with a look of total confusion on his face and said nothing. Running Feet came to the other side of Alex with some cooled broth. She fed him several spoons full. As he swallowed the broth Alex kept looking around the cave as though he was searching for something while seeming to be deep in thought. He recognized this woman as the one who had sat by the fire.

Andre said, "You are welcome here until you have gained your strength back. However, while you are here I insist upon knowing who is in my camp and why you were nearby in the first place. I have gathered from my women that you and others were in a fight with some Indians. Where did you come from, where were you headed and why did your party leave you?"

With much confusion written all over Alex's face he looked at Andre and said, "I don't know."

"What do you mean? You don't know. You don't know where you were going?"

"I mean I don't know anything. I don't even know who I am!"

With a look of dismay Andre leaned back and stared at Alex before saying, "Looks like that rock you hit caused you to lose a lot more than just some of your blood. Running Feet, bring our guest some more of that stew." Alex ate a couple of bites and then drifted back into a troubled sleep again.

Andre and Soft Dove were walking back to the site of the battle. Andre commented on how well they had managed to conceal the tracks of the horses and the travois that lead to camp. He taught his squaws to be alert when he was gone and take extra precautions. Andre had developed an amicable relationship with the Indians that lived nearby. He spoke some of their dialect and was in full command of sign language. He felt that they were safe in this location, but more and more the indigenous people were feeling the push of the white man into their lands. The unrest aroused in some of the braves who traveled through this area because of the infringement of settlers on their land could be very dangerous for anyone. He felt certain this is what had happened to Alex. Somehow he had managed to keep his scalp and that was amazing.

Soft Dove took him to the location where the fight appeared to have started. Andre hoped he might find something that was lost or left that he could take back and show Alex. Something that might jog his memory. There was not much sign of a battle at all after all the rain that had come through the area except for a few recently broken twigs of brush and damaged tree bark. If you weren't really looking you would not know anything had transpired here. It was almost as though the rain had taken all of Alex's history away with it as it ran into the creek and then flowed on into the muddy Missouri River.

Soft Dove next showed him the spot in the gully floor where Alex was lying unconscious. Andre asked her to describe the clothes Alex had on when she found him. She told him he only had on his shirt and pants. She then told him about the bleeding. How she was afraid to move him without attempting to stop some of the flow of blood. Soft Dove explained how she had cut the shirt and pants in strips for bandages.

Andre asked her, "Where are the remains of Alex's clothes?"

Soft Dove replied, "They were so bloody Running Feet burned everything after we cleaned his wounds and changed the bandages. We were afraid the scent of blood might draw the wolves to our cave."

"Did his shirt or pants have anything on them to indicate it might be a uniform?"

"We saw nothing. His shirt only had a few buttons sewn on it. We did save those."

They searched around in the ravine to see if anything might have been overlooked. They found nothing.

Andre said, "It looks like if there might have been anything here to help identify who was fighting against the Indians it was either taken, buried in the skirmish or washed away. Let's head back to the camp." He placed his hand over her protruding stomach and said with a big grin on his face, "I hear our papoose saying he wants something to eat. We are both looking forward to more of yours and Running Feet's good cooking."

Soft Dove smiled at Andre with affection and said, "You know it is Running Feet whose cooking you like better than mine. So do we." she said as she patted her swollen stomach. They both had a good laugh and headed toward the cave.

While they were returning to camp Soft Dove said, "I do not think the man will be well enough to leave alone when it is time for us to return to the south in a few days."

Andre said, "Do not worry my Little Dove," as he sometimes affectionately called her. "We will wait until our stranger is strong enough to go with us if he chooses. He may want to strike out on his own in search of his identity."

He secretly hoped he would join them. As much as Andre loved the wilderness and the solitude of trapping, he often wished he had a man around to help him. The beaver was plentiful, but he could only manage so many. But even more than that he would like someone to converse with where there were no language barriers. A man had a lot of time to ponder things out in this country. It was good to have someone to talk to about them.

When they reached the camp, Running Feet had finished cutting the deer meat Andre had brought back into strips and had it placed on the drying racks with a fire going underneath. She was scraping and cleaning the skin. It would be used to make a tunic for her or Soft Dove to wear. There was a delicious smell outside coming from chunks of the meat that had been pierced with a thin stick and were sizzling and dripping over the fire. As soon as they stepped inside the aroma of a stew permeated the cave. Andre sighed with contentment. He went to his mat which Running Feet had placed near the fire while they were gone and sat down. Running Feet handed him a bowl of the stew. Andre finished his stew and lit his pipe. He was enjoying just being back in his cave as he sat and watched flames dance in the fire.

Soft Dove found the two buttons that she took off of his shirt and gave them to him to look at. He saw nothing that would distinguish them from ordinary buttons. They would be of no help in finding out who their patient was.

Soft Dove was very much in love with husband. When he had told her this past winter that he was taking another squaw as his wife, she had become very angry. She recalled the fight she put up with Andre.

"It will be better. You will see." Andre had replied.

"Who filthy squaw live in teepee?" she had screamed at him in French. She used the broken French she knew when upset with him.

"Her name is Running Feet. She will free you from much of the work and can do all of the cooking."

"Now, you no like my cooking?" She had flared back with her hands and mouth moving rapidly.

Andre knew his decision was going to upset Soft Dove. Andre did love her and never wanted to hurt her, but they really had needed help. Not only that, but Soft Dove was not the best cook in the world. She did try Running Feet was an excellent cook. He had discovered this while eating with the family that held her captive. It was not uncommon for trappers to have more than one squaw and when this Indian slave had been offered to him in trade, he had felt sorry for her more than anything. But the taste of her cooking had sealed his decision. Running Feet had been physically and verbally abused and belittled by the Indian family she had served. He had not expected any hesitancy on her part to live away from those people. He was right. When it was time to leave she had willingly followed him out of the dwelling without so much as a backward glance.

He had told Soft Dove about the cruel treatment Running Feet had endured. He had known Soft Dove would change her mind when she realized the help Running Feet really would be. He also knew it was lonely for her without someone from her people to talk with, even though she never once complained. They were not from the same group, she and Soft Dove, but were both a part of the same people. Andre had taken Soft Dove by her shoulders and held her far enough away from him that he could look her in the eyes.

He said, "Woman, stop this senseless chatter. I am going now to get Running Feet. You will see that she is not dirty, but very clean like you. She is a great cook and will take a lot of the work from you. Life will be better for you, for both of us Soft Dove."

Soft Dove had calmed down and the fire that was in her eyes was now replaced by pain. She had reverted back to sign language.

"You think only of your stomach and new company for your sleeping mat. For you it is better. It is not good for me. It is bad." Soft Dove had jerked herself away from his grasp and had run out of the warm teepee to the cold snow covered ground. She had run for the privacy offered by the trees in the forest. She remembered not wanting him or anyone to see the tears she had been unable to stop from falling. She had cried with abandon and had let her eyes empty themselves. When the tears had finally stopped Soft Dove had known she would not speak of her unhappiness again. Somehow she would find a way to share her man without anger. She had gone back to the teepee. Andre was gone.

Soft Dove had sat staring into the fire. The teepee flap had opened and inside had stepped the new woman. Soft Dove had noticed that she was short where she was tall. Just as Andre had said she had been dressed in a clean tunic with her hair neatly braided, clean and shining from the bear grease she had applied. The squaw had stopped as soon as she was inside and looked at Soft Dove then dropped her gaze to the ground. Before she had done that Soft Dove had seen the result of the beatings and inhumane treatment Running Feet had come to know as a part of her existence. She also had seen in those brief moments that the new woman was not expecting anything to be different. She had stood there with her head down waiting for something to be thrown at her. Whether it was a fist, hand, foot or loose item lying about she waited. At the very least Running Feet had known there would be words of hate assaulting her ears.

Surprising to Soft Dove, after seeing the fear in this woman, her built up anger had dissipated and was replaced by compassion. She had walked over to the woman. Running Feet had been unable to keep from cringing as she drew near. Soft Dove had reached out and lifted her chin up. She had begun to communicate with her in her native tongue and with sign language,

"Hold up your head, woman. We are the proud squaws of our man, Andre. We do not walk with our heads bowed in fear and shame. Our man is kind and a good provider. We will share in the keeping of peace and happiness in our home. He tells me you are a good cook. Is this true?"

Running Feet had looked back at Soft Dove and with hope in her voice had answered, "Some have said I am."

"Good. See what you can do with that stew."

Soft Dove had shown her where she kept the herbs, dried vegetables and roots. It hadn't been long before the pot that had been simmering over the fire turned into an aroma that had caused Soft Dove to anticipate food more than she could remember since her mother's cooking. Andre had been right. His new woman could cook. Not only that but they would have no trouble communicating.

Soft Dove remembered thinking that the hardest part of having another woman in the teepee would be when the night time came and he chose Running Feet's sleeping mat and not hers. Many days had passed since that first night and Andre did not do so. When she finally had asked him why she was surprised but very happy with his answer.

"You are my wife. I do not need nor want more." Andre had told her.

Before Running Feet came Soft Dove had all the chores to do herself along with preparing the meat from a fresh kill and then cleaning, scraping and pounding the skins of many of the animals to make them soft for clothing. Running Feet like Soft Dove was not lazy. She too wanted herself and their camp clean and neat. It was customary for the first squaw or wife to direct the newest one, but almost from the start Running Feet knew what needed to be done and did it. She had completely taken over the cooking.

Because of her help, Soft Dove had more time to spend searching for and collecting her herbs, vines, plant leaves, spider webs and roots she could use for their medicinal needs. She was not sure sometimes how she always knew which plants to use. Her grandmother had taught her a lot, but there were so many she could not remember being shown or told about. Soft Dove and Running Feet had become close friends. Both of them had been very much in need of one. As they had worked through their chores each day they became familiar with one another's past. One day when they were at the creek sunning themselves after bathing Soft Dove asked her friend how she got her name.

Running Feet had told her, "It was given to me when I was a baby. My mother told me that when I was not bundled or in the cradle board that my feet and legs were constantly moving as though I was running. She said she and my father would laugh watching me and call me Running Feet. After I started walking my steps soon turned into a run. My father and mother had decided that Running Feet was to be my permanent name. How did you get yours?"

Soft Dove told her about a dove with a broken wing she had found. She had brought it home to the teepee crying. Her mother had bound the wing without much hope that it would survive. It did. They had kept the bird and it soon became a pet. Soft Dove was always picking it up and rubbing its head and feathers. She would say how soft the dove was. She was happy to see in time that the bird could fly again, but when it flew away and did not return she could not hide the sadness of knowing she might not see it ever again. Her grandmother had consoled her and said she thought the dove might come back and visit.

One day she was playing outside the teepee alone. Suddenly a dove landed on the ground in front of her. Soft Dove knew it was her little friend, because the dove let her pick it up. They visited for a few minutes and then the dove flew off. Soft Dove ran in the teepee shouting to her Grandmother that her bird had come back. Her grandmother listened to what had happened and then gave her the name of Soft Dove.

Alex was fast becoming stronger each day. He was now able to sit up for much longer periods of time. The women were at the creek fishing when Andre stepped through the door and saw Alex propped and looking at the fire.

"Well hello there, Friend. You look a lot better today. I see some color in your face. I hope you don't mind my calling you Friend. I just can't seem to get comfortable with calling you Mister. Of course, if you have a name you prefer just let me know what it is."

Alex spoke up and said, "Andre I like that. However, it is you three who have been friends to me. This I won't forget. I don't know how I can ever repay you, but I will find a way when I regain my strength."

The name had stuck and everyone was comfortable with it. They all understood without having to discuss it that Alex did not want to dwell openly too much about what he could not remember. All three also knew he had hopes the memories along with his real name would return to him.

CHAPTER 17

Agatha stood with her big brown eyes larger than usual and her hand pressed to her mouth as Edmond told her what had happened on their mission.

When he had finished she said, "Edmond you have to try to find him. Oh, dear Lord. We have to get to Grace right away before she hears about this from anyone else. She will need you to tell her."

They found Grace in her flower garden out back. She was sitting with a bowl in her lap shelling dried peas. When she saw Agatha and then Edmond come through the gate she knew something was wrong. The look on their faces caused her heart to fall to her feet. She bent and placed the bowl of peas down on the ground and stood up. However, she felt faint and had to sit back down.

Before Grace could get to her she said, "Where is he? Where is Alex?"

Edmond began to tell her what had happened starting with the stop at the creek. He told her how he had left him to join the others and Alex was still standing at the creek by his horse. He told her that he was the last one to finish before joining the other soldiers.

"That's the last time I saw him. Just as I reached the men is when the ambush started. We had anticipated the strong possibility of such a thing happening when we approached the creek, but certainly did not see it coming in that location.

"We had to retreat back across the creek. Our casualties were heavy. Eight of our men were killed, another three seriously injured and Alex missing. We made such a hasty retreat, we did not notice he was missing until we had ridden a good distance from the attack site. Once we were certain the Indians weren't still close in the area we went back to the site and searched for him, but did not find a trace of him or his horse. We can only assume he was captured and taken as a prisoner. Grace, you know if Alex can he will get back to you."

Grace looked at Edmond and even though neither one of them said it both knew the chances of that happening were not very good.

As they had been saddling Agatha's horse before going to see Grace, Agatha had asked Edmond, "What do you think the chances are of finding him alive?"

Edmond had told her the truth. "Agatha, most likely they are torturing him to death right now in a slow and cruel way. I pray if that is the case that he dies quickly. If we are lucky enough to find him, most likely depending on what tribe took him there might not be much left to find. Especially if they have cut off body parts and the wolves have found what's left."

Agatha had sat on the bench beside Grace with her arm over her best friend's shoulder and said, "Grace, you must hang on. There is a search party that has already left the fort and Edmond will be joining it. You know Edmond will find him, if he can be found. He could be back home in a few days."

"Agatha, I never talked about it, but the fear of him not coming back from a mission was always just under the surface each time he had to leave. I would fight to keep those thoughts from rising all the way up.

Somehow, I felt by not thinking about it that alone would be enough to keep it from happening. Isn't that crazy?"

"No Grace. It is not for I do the very same thing."

Rosa and Agatha spent as much time as they possibly could with Grace while some of the men searched for him. Hannah did not know what had happened yet. She and Francois had decided to marry when the house they were building was completed. Hannah had gone to St. Louis shopping for furnishings. She had intended to spend up to two weeks if needed to have first pick of what was coming off the boats when possible.

Agatha and Rosa had brought some soup and bread they had made and were sitting with Grace watching as she nibbled and sipped out of consideration for her friends. She was not hungry and did not feel that she would ever be again.

After the table had been cleared and they had all walked out on the front porch Grace said, "Wait a minute you two." Both stopped and turned. Grace reached and took a hand from each. She said, "You are so dear to me. I will never forget the way you have shown your love through this nightmare. But, it is time you get back to doing what is most important in your lives. That is taking care of your families. I do not want to see either of you until Hannah gets back and we can get together to start her wedding dress. I have to start keeping myself busy until Alex returns. I promise that I will eat. I want to be healthy in case Alex is hurt. If he is he will need my strength" Agatha and Rosa waved goodbye from the wagon as they left.

When they were certain there was no danger in Grace hearing them Agatha turned to Rosa and said, "Well how do you think she is doing? I am worried for her, because she has not spoken of the possibility of Alex's death since Edmond and I came to tell her what happened."

"You know she is strong," Agatha. It is going to be a long while before we start to see our Grace come back, but she will."

The days passed and there was no sign of Alex anywhere. Grace was hurting in a way she could not believe a human could hurt and continue to breathe. The search party had returned after a month long trip. They had found tracks they followed toward the south for several days until they too had vanished after a heavy rain. Their orders had been to return if no sign was found after three weeks.

It had now been almost six months since he had been missing. Grace sat at her writing desk with her journal open in front of her and pen in hand. This journal she had been keeping since she was a young girl. She had not been able to write in it at all the first few weeks that Alex had been missing. She sat now holding her pen in one hand and holding her necklace in the other. It was gold and in the outlined shape of two five point stars diagonally touching. Alex had given it to her on their last anniversary. When he had given it to her he had said, 'Grace, you sometimes call me your shining star. You, are mine. Because of you there is now much light in my life where there had been little to none for most of it. Thank you.' He had put it over her head. Grace had not taken it off since.

"Oh Alex," she whispered, "Where are you? How can I be on this earth if you leave it without me?" When she said those words, immediately she remembered the sowing circle talking about Enoch who was on the earth three hundred sixty five years and walked with God three hundred of those years. Then God just took him. She pulled out her Bible and found the reference in Genesis 5:24. Grace felt more than anything that Alex was not dead. He was just like Enoch and was just not. Not here with her anymore, she thought. She knew if he had died she would know somehow. Yet, letting herself believe that he was alive and had not returned to her was some form of insanity. She kept telling herself, if he were alive he would be here or at the very least have sent word of his whereabouts.

"Grace," she said out loud, "You have to get a hold of yourself."

How in the world was she supposed to do that she wondered. Very few nights passed that she did not dream of Alex. The dream repeatedly consisted of nothing except she could hear Alex's voice calling for her. There was nothing more in the dream. She would wake up sometimes crying while still hearing him call her name. Many times in order to go back to sleep after this happened, she would imagine Alex was on one of the stars she could see up in the night sky. She would close her eyes and imagine an array of stars. She would pick one to focus on. Before long it was as though she had gone to that star. She could see him sitting by a fire talking with another man she imagined to be Enoch. She would think to herself that if God had taken Enoch, he could just as easily have taken Alex too. Grace would imagine that they were planning another trip back to earth. How they might do this, she could not fathom. She knew it was not rational, but every time she did this she would drift off into a restful sleep until time to get up and start another day. Grace entered these thoughts and her repetitive dream in her journal.

She then closed it and picked up The Sowing Circle journal. The last time the group had met they realized that they were definitely asking questions that continued leading to more. The list of questions for the group had grown into quite an impressive collection.

It seemed that most days Grace could not be still and concentrate on any one thing for long unless it was a mundane chore that had to be done. Still at times she would find she had walked away in the middle of making bread or another project only to discover it later and then finish. She would not remember having walked away. Today she was determined to be more focused. She picked up the journal and read the list of questions from Genesis Chapter 6.

- *Who were the sons of God that took daughters of men for their wives?*
- *How many sons does God have?*
- *What happened to the Giants that were on the earth during this time and later?*
- *Who were these children of the sons of God and the women of earth that became mighty men of old also known as men of renown?*
- *What happened to these beings?*

Grace remembered that Rosa had told them about a story her mother's people had passed down for many years about these giants that were almost twice as tall as the Comanche. They were said to have been a race of white men who ruled over all the land from the high places. She said other tribes had spoken of Giants as tall as full grown trees her mother had told her. It was said that they could stand with one foot on one side of the creek and the other on the opposite side. Agatha told them about hearing her parents tell of a black race of giants spoken of and passed down by their Scottish and Welsh ancestors. Grace could not remember hearing about the giant people, but would ask her parents about it when she could.

She heard Agatha calling her and knew it was time for their next meeting. They were actually going to be sewing today. Earlier Grace had lowered the quilt rack from the ceiling and placed their chairs around it. When she walked in, Agatha and Hannah were already sitting with their needles and thread in hand and beginning to quilt. Rosa was bent over her sewing bag and fussing about not finding her thimble.

"Here Rosa, use one of mine and return it when you find yours." Agatha said. Their fingers were close in size and it fit perfectly.

Before Grace sat down she said, "I was just reading our list of questions from Genesis 6. Before I get my sewing things out does anyone have any more thoughts on this?"

"I do." Said Hannah.

"In that case," said Grace. "Let me get to my writing desk where I can take notes. Guess you noticed I moved it closer where I can hear everything that's said." With that she sat down, opened her ink jar, the Sowing Circle Journal and looked up at Hannah after she dipped her quill pin in the dark ink.

"This Chapter 6 in Genesis just totally confuses me." Hannah said. She got up and walked over to Grace's desk and picked up the Bible. She then went to the table, sat down and opened it to Chapter 6. "God the creator of all says he can't continue to deal with man and shortens our time to one hundred and twenty years. Then he talks about the giants that were on the earth then and after that and the sons of God having children with the daughters of man. These children became mighty men it says. Were the giants the sons of God or was this two different types of men? If they were giants how in the world would a woman be able to get pregnant with a giant and then give birth to a giant baby? Where did these sons of God go? What about these children that became men of renown? What happened to them? Was there a separate race of people that were giants? If there was where did they come from?

"You know Chapter 5 starts off with the generations of Adam listed through to Noah. All these men lived for hundreds of years. Most of them were closer to making it to a thousand years. Enoch was the only one who lived a short time compared to the rest. He lived three hundred and sixty five years and then was not for God took him. He walked with God three hundred years before he took him. Compared to the others he would have been a very young man when this happened. I really wonder what was so special about Enoch that

God wanted to keep him with him and did not let him die as the others had. Why does the Bible say he was not? Did he just vanish or go up in the sky with God? I just find this really fascinating."

Hannah continued, "God saw the wickedness of man was great in the earth and every imagination of the thoughts of his heart was only evil continually. He then said he would destroy man and beast, the creeping thing and the fowls of the air because he was sorry that he had made them. Hannah got up and walked over to where Rosa and Agatha's babies were playing on the floor. "Just look at these precious beings. Do they look like their thoughts are evil? Weren't there babies and innocent children on the earth then? How can babies be destroyed because they have evil thoughts? Why destroy them and every living creature except Noah and his family? If God knows everything wouldn't he know how these people would turn out before he made them? If so, why make them in the first place? Agatha had brought her Bible today and was sitting with it in her lap. She said, "Noah had found Grace in the eyes of the Lord. He was a just man and perfect in his generations. Noah walked with God just as Enoch had, but unlike Enoch he was not taken and lived nine hundred and fifty years. I wonder how Noah managed to be the only perfect one out of all the people."

"You are right Hannah," said Agatha. It doesn't make sense. There were obviously many people in the land at this time. Just go back and read Genesis 4. When Adam and Eve's son Cain killed his brother, he was thrown out of the garden. He then went and dwelt in the land of Nod, had a wife and son named Enoch. He built a city and named it after Enoch. This is a different Enoch than the one God took. Four generations later Enoch's descendants became the fathers of tent dwellers and those with cattle, handlers of the harp and organ and others artificers of brass and iron.

"What kind of God creates everything on earth and then decides to destroy everyone and everything except for one family and two of all living creatures that he puts on a boat?

"Why would the Creator decide to destroy everything in a flood?

Rosa said. "He created heaven and earth in six days. Why did he have to drown mankind to start over with Noah? It doesn't look like it did much good to start over as there is still so much evil abounding in this world today. The more I read the stronger I feel that this story has missing parts. At times it seems as though it is somewhat like our quilt before it is put together. There are a lot of pieces in different sizes and shapes, but when it's together it makes a lovely pattern. Maybe some of the pieces or parts of this story were lost."

Grace who was trying to get everything down stopped writing. "You know, if you haven't read the very beginning of the Bible, you might want too."

Hannah said, "What do you mean the very beginning. We have. We started with Genesis 1:1."

"Yes, we did. But before that there is a part that talks about the writing of this Bible and the translating of it into English that is quite lengthy. We all have it in the front of our 1611 King James Bibles. I decided to read it all the way through and found it tedious in parts, but fascinating, interesting and informative in others. Let me see. Here's my notes I have made so far. Would you like to hear them?"

"Yes." They all said in unison as if someone else was there with a directing wand that had cued them to speak.

Grace started reading her notes. "The Book of God, as the writer of this introduction calls it was first written in the Hebrew language. An Egyptian king named Ptolome Philadelph procured seventy interpreters to translate the Bible out of Hebrew and into Greek. The Greek tongue was well known and familiar to most inhabitants in Asia, many places in Europe and Africa also.

"This writer wrote that it is certain that the Translation was not so sound and so perfect, but that it needed in many places corrections. Following after the seventy and not long after Christ there were it seems up to six more editions or translations of the seventy learned men's work.

"These seventy were referred to as prophets by some, but were eventually considered interpreters. They did many things well as learned men, but some stumbled and fell through oversight and ignorance. The writer says that at times they added to the original and other times they took away. There is quite a bit more, but this is all I managed to get through and take notes on."

The women all looked at each other and said nothing more. They put on their thimbles, picked up their needles and began to push them down or pull them up through the quilt with the threads heard clearly as they obediently followed the needles. Both babies were curled up and sleeping on the blanket Grace always put out for them. She did not join them at the quilt rack. She went back to her journal and continued writing. The women continued their quilting with each one apparently in deep thought.

Agatha found she could not concentrate on the quilting and walked over to the table and sat down with Grace's Bible opened in front of her. She went to the introduction and started silently reading.

Rosa finally spoke again after a deep sigh. "My mother told me that one day the Great Spirit collected swirls of dust from four directions to create the Comanche people. She also told me there was a time when many wise men were warned of a great flood in their dreams. In these dreams all the people were drowned they said. The wise men were afraid and called a council to decide what to do. One of the wise men suggested they build a great raft to put the people in when the rains started.

"The ones who believed the dreams worked hard to get the raft built. The people who did not believe in the dreams laughed and were idle while the great raft was being built. When the rains came the builders took food they had collected and climbed in the rafts with their families while they waited for the waters to rise. When the waters rose the people who had not believed had climbed the highest mountain, but it was soon covered too. They drowned. My mother told me that there are many more stories of creation and this great flood from other tribes, but this one was her favorite."

It seemed as though each of the women were like a tea cup filled to the rim and if one more drop goes in the cup it will run over. Their heads were so full of questions there just wasn't room for one more right now. Each felt like they might explode if they dared to voice another one. Instead they sat quietly as Grace went back to her writing and Agatha continued to read. Hannah and Rosa continued quilting.

CHAPTER 18

Alex had found a spot on a huge boulder where he liked to sit on the hillside and look out over the little valley and the lake below. They were in the middle of Osage country a three or four days ride south of the Missouri River and about the same distance west of the Mississippi River. The closest Post was a few days east toward the Mississippi at Cape Girardeau.

To get to this spot where he could enjoy the view was quite a climb for Alex with his leg still a bit out of sorts. He didn't complain because the reward was well worth it. This place that Andre had picked out to build their home was so beautiful at times it felt magical. He watched the smoke drifting from the chimney and knew Running Feet had something delicious simmering over the fire. He could see her outside working in the garden. She was preparing the soil so it would be ready for the seeds of corn, beans and squash she would soon be planting. The sky was a crisp blue without a cloud to be seen anywhere. The sun was warming the days now, but when it set the cool night air would be back.

Soft Dove was down by the lake washing clothes. She had hung the baby in the cradle board up on a tree branch nearby. Andre was casually strolling toward the lake. He stopped and squatted down near Soft Dove. Alex looked at them and wondered if there had been someone in his life he had loved as much as those two loved each other. He was pretty certain the light haired woman with the double star necklace he kept seeing in his dreams was the key to answering that question. She always looked as if she was searching for something or someone. He could never understand what she was saying. Her words were muffled and reminded him a little of the sound made when someone was trying to talk underwater.

Today Alex had come up to the rock to be alone. He wanted solitude to think about the offer he had accepted from Andre this morning. They had just finished breakfast and walked down to the lake.

"Friend," Andre had said, "I have been thinking about your situation and it appears to me that it would be a whole lot easier to strike out on your hunt for where you came from if you had a little money. Soft Dove, Running Feet and I have all agreed that we would like for you to join us for as long as you like. As soon as you are up to it we can head out and do some trapping. Of course, you will get a fair share of the profits. You don't have to give me an answer now. Think about it a day or two if you like."

"I don't need to think about it. I accept your offer and am ready to go whenever you say." Alex extended his hand to Andre. They shook on it while grinning at each other. "Thank you, Andre."

It was hard to tell who was happier with the arrangement. Andre because he would have that male company he missed or Alex who now would have some direction to go in rather than days passing with no plans for the future and no memories from the past to guide him.

"Soft Dove tells me your leg should be as good as new in another week or so. I say let's head out then and trap our way toward Cape Girardeau. We probably won't get a big load, but it will fill some space in them empty pockets of yours and get enough to purchase a knife, gun and maybe a good horse or at least another pack mule. Anyway, if we wait a few days that will give me some time to clear out more land. The women are having a fit to expand the garden."

The men worked cutting the trees and burning the stumps out. Soft Dove and Running Feet helped quite a bit in removing the rocks they could carry and threw them in a pile that grew in size each day. It was very time consuming just getting the fire wood cut up so the women could haul it to the cabin and stacked to dry. Almost two weeks had passed, but the women were happy with the expansion of the garden area. There was enough wood to last through the summer and a good portion of the next winter when they finally finished. The men decided to leave at daybreak the following morning.

Everyone noticed that Alex seemed to have been lifted in spirit since Andre and he had agreed to trap together. He had actually been whistling that afternoon as they were getting ready for their trip. Alex had very little to pack, but Running Feet gave him a leather pouch with a strap long enough that he could put it over his head and across his chest. He really did not have anything to put in it now, but knew once he had a gun again it would be used for powder and balls. She also gave him a bow and some arrows that she had made. He had seen her making them, but thought they were for her use when she hunted.

Alex was trying not to show how excited he was about finally having a plan in place. He was not sure if he was a dancer before, but felt like dancing a jig. He just could not stop whistling as he went about collecting his gear for the trip. He put his bow over his shoulder along with the quiver of arrows. He had decided he would practice using them along the way when they stopped and made camp. Strangely the bow and arrow seemed very familiar to him as he sat mounted and waiting for Andre.

He wondered if maybe he already knew how to use them. Might as well see he thought and started to dismount. Andre came out the door and he decided to wait. They were only taking one horse and the pack mule. Andre said they could take turns riding and Alex should take the first turn. Soft Dove and Running Feet who was holding the baby were standing just outside the door.

"See you in about two weeks." Andre said as he looked at Soft Dove. He took the lead with the pack mule while Alex followed behind him on the horse as they headed toward the rising sun and the general direction of Cape Girardeau on the Mississippi River.

The first day out they spent traveling following one trail then another. The next morning they were headed to an area Andre liked to trap. He told Alex it was an area where several creeks and streams fed into a big lake. Andre said he thought it was really the start of a river that went underground. He had fished on the lake and said it was mighty deep. The Indians called it the lake with no bottom. They had actually turned more toward the north northeast in their travels. They came upon a wide trail that looked like it saw quite a bit of traffic to be so far out in the wilderness. Andre told Alex it was a mining road that went from the lead mines on into St. Genevieve. He said they would follow it for a small distance before breaking back to the south a little heading toward the lake area.

When they had started out this morning, Alex had insisted Andre ride the horse and let him walk today. He said his behind was worn out from sitting all day yesterday on it. He still had not practiced with his bow and arrow yet. It was almost dark when they stopped yesterday and made camp. This morning both were anxious to break camp and get closer to where they would start trapping. He fully intended to try it out when they stopped for the night.

There were no teams pulling wagons loaded with lead coming through. Alex and Andre seemed to have the road to themselves. Andre was taking advantage of not having to dodge limbs and brush as they walked and rode. He was busy telling Alex about the techniques he used to get the beaver pelts. He knew his friend would have no trouble catching on, but thought just hearing about the process would help prepare Alex for what to expect. He was focused on the telling and Alex on the listening. They had just entered a grove of cotton woods when the first shot came. Alex dove for the ground and Andre jumped from the horse and hit the ground too. The second shot barely missed Alex's head and hit the tree right beside him. They immediately crawled for cover in some bushes on the side off the trail and behind a big rock. Alex could see the blood oozing from a tear in Andre's shirt on his arm.

"Did you see where it came from?" whispered Alex. He was not even conscious yet that he had grabbed his bow and had an arrow in it and ready to draw. "I'm thinking from behind us and on the other side of the trail."

"Me too," said Andre.

"I'm going to ease back and see what I can find. Are you going to be all right?" Alex asked.

"Yeah, it's just a knick. You want to take my gun?"

"No, you might need it. I am fine with my bow." Alex said. "It feels real natural and familiar."

Alex very slowly worked his way away from the trail a short distance then turned parallel to it. He carefully and quietly eased his way in the direction they had just come from. He knew not to get in a hurry and alert the shooter to his location. It seemed to take a long time, but he had gone about fifty feet when he came across a stone about the size of an apple. He stayed low to the ground and was crouched behind another boulder alert for any sound or movement human made. He looked up and around just to be sure no one was up in a tree. He realized he was seeing a small area or opening in

215

the trees where there were no tree branches between him and the sky. He took the stone he was holding in his hand and tossed it in a high arc across the trail and back toward Andre. When it started hitting tree limbs on its way to the ground the shooter stood up from behind a tree and fired in the direction of the sound. He immediately stepped behind the tree and reloaded his gun. He then leaned back against the tree with his head turned to the side. He was holding his gun with the barrel aimed toward the sky held close to his body getting ready to make the next shot. He was no more than twenty five feet from where Alex crouched. He would have seen Alex most likely if he had not been so focused on the area where he had first started shooting. Alex stayed behind the cover of the big rock and listened to see if he could hear anyone or anything else. He felt pretty certain the man was alone. He took off his coon skin hat and put it on a stick which he eased back against the rock. It was a little over a foot away from him and to his right. He knew the man would be able to see most of the hat sticking over the rock.

"Mister," he said. "If you want to see another sun rise, I suggest you throw that gun off to the side and be quick about it."

Alex's coon hat went flying through the air behind the unseen fast moving ball that had put two holes through it and was now most likely lodged in a tree. The shooter's gun was empty. He would have to reload. Alex stood and released his arrow. It went straight in the man's heart. The man looked stunned and seemed to be staring at Alex as though he was going to speak. He was dead before he made it all the way down to the ground.

"Come on out Andre." Alex shouted. "We won't be having any more trouble from this fella."

While Andre was walking up they heard horses approaching fast from the direction of the mines. Both of them stepped off the trail out of sight. When the horses came into view it was a small party of soldiers from the Post at St. Genevieve. Alex and Andre stepped out in the trail both with arms raised. Andre had left his gun in the bushes. Neither wanted to take a chance on getting shot for who knows what reason.

The obvious commanding officer of the group spoke up and said, "Gentlemen, do you mind telling me what is going on here? We heard shots."

After they had explained what had happened and found the dead man the leader told them about the man. It turns out that their shooter was a wanted man. The soldier in charge said he was a murderer, thief and deserter in that order. They had been tracking him for a while. The soldier had gone into town and while drinking a lot of whiskey had lost all his money in a poker game. When it finally broke up instead of returning to the Post, he had waited for the winner to come out of the Inn. He attacked him from behind, stabbed him to death and robbed him. The soldier went on to tell them the shooter didn't stop there. He then took the man's horse, gun and camping gear. The soldiers had found the horse lame about a day's ride back and figured he might try to sneak back in closer to town and find another one to replace it.

While the soldiers were getting the dead man ready for travel and collecting the stolen gear, Alex and Andre had gathered up the gun, mule and horse. The soldiers saw the traps and camping gear loaded on the horse and mule and were satisfied with their story that they were two trappers ambushed by the dead man. They headed toward St. Genevieve. Alex and Andre had traveled a ways before either said anything

Finally Andre said, "Well that was as interesting a morning as I have passed in a long while. We are both mighty lucky that he wasn't the best shot around. He still got way too close for my comfort. When I heard that first shot after you had doubled back, I thought I had lost my new partner, but then I heard you saying something.

"By the way, what were you going to tell them boys your name was if they had bothered to ask?"

"Well, if it had come up I was just going to tell the truth and then introduce myself using Absence Jones as a replacement name for the missing one. If they had not had their minds on getting back to the Post for some good food and whiskey they might have noticed I did not have a gun nor a horse. Sometimes, the truth as strange as it may sound makes the most sense. Absence obviously fits right in with the loss of my memory. It feels right for now."

"Absence, my friend," says Andre, "whatever was in your past it included the use of a bow and arrow. I think you were close to having that thing loaded and ready to draw before you hit the ground."

Alex did not remember that he had been taught by an Indian who lived near the post. He had worked as a scout for the Army and like Alex had spent many hours at the Post with very little to do. Alex had approached him and asked if he would teach him how to make a bow and arrow and how to use it.

Alex was glad they were near the lake and did not have far to travel. Alex was leading the pack mule and following Andre on the narrow and sometimes dense trail. It seemed to be opening up a little. At least brush and small tree branches were no longer hitting him in the face.

Alex began to hear the distinct sound of something rhythmically hitting the ground. It really made him think of Running Feet when she was digging in the garden. Before he could say anything about it, Andre who was in front of him a short distance on the horse made an abrupt right turn and disappeared into the forest.

Alex could now hear women's voices. When he reached the spot where Andre disappeared from the trail he was standing in front of some poles covered with running bean vines that were hanging full of blooms. He turned to the right as Andre had.

He realized they were at the edge of a clearing with a huge vegetable garden in it. As he followed the

trail around the edge of the garden to his left he could
see the bean vines were one of many standing among
what looked like squash vines running across the ground
in a fairly large area. Intermingled were green stalks of
corn dotted throughout the garden. He could see Andre
talking to several of the Indian women on the other side
of the garden. When he reached Andre, Alex knew what
he had heard. Most of the women were using a bone tool
to dig out the dirt and loosen it. A few of the workers
were young girls who were holding a long stick with a
pointed end. They would stick the point in the loosened
dirt, rotating it a little to make an upside down cone
shape and then drop a seed in it from a pouch that was
draped across their shoulder and hung down to their hip.
The women who were digging would then gather the dirt
back over the holes and push it gently down leaving their
seal of handprints clearly visible in the moist earth.
Watching this Alex could not help but think his past life
was like that. It had been buried, covered over and sealed
with the hands of fate.

When Andre stopped talking to the women, he
looked at Alex and said, "We had such a scare this
morning I forgot to tell you we would be camping here
with the Shawnee tonight. I like to stop by when I am in
the area and ask permission of the chief to trap around
the lake. This land was given to them in a land grant a few
years back before Napoleon sold it to the United States in
the Louisiana Purchase. The lake and area right around it
is not on the Shawnee land grant, but I like to have their
permission anyway. The chief and I are friends and I
want very much to keep it that way. The government is
talking about pushing them off the land and further
south or west. The chief says he is not leaving this land,
but many of the band have already left. His woman says
he is out hunting. She has received word that he will be
returning this afternoon."

They left the garden and entered the village. It
consisted of cone shaped dwellings about ten feet high

with a larger one in the middle that would hold a lot of people. The frames had been covered with birch bark and secured in place with rope. Alex had seen some of the women making rope from hemp as they had entered the village. Others were weaving what looked like mats from the hemp. After they had set up camp and secured the animals one of the men came up and told them the Chief had invited them to eat with his family in the large center dwelling.

They were sitting with the chief and several other men of the village enjoying a really good meal. The chief's hair hung long and straight. He had a leather head band on with some feathers attached which dangled loosely on one side of his head. Andre had told him if he saw a Shawnee with a shaved head except on the top that was a mark of a warrior. None of these men had shaved heads. What had really caught Alex's eye was the bear claw necklace he was wearing. The claws were big and long. The chief caught Alex staring at them and explained that he had helped kill a bear in his youth, but these claws were a gift from a trapper friend of his.

The women who were serving the food had obviously dressed for the occasion. Alex assumed they were wives and daughters of the men gathered around the fire. Their tunics, skirts and moccasins were decorated with many colored beads in varying sizes. Each woman wore a beaded band tied around their forehead. The art work was intricate and very pleasing to look at. While the chief and Andre talked, he was surprised that he was understanding quite a bit of the Shawnee words. He wondered where he was and what he was doing when he had learned them.

After the meal the women cleared the food away. One of the younger women was obviously interested in Alex. She was looking at him in a way a man could not mistake. He knew he could sleep with her if he chose, but something was holding him back. He deliberately kept his gaze from locking with hers. However, he could feel his body responding to what she was offering and had to really focus his thoughts away from her. He was glad they were sitting in the bent and cross legged Indian fashion. He did not feel like the teasing that would have ensued if the other men knew what was happening to him.

Long after the women had left the lodge Alex finally told Andre he had to get some sleep. He thanked Black Bob for the good food and company and left. He had passed several of the dwellings, but their entrance ways were closed and it appeared that all were asleep. He could barely see the outline of one ahead when the flap opened as he was approaching. There was still a glow from a fire inside and he could tell that someone had their head through the flap peering out. When he was a few feet away he realized it was the woman who had stared at him with the inviting look in her eyes. He stopped and stood still just looking at her. She was beautiful. He did not need to remember anything to know he was missing the feel of a woman. He stepped forward and entered through the flap she held open for him. He helped her shut it behind them. She reached out and took his hand as she led him to a sleeping mat.

After they had both satisfied their physical needs, they spent most of the night talking. With his broken Shawnee and using sign language they were able to learn a lot about each other. It seemed that both of them had needed way more than just the physical intimacy. She told him her husband had been killed shortly after they were wed. His family had no other members in the tribe except for a cousin. Usually in her situation a woman would live with the closest relative of her husband. The cousin's wife was extremely jealous. She explained to Alex how she knew she did not want to be living with an angry jealous woman every day. She decided to stay where she and her husband had lived. Some of the men in the tribe saw that she had fresh meat to eat. Her vegetables were plentiful as before, since she worked in the gardens. She also liked to forage in the forest for nuts, berries and roots.

She told Alex, the women of this tribe did not hunt or fish as a general rule. But because she was alone she was allowed to fish when she was not needed elsewhere. She was hoping that the men would teach her to use the bow and arrow to hunt, but so far that had not happened. When she could, she watched as the men made new bows and arrows. She had figured out what materials they used and had started experimenting with the making of her own. She would sneak off from the camp and practice, but was not satisfied with her results. She told Alex she would keep listening to the men talk about their hunts and the making of their weapons until she had one that would work. She did not like being dependent on the tribe for all of her meat. She told Alex when she was away from her dwelling she always kept a few rocks in a pouch she carried. A few times she had managed to throw one accurately and kill a rabbit, but she had not become consistent with that either.

He was surprised at how he opened up to this woman and shared what had happened to him. He realized he had needed to talk about it all after he started and could not stop. When he did finally stop and remained silent the woman reached out and put the palm of her hand over his chest.

She said, "My friend, we are more alike than we realize. The Spirits that travel in the winds have put us together for this short time, so we could help each other. We both have lost our past lives, just in different ways. I remember mine and you remember nothing. Either way they are lost to us. If we never meet again I will think of you often as the man who lives in the land of no memories. Do not worry. It will not always be this way. You are making new memories to replace the ones you have lost."

Just before sunrise, Alex dressed. He and the woman stood facing each other. Alex took her hands and held them in his close to his chest for a few seconds as they looked in each other's eyes. Neither said anything. He released her hands, turned and left the dwelling.

Andre was already up sitting at the fire and waiting for the coffee to make.

He said, "Thought you might need a cup. I know I do. If you are ready let's head on to the lake. It is less than half a day's walk and we can get our camp set up, catch a few fish and eat before we start working. I am still full from the feast last night."

"Sounds good to me." Alex was glad he had not asked him about the woman. He wanted to enjoy reliving the experience in his mind as they made their way to the lake. If they should come back this way, as he felt they would, he thought he would want to see her again. Until he knew for sure that was the case, he preferred keeping their time together to himself.

CHAPTER 19

Grace sat in her beloved garden. She had planted yellow poppy, false garlic, squaw weed, red buckeye and periwinkles among many other flowers. The garden was fenced or walled, whichever way you chose to think about it. Running roses intermingled with various blooming vines climbed to a height well above her head along all four sides of the garden. Where the gate stood Alex had built her a crude but effective archway which was covered in morning glory vines filled with their deep blue blooms. There was an oak tree nearby that protected her garden from the heat of the sun most of the day. The result had created an enclosed area of color you would be hard pressed to find anywhere else west of St. Louis.

She was thinking about the earlier times she had come to sit here and found a swath of her flowers eaten. Sometimes there would be tracks of one deer and other times there was evidence of more. Grace would always repair the damage as quickly as possible by salvaging what she could and sowing seeds for new flowers where needed. Alex had built her a fence around it to keep the deer out, but they soon discovered it was not high enough to keep them from jumping over it.

Grace smiled to herself as she recalled how she and Alex had come in the garden one late afternoon when it was in full bloom only to find the damage left by the feasting deer. Alex had just left the fort and was still in his uniform.

As soon as he had seen it he had grabbed his hat off his head and slammed it on the ground and had said, "Danged it, Grace. I am not going to let these fence jumping, flower eating, big eyed beautiful creatures keep having their desserts from your garden." As he had been busily brushing off the grass and dirt from his hat, he had said, "The fence is going higher." With that said he had left the garden and stormed in the house where he grabbed pencil and paper. He then had plopped down at the table and began to figure out how and what he would need to increase the height of the garden fence.

Just as she had this morning, she and Alex had often come to the garden with a cup of coffee in one hand and a biscuit with ham in the other. It would be one of those mornings when he did not have to rush off to the Post. That was some of her most favorite memories. Usually any problems or matters of irritation had been left to another time. If they had not been and needed to be addressed they had dealt with them in an atmosphere of tranquility. Most times they had just sat and enjoyed the morning together while listening to nature's sounds.

Grace sat holding the most recent letter from her mother in her hand. As in the other letters from Catherine, she asked Grace again to consider moving to New Madrid. Up until today it had not been a consideration. Grace had kept her sorrow from completely overtaking her with the passing time and by continuing to believe Alex would return to her. She would see him returning in her mind. It was always the same way each time. She was standing in the middle of a street. He was walking toward her in the last hour of the sun's light. She could never see his face only his form, but she still recognized that walk and knew it was him.

Today for the first time she actually began to seriously think about moving to New Madrid. She really did not want to leave her home in St. Charles. However, the thought of a new place with new faces and new beginnings was starting to gain her interest. More than anything she longed to be near her parents again. It would be terribly hard leaving her friends. Agatha, her sister in heart, she just could not think about a lot of days without her company. With Agatha's expanding family there was not a lot of leisure time anymore for them. It was a rare occasion for them to meet at the river spot. Grace still went there often, but knew that would not continue for long. The town had purchased the lot and was getting ready to construct a government building there she had heard from several people.

Here in St. Charles Alex was everywhere she looked. It was time to go where he was not a part of everything she saw, felt and heard. Grace knew her parents could use her help. The thought of being with them lifted her spirits immensely. She decided she would discreetly listen out for someone who might want to buy her place. She might even rent it for a while and go see her parents for a long visit. She decided not to say anything to the girls just yet. She knew how these days her emotions and her mind could run in totally opposite directions from where they had just been a few hours before. For now there was nothing to be done, except to bide her time and say nothing about what she was thinking.

The bell on the door jingled as Grace entered the mercantile and now officially the Post Office.

"Good morning." she said to Mrs. Hawkins. "Have you received any new patterns?" asked Grace.

"No, but there's a letter from your mother."

Mrs. Hawkins nose seemed to be almost twitching with curiosity. She suspected there must be some news of interest in this one. It was taking all Grace could do to keep from giggling in her face. She so reminded Grace of a mouse test sniffing a crumb of bread with its little nose twitching and whiskers wiggling in the air before eating it up. Grace was surprised herself to receive another letter so soon from her mother. It had not been quite two weeks since her last one and she prayed nothing was seriously wrong with either of them.

Millie who was also in the mercantile this morning spoke up with that nasally whining voice and said, "Grace, I certainly hope you're Mother has not written bad news."

"Thank you Millie, but I am sure everything is fine."

"I will be sure to let you know if there is anything seriously wrong."

Grace was right to be concerned. Catherine wrote that a fire had destroyed most of the hotel. It would have to be completely rebuilt. She wrote that Charles was considering not rebuilding at all, since they had started building and ordering stock for her new specialty shop Catherine was anxious to open. Catherine wanted him to rebuild and expand the hotel. With his saw mill the cost for lumber would be minimal. Her concern now was for the employees. They would be paying them as always for a while until they found work elsewhere or stayed on if they decided to rebuild. Her plan had been to start the new business since it would not take so many hours to manage and promote one of the staff at the hotel to help oversee it. Now this fire had disrupted everyone's life. She did not know if the employee she hoped to promote would stay now. If they should leave she thought it might be a big problem finding someone else. Of course, all this would not matter if they did not rebuild.

Grace hurried toward home barely escaping being rude to a couple of people that spoke to her. She was anxious to get there and read her letter again. After she had done so, she immediately replied to her mother letter and told her she too hoped her father would rebuild the hotel. If he did she wanted to help run it. She wrote she was ready for a change and the long hours would be good for her. She also wrote that she would be arriving in New Madrid within a month either way to help out as best she could. Even if they did not rebuild she knew she could be of help somewhere. As soon as she had delivered the letter to the mercantile for posting, Grace knew this was the right decision. The challenge of possibly running a business in the near future excited her more than anything had in a long time. She could almost hear the voice whispering behind her that this was the right direction.

The days since she had written to her mother had flown by. Grace had a little trouble focusing on the sowing circle, knowing this would be their last planned meeting.

"I summarized the notes from our last meeting." said Grace. She began to read them.

"The Book of God, as the writer of this introduction calls it was first written in the Hebrew language. Seventy interpreters translated it out of Hebrew and into Greek. The Greek tongue was well known and familiar to most inhabitants in Asia, many places in Europe and Africa also.

It seems that in one translation of the Old Testament from Hebrew to Greek there was a group of seventy that did the job and were selected by an Egyptian king. Admittedly by this writer they made mistakes, omitted and added to their translation and fell short by oversight and ignorance. After them there were six more translations of the seventy men's work. It is not told to us here how many men worked on the six other translations before this one. It appears there was a disagreement as to whether the seventy men were prophets or interpreters for a while, but because of mistakes, omissions and additions were deemed interpreters. Then, of course, they and the other translators were followed by this group of scholars which gave us the King James Version. I have read elsewhere that there were over forty men chosen for

King James who worked on this translation we now have. I can't remember the number exactly."

Agatha said, "This was a little difficult for me to read. I found myself having to read and then read again the material to understand what the writer was saying. Some parts I had to read more than twice. It is very wordy."

"Glad you told us that." Hannah said. "I was having the same problem and beginning to think I was a little daft."

Grace continues, "This writer goes on to say a few hundred years after Christ there were many translations into the Latin tongue of the Law and the Gospel. Many countries in the West, South, East and North spoke or understood Latin since they were a part of the Roman Provinces. The Latin translations were too many for all of them to be good according to Saint Augustine. Whoever that was. Guess we could ask the Catholic priest here in town. I don't remember anyone in our church talking about this Saint." Grace says, "Anyway continuing on from my notes, because the Latin translations of the Old Testament were not of the Hebrew stream but of the Greek they were deemed not clear so must be muddied. Then a Saint Jerome translated the Old Testament yet again from which language I am not sure, but assuming Hebrew. It gets confusing as to who and how many are translating from what to what if you don't write it down and then that is still not so easy to keep up with."

Hannah said, "It is interesting that the writer seems apologetic and goes to great lengths to explain the errors, arguments, omissions, changes, amendments and corrections. It is also interesting to me that he points out the actual burnings of Rome by the Galles, the burning of Rome during Nero's reign and the actual intended burnings of other translations. I really do wonder what was burned in those times and others that we will never know about."

Agatha added, "Because the history given here of the many translations and the burning of libraries, not once but several times really makes me wonder just what we are missing. It is written in this introduction that things were changed, added or omitted. At this point for me it is pretty clear why or how the Bible can sound like parts are missing while others have been added that don't fit. Anyway, I for one am going to continue reading and studying, but with my mind open. I will no longer be believing everything shouted at me by a man just because they say they have been called by God to teach his word.

Hannah said, "I am going to do the same thing, Agatha. Keeping your mind open is mighty important. If you don't there is so much that can be missed. I am so glad we have these times together, but we still have to remember how dangerous what we are doing is. We must not forget to be careful and keep it to ourselves. I have been called many names being in my business, but a witch has not been one of them and I hope to keep it that way."

Grace said, "Agatha will you stay behind so we can go over all the notes.

"Of course, I need to feed my hungry little one, anyway. This will be a perfect time to do both." Agatha knew Grace was using this as an excuse to talk with her in private, because they had gone over their notes a couple of days ago.

After Hannah left Grace went to the well on the back porch and pulled a bucket of water. She had enough in the kitchen to make a fresh pot of tea, but was stalling. As she slowly pulled the filled water bucket up to the top of the well, she gazed out over her back yard at her garden, the wood pile, her hen house, the smoke house and finally the trail leading through the woods and down to the creek. Grace knew she would miss these things, but she would replace them with other things when she reached New Madrid. She only had one problem now with her decision to leave and it was to tell Agatha about it. She sighed deeply as she picked up the bucket and walked into the kitchen.

"Let's sit out on the front porch. I want to tell you something that is very hard for me to say."

Agatha held up her hand palm out and said, "Grace, you don't have to say it. I know you are leaving. We all do."

Grace's eye became huge with shock.

"But how can you know. I only talked to the manager at the bank about a possible buyer for the house just recently. That was done in the strictest of confidence."

"You know how it is here. Probably someone in the bank heard something about your house selling and put two and two together. I don't know. We only found out this week and all of us agreed to wait and let you tell us when you were ready. It put me out of sorts completely for a couple of days, but I understand why you have to go, Grace. I really do. You need to be with your folks now and it sounds like they really could use your help. There will be a big empty place in me for a while, but I know we will see each other again one of these days. Besides, you know we are going to be writing each other. We can still keep our sowing circle going. You will just be participating by mail. The only important thing we don't know is when you are leaving. Have you picked a date yet?"

"Yes, I plan to leave a week from tomorrow. I know it sounds sudden, but I had to keep the time short and filled with the things necessary to make a move. I was afraid I might waiver in my decision after telling my Mother I would come. When she found out I was coming she sent a letter back saying that New Madrid had just finished building a school and needed a teacher temporarily until they can locate a permanent one. She thinks it will keep me busy while the hotel is being rebuilt. I agree with her. I am going to send ahead overland to St. Louis what possessions I want to take with me. I have decided to leave the furniture with the house. It will be easier to find a renter or buyer for that matter.

"There are some books in the Devereux library that belong to mother. They had planned to ship those along with me to New Madrid years ago, but meeting Alex changed all those plans. I will get those and maybe borrow some of Mr. Deveruex's collection. I remember he had several that I think will assist us in our studies. He has quite a library and has offered to share any that would be of interest to me personally or for the school. It will not be difficult to get them back to him as there is so much land and river traffic along the Mississippi River to St. Louis from New Orleans.

"I had thought about taking the Kings Highway from St. Louis to New Madrid. It will take longer overland, so I am going to ride a flat boat down the Mississippi. I understand there are several now that are equipped to take passengers. It will be a nice adventure and I will have the opportunity of moving about while traveling. The idea of sitting through a bumpy ride for days does not appeal to me.

"I am so thankful that Alex insisted on putting aside a portion of his pay each month. With that money and what is in the bank at St. Louis I should fare well until I have more permanent arrangements in place. There will be money coming in from the house in the future also."

"Well, you must know that we three are insistent we have a special get together before you leave."

This time when these two special friends parted there were no tears. They both knew they had already been shed.

CHAPTER 20

The Indian woman stood in the trail that wound through the woods. She was watching as the last one of her tribe disappeared from sight behind a big cotton wood tree. The excitement of giving birth to her child did not totally block the anxiety she felt as she stood there now totally alone. It didn't really matter how she felt or what fears she might have. It was the way of her people and she would honor that. She had hoped with everything in her that the baby she was carrying would be born before they left their temporary camp ground and headed north to their permanent home. It was not to be. The tribe had traveled four days from the camp and now on this fifth day she had to stop. The pains had started and she knew she had no choice but to stop and prepare for the birth of her child. She would be alone until the baby was born. Afterwards, she and her baby would catch up with the tribe. She had been searching for just the right place. Moments before finding this place they had crossed a little stream and walked a very short distance when she saw it. She inhaled deeply of the air for her choice was a pine thicket. The ground was smooth and covered by a thick blanket of pine needles. This was the perfect spot for her baby to be born. She inhaled deeply again and thought how much she loved the smell of the pine trees.

The large bundle she was carrying seemed to be awfully big for her. It was secured across her chest and hung down her back. Over her forehead and down each side of her head was a strap attached to her baby's cradleboard. The cradleboard was hanging out and over the top of the bundle which made her look as if she might fall backwards at any moment if she had a misstep. In addition to the load on her back her huge stomach was protruding in the front. From a distance she looked like a moving mound on two stumpy little legs.

She had planned well for her baby's arrival. She did not tell anyone of the women in her tribe, for it was not their way, but she was uneasy about being left alone. Her closest friend that she always talked to had recently married and left with her husband to join his people. There was no one else she would have talked to about this feeling of uneasiness she just couldn't seem to get rid of.

This was her first child and she had spent many a night thinking about what she might need if things did not go smoothly or quickly. As a consequence she had packed a few more things than was normally done. The other women had tried to talk her out of packing so many things for the delivery, but she had not listened and stuck to her plan. Admittedly the last four days on the trail had been extremely tiring carrying the extra weight.

It had been looking as though it was going to start raining any minute all morning. The clouds were dark and low as they passed overhead. She decided to build a shelter from the rain whose arrival was imminent. That was another good thing about pine forests. There were always broken limbs on the ground that could be used for a temporary shelter. This would lessen the time she needed to prepare. She found two trees a few feet apart with forks low enough that she could reach them. She took off her cradleboard and hung it on a tree nearby and then removed the bundle and placed it on the ground. She had to be very careful with her cradle board, because she was carrying hot embers from the morning cook fire in a buffalo horn. She also had inside the rabbit skins she had prepared to wrap the baby in along with the smoke treated moss to put in his cradle board for a diaper. She had packed more moss in her bundle to use as packing and pads for herself and the baby after the birth.

After having gathered several limbs she placed the ends of the first limb in the bottom forks of the two trees she had picked. The limb was almost level with the ground. Next she took two limbs and leaned them from the ground up to each end of the limb protruding from the forks and tied them with some woven hemp. Before building the roof of her shelter, she took her two thick birthing sticks she had brought and pounded them in the ground where they would be under the roof once it was completed. Between the two sticks she dug a hole she would squat over during the last part of her labor as she gripped the sticks. She found leaves and put them in the bottom of the hole. They would be used to catch the baby. After that it was just a matter of stacking the other limbs one on top of the other all the way up to the supporting branch. Normally she would have found a vine to tie the bottom limb on the ground to the slanting poles keeping it in place. Since the rain was so close to falling she did not want to use the time searching for one. She used a couple of good sized rocks she found lying nearby and placed them up against the bottom limb for stability. For a roof it was easy to scoop up the fallen pine branches with needles and place them on top of the lean to. They would not keep all the rain out, but most of it. She took the time to make an extra thick layer of brown needles for her roof and then placed some long green pine branches she broke off over the top to help hold them in place. These she tied with the last of her hemp from her bundle.

By the time she had walked to the nearby stream and collected water in her leather basket and gathered some dry wood for a small fire the rain had started. She hurriedly pulled her cradle board and pack in the lean to and started a fire in another shallow hole she had dug. The heat felt good. She squatted over the hole where she would stay when the pains were closer and grabbed the birthing sticks and pulled and pushed on them. They did not move. She had to make sure they were buried deep enough to hold when the pains became harder. They felt strong and secure in the ground. Having watched and helped with two births in her camp, she knew what to expect and was anxious to hold her baby.

The father, a white trader may not ever be seen again by her. He had come through their camp only the one time wanting to trade for pelts. The trader had taken a fancy to her.

Her father had traded her for two nights in order to get extra whiskey. Her value had been determined to be only equal to a jug of whiskey. She was determined her baby would be loved and never made to feel as she had. It was her first and only time she had been with a man in her fifteen summers.

The pains had slowed a little, so she took the time in between to lay out her sleeping mat. It was now getting over into late afternoon. She would not be leaving her little shelter during the night. She took her cradle board and removed the skins that would be used to clean and wrap her baby in. She padded the cradle board with some of the moss. Now when the baby came his space was ready for him. It appeared that it might be a while before that happened, so she ate a few bites of pemmican made with dried meat and berries for strength more than from hunger. The woman lay down on her mat and waited for the pains to become closer together. The warmth of the fire and the falling of the rain lulled her to sleep. She awoke cold and in intense pain, with a dream vivid in her mind. She waited until the pain passed. It was dark and the fire was almost out, but she managed to get a good flame going again. She squatted between her birthing sticks and grabbed hold waiting for the next pain to come. The dream flashed in her mind again. She was seeing herself and the baby as if she was looking down on them both from a few feet up in the air. She was lying on her side. The baby was in her arms crying for her breast, but she did not move him closer so he could suckle. In her dream her sweet baby's face and little head were so red from the crying but her face seemed to have no color at all. She shivered as though she were outside the shelter in a freezing cold wind and then the next pain hit.

The labor pains lasted until just before sunrise. The baby came at last. She cut the umbilical cord and tied it. She bathed her precious baby boy, wrapped him snugly and held him to her breast for a few minutes. She watched him as he hungrily suckled and loved him instantly. When he had drank his fill and was sleeping, she took her bone shovel and covered the placenta in the hole using the loose dirt from both holes she had dug earlier. She cleaned herself and then packed the birth canal as best she could with moss to stop the bleeding. She knew she needed to pack more moss, because she could feel the blood oozing down her leg, but for now she could do no more than lie down with her baby in her arms and let him suckle. She would go to the creek for a good bathing of herself after she fed the baby and rested for a while. Afterwards they would catch up with the tribe. The baby was sleeping now. She wished her mother was here to help her, but she had gone to the spirit world many winters past. It was strange, but very comforting for she could hear her mother clearly calling for her as she drifted away with her baby still sleeping in her arms.

The rain had stopped. Alex and Andre were walking through the woods on a barely discernible trail that lead to an area close to where they had camped. Soft Dove, Running Feet and the baby had come with them on this trip and were waiting for them. Andre's horse carried a deer draped across its back. Alex was leading his horse. He walked a lot to continue strengthening his leg. Even though there was no pain for well over a year, it was as though deep inside the bone there was still a spot that he could feel when he had to put any heavy strain on his leg.

"You know Friend, I can remember the day not too long ago when we would have had at least two and more likely three white tail after a morning's hunt.

"Well, at least we got a buck, even if it wasn't a white tail deer." Alex replied.

"That's true and I am happy for the fur and food, but we could trade a white tail for a lot of beaver pelts with the Indians. I say let's head out toward...... Andre didn't finish, but stopped talking the moment Alex held up his hand. "What is it?" he whispered.

"I hear a baby crying."

"I believe you do." said Andre as they stood listening to the sound.

It only took them a minute to find the baby and his mother. As they stood looking down at them Andre said, "She is awfully pale and has lost a lot of blood from the looks of things." As he was saying this Alex reached down and picked up the crying baby.

"That's some mighty healthy lungs you got there, Little One," he said quietly to the baby as he gently jostled him up and down in his arms. The baby stopped crying.

"I am not sure we need to be jostling this woman on a horse to get her to camp. I am going to take your horse and go get the women. If there is anything to be done, they will probably know what it is." Andre said. He mounted the horse and rode as fast as he dared through the undergrowth in the forest toward their camp. He knew the young woman was near death.

While he was gone Alex gathered what dry wood he could find and manage carrying the baby at the same time. When he had enough to start a fire he took the woman's leather water basket and gathered more water. He heard the horses coming before he could see them.

Soft Dove dismounted and ran to the limb where the empty cradle board had hung. She took her baby's cradle board off her back and hung her baby there. By this time Running Feet was at the lean to and was examining the woman.

Soft Dove squatted beside her and after a few seconds said, "There must be something else that has to come out. She has lost too much blood and is still bleeding. First we have to get her hips up. Let's roll her on her back. Andre, please lift her hips while we get this mat rolled up under her." She reached in her pouch and pulled out a small soap root. She grabbed two small rocks and pounded it. When the liquid started oozing out, she rubbed it over her hands and cleaned them up to her elbows with the water Alex had brought.

Soft Dove was able to remove what she hoped was the last of the afterbirth. The bleeding did slow down. Soft Dove did not know if they had reached her in time. The young woman's pulse was still awfully weak. She and Running Dove cleaned the girl and repacked her with some of the prepared moss still lying where the girl had last placed it. Running Feet was preparing a tea which Soft Dove hoped would be strong enough to overcome any infection that might be trying to take hold. After it had cooled they managed to get a few sips down her. The baby had awakened and started wailing. They placed him in his mother's arms and let him nurse. Both women hoped that the mother and child's physical contact would give them much needed strength to survive.

Alex and Andre had rigged a travois with what they hoped would be limber enough tree limbs, but not too limber. They would help soften the jarring of the ride back to camp. Soft Dove wanted to wait to make the return trip just before dark to give her as much time to rest undisturbed as possible. They packed all of her belongings in the meantime and packed the baby in his cradle board.

They put the woman on the travois with her feet toward the rear of the horse and her head closer to the ground. Alex said he would carry the baby. Running Feet showed him the best way to secure the cradleboard to his horse. No one said anything about Alex wanting to carry the baby. Andre had already told them about their first meeting when Alex had picked up the baby and seemed to calm it somehow.

CHAPTER 21

Grace walked out the back door. It was late afternoon and the last day she would spend in this cabin that had been her home for ten years. Another part of her life was passing. Four of those years had been without her Alex. She stopped at her well on the back porch and lovingly ran her finger tips across the ledge. She let her eyes wander over the back yard to the garden she loved and the path that led through the woods to the spring. She let the bucket down and gazed at the buildings Alex had built: the hen house, the smoke house and sitting off to itself closer to the woods than the cabin sat the outhouse. She pulled the pail out of the well and poured the water in a bucket that set by her side. She was collecting water for her last bath from her treasured well. Agatha and Rosa had planned supper for her and Edmond was picking her up in an hour. She took one last look around and carried her pail of water through the back door. She closed it for the last time.

She felt relief again for making the decision to move on with her life. This morning after packing her lunch, cleaning her breakfast dishes and putting them away for the last time she walked over to the front door and turned looking all around the house slowly taking it all in. She could not help but notice the things missing, especially her writing desk which had been sent on ahead with the other things she was taking. After a minute or so, she picked up her valise, went through and closed the front door, walked down her stone path and under her rose covered gate closing it behind her.

Grace stopped and stood there for a moment just looking out over the street toward the river with her back to the house. She had known deep within her it was the last time she would ever be in this spot. She turned and headed down the street toward the dock and her new life. She did not look back. She was not able to, because she knew she would see Alex and he was not there. Old man moon was shining in all his glory and lighting her way.

When she reached the dock she saw two boats and several wagons waiting for their merchandise to be loaded for transport to St. Louis. One was ready to leave, but she did not see any sign of passenger accommodations. It looked as though it was strictly used for cargo. The one she had planned to take was still loading and from the looks of things would be doing so for a long while. On impulse she approached the pilot of the other boat that was ready to go and asked if she could pay to ride to St. Louis. He told her he was not situated to take passengers. Grace being anxious to get started and very persuasive convinced him to take her anyway. They had been moving through the water before the sun had risen completely over the bank of dark clouds on the horizon. It's reflection off the high clouds with the dark red and orange was a sight to remember.

This was a rectangular shaped flat bottom boat. About a third of the boat toward the back had an enclosed area but still allowed room on either side for the crew to walk back and forth with their oars or poles depending on whether they were going up river or down. There was a small sail that was down now as they seemed to be traveling into a light head wind. Grace was amazed to find she was being accompanied on this trip by crate after crate of squealing pigs. They were not exactly happy with their accommodations and were wanting to be back in their pig pen happily wallowing in the mud and stink of home.

The pilot had provided a seat for her at the front of the boat as far away as possible from the pigs. Generally the breeze blew from the front of the boat and she did not have to breathe the horrid odor. When it briefly changed directions, she was surprised at how long she could go without taking a breath and then only through her mouth. She knew the pig farmer and his family who lived near St. Charles and was happy to see that they were able to start marketing in St. Louis. However, she wished more than once that she had waited for the other boat to depart which she felt certain had a better smelling passenger list and none with four legs.

They had been moving through the water before the sun had risen completely over the bank of dark clouds on the horizon. It's reflection off the high clouds with the dark red and orange was a sight to remember. Now that she was really on her way Grace mentally chastised herself for her hastily made decision as she once again held her breath until the head wind regained command of the moving air. She realized too late that she had heard the animals squealing as she had so masterfully persuaded the captain into taking her on board. She was so excited about leaving that she had not consciously thought to check the direction of the noise. After they had been traveling a few hours she was becoming more accustomed to the odor. She noticed when the wind did occasionally blow from the rear of the boat and the odor assaulted her it didn't feel as though it would knock her off her seat. Grace still had to hold her breath, but it was getting easier and easier to deal with. She consoled herself with the knowledge that she wouldn't be on the boat very long anyway. Even with the slight head wind they would be in St Louis hours before supper time.

The captain had come up to the front and talked with her for a little while. He explained that he was one of the first flat bottom boat owners to set up a regularly scheduled run between St. Charles and St. Louis. He had started out making runs between St. Louis and St. Girard on the Mississippi River, but there was so much more boat traffic he had decided on this course. It had worked out well for him and his crew.

Everything Grace wanted to take with her had been sent on ahead by land to the Devereux's residence. All that traveled with her was a small valise, a parasol and her purse of course. Other than having to continuously hold her parasol over her head to protect against the sun and the occasional whiff of the pigs, Grace was quite comfortable. She was enjoying the sights on the river. She loved seeing the animals and birds drinking from a water pool left on one of the islands they passed or an animal at the river's edge having a drink. So far she had seen a fox, skunk and wild boar. The captain had told her these sand islands could be gone the next day the way the river current shifted. In the late morning the sky clouded completely over and it cooled the air. This time of year a spring shower was usually nearby.

Grace could hardly believe her eyes when they reached the edge of St. Louis. The town had grown immensely since she had seen it last. There were new buildings all along the bank of the river. The dock had been expanded. She was shocked to see how many boats were there. The market that she had so missed was huge compared to what it had been when she lived here. She decided to stroll through before engaging a carriage to take her to the Devereuxs. She could still hear the gypsy couple singing as they had that day she met Alex. His eyes shined as brightly in her mind today as they did then. His smile had not dimmed. It did not make her sad today. She was glad she could still see him so clearly for she did not relish the day when she could not.

The Devereux family had all gathered for her return except for the oldest daughter who had married and was now living back east. It felt so good to be with this family again in their big rambling house. As happy as she was to be here, she only planned to stay two nights and then be on her way to New Madrid. Tomorrow she would make arrangements for her belongings to travel on a more passenger oriented boat. Mr. Devereux informed her that he had taken the liberty and already secured her passage to New Madrid on one of the boats that would be leaving day after tomorrow.

"I will repay you. Please tell me how much the passage cost."

"No Grace," said Mrs. Devereux. "Please, we want to do this for you. After all you have always been like one of our children. We also have made arrangements for you to have a separate supply of water on board to use as you wish. It is clean enough to drink, so you won't have to be sharing the water and dipper with goodness only know who. Sometimes I see these men walking down the street spitting their tobacco juice and it dribbling down their chin in those nasty looking whiskers and well I don't want you having to worry about such nastiness in your water. I also had the maid to gather you up a dipper, small pan, some soap and bathing cloths along with a bath towel. They should make your trip a little more comfortable.

"It will be docking tomorrow morning if you would like to go have a look. If it doesn't suit you, you can always extend your stay with us until you find another one to your liking." Mrs. Devereux said.

"I know it will be perfect even before I see it. I will have a look through my things in the morning to see what I will need to unpack to have close with me for the trip. I understand some of these boats have managed to become quite accommodating for river travelers."

Grace walked over to where she sat and gave her a long hug.

"You have always been so good to me."

Mr. Devereux had given her an envelope shortly after she had arrived with the money her parents had left for her. "I hope you will be happy to know the original sum your parents left has doubled. I made a few investments that paid very well." He had told her. She had no idea how much her parents had left for her. When she went to her room to retire for the night and opened it, she was pleasantly surprised to count out over $600.

Grace awakened early and had breakfast with the staff. Everyone that worked there when she was growing up was still there. A couple of new ones had been added to make up for the aged staff's decrease in duties. They all made a fuss over Grace and lingered at the table longer than usual before beginning their daily chores. Everyone had a good time sharing their different memories of Grace and the children's shenanigans they were always keeping hidden from the parents they thought. After she finished preparing for her journey Grace headed to the market. She did not plan to shop, but wanted to experience it one more time before leaving St. Louis. After she had her fill of the noise and the people she moved toward the dock where it was noisy too, but in a different way.

She began to search for the boat she would be taking called the Mary Mae. It did not take long to find for she knew it was a flat bottomed boat in a rectangular shape. The Mary Mae was easy to spot in its bright red and white colors. She did not have to go on board to decide she was definitely happy with Mr. Devereux's selection, however she did see a man she guessed to be the pilot seeming to be directing the loading of cargo. She went up to him, introduced herself and asked if the boat was still leaving at 7 am tomorrow. He assured it was. She turned and headed back to the house ready to spend some time in the library.

Grace had spoken with Mr. Devereux the previous evening at dinner about the interests of the sowing circle and their mound of questions that constantly came up. She knew she could talk to him about it, because he had a mind that was open and not controlled through fear. Grace remembered when she was approaching adolescence that some of her favorite evenings were when the family dined with the Devereux family. He and her mother especially had the most fascinating conversations about various subjects. She tried to catch every word when they talked about the history of Europe. There were so many wars with thousands of people killed in the name of a religion. Grace would go to bed many evenings with her mind whirling and filled with questions. She had then started spending more of her free time in the library. Mr. Devereux's fatherly manner could not help but caution her about the subject. He told her to be very careful with whom she talked to about this in a new place. Grace assured him that they were all well aware of the danger involved and were extremely careful to prevent being accused of witchcraft.

He made her promise to take advantage of his extensive library which included several books referencing history and religion's influence in events of different time periods. Grace had agreed that she would take a few of the books that might help them with their study. She told him she would have them shipped back to him, if she was unable to return them herself.

Grace went to bed that night filled with imaginings for her new life. She had begun to work out in her mind lessons she wanted to share with the school children in addition to the regular reading, writing and arithmetic. Of course, so much would depend on how much of her time would be taken up with some of the children who were behind in their education or might have special needs to be dealt with. She would know this soon enough. When she realized how much money she had on hand, she had purchased a few school supplies of her own to take with her. She went to sleep seeing children drawing the outline of different countries on the chalk board.

CHAPTER 22

Alex could not believe he had become so attached to this little baby boy. It seemed that from the moment he picked him up their paths were meant to cross. Soft Dove and Running Feet had worked diligently trying to save his mother, but she had simply lost too much blood by the time they found her. She lived only a few days after that. Alex picked a spot to bury her that they could easily find again. Alex told them he wanted the baby to be able to find it when he was older if he wanted. It was close to a water fall on a creek that ran near their camp.

Soft Dove had been able to nurse him since her little girl was old enough to be weaned from her breast. Everyone doted on him just as they did the other child, but it was Alex who spent every moment he could holding him, playing with him and talking with him. He named him David.

Alex and Andre had walked down to the lake. Alex had built a bench near the water and they sat there talking with David in his lap.

Alex said, "Just as King Saul loved David greatly, who was not his son, I love this little David the same way. I do not know how I can feel so much for this baby boy,

Andre. The why of it I don't guess really matters. I just do and intend to take care of him always."

Little David was sitting with his back to Alex's chest facing the water also. He was now walking a few steps without falling. He usually did not want to sit for long in Alex's lap unless he was sleepy, but today he seemed content.

He leaned to one side, turned his head up, reached out his little hand and touched Alex's chin while smiling.

He said, "Puh Puh".

Alex turned him around and tossed him in the air as David squealed with delight. He said, "That is right, David. I am your Papa."

Running Feet called them in for supper.

As they walked up to the cabin Alex said, "Andre, I need to pay another visit to the Shawnee camp." This did not surprise Andre as Alex had made several trips back since his first visit with this tribe. Andre knew he was going to visit the woman called Falling Waters.

He left after breakfast the next morning. Alex wondered if Falling Waters would be shocked at what he planned to say to her. Even though they had been together only a few times it seemed to him they had known each other for years. When he reached the garden he did not see Falling Waters working among the women. He did not stop, but continued on into the camp. He stopped at Chief Black Bob's dwelling after he saw that Falling Waters was gone.

Alex left the camp and decided to see if she might be at the creek. He was ready for a bath anyway. If she wasn't there he might do a little fishing while he waited for her to return to camp. He found her lying on a flat rock by the creek soaking up the sun's warm rays. This was where she came most often to bathe and swim when she did not want company. Her tunic was lying over some bushes drying along with her moccasins. She had combed her wet hair with her fingers and then lay on the warm rock on her back with her feet together and legs extended. She had fanned her almost dry hair out around and above her head. Her eyes were closed and she was thinking of Alex. Even though no words of loyalty had been exchanged between them, Falling Waters already thought of him as her man. He had only returned twice, since he had found the woman and the baby. It did not matter. She knew he would be back and she patiently waited for his return.

In the spot where she lay was in front of a rock bank about twenty feet high. Alex had been able to get to the edge without her hearing him. When he spotted her he thought how beautiful she was. He could not help but stand and stare for a few moments, then eased away a slight distance and noisily announced his arrival by calling her name.

Falling Waters opened her eyes not sure if she was hearing Alex or dreaming. When she was sure it was him she jumped up and ran to where he was working his way down the bank.

"Absence, I am dreaming of you in my mind and here you are."

When Falling Waters spoke his name it always sounded as though she was calling him Ahb-sen. He liked the sound of it and did not bother anymore to correct her. Alex picked her up and headed toward the water. Falling Waters was laughing and kicking as they fell in the water and went under.

As always after not seeing each other for a while, their lovemaking was intense. Afterwards, Falling Waters playfully helped Alex bathe. While his clothes were now strewn across bushes along with Falling Waters they lay quietly beside each other.

"Absence, what troubles you?"

Alex sat up and so did she.

"Do you remember what I told you about the day Andre and I found the baby and the connection that seemed to be there between us?"

"Yes. He is what you talk about the most now."

"Well, I have been thinking. I don't even know if it is the right thing to do. There may already be a woman that I am married to in my past. I may be a father too. I just don't know. I only know that I love this baby and I love you too. You are both here now and I want to be with you. We can make a family that came from loss into a family filled with love for each other. Falling Waters, would you like to come and live with us both? I have given the baby the name, David and declared myself his Papa. Would you want to be his mother?"

"Yes, Ahb-sen. This has been in my heart since the first time you told me about him."

"I have already talked with the chief and asked for you. He has given his permission as long as it pleases you. We can have a wedding ceremony here with your people."

They sat until late afternoon talking about their future together as a family. Falling Waters asked Alex if he would object to wearing a white skinned wedding tunic and leggings she had made for her first husband as there was no time to prepare a new one. She said she would alter the bead work on it and on her white tunic also. Alex did not have any objections if it would make the day more special for Falling Waters. He knew that was the right answer by the way her eyes had lit up even more.

He left for a quick trip to Cape Girardeau. He told Falling Waters to make arrangements while he was gone. He did not tell her, because he wanted it to be a surprise, but he intended to buy her a horse and a knife for the chief as gifts. When he arrived in Cape Girardeau the man he wanted to see that sold horses was gone. His wife said he would be returning in the mid to late afternoon tomorrow. That would extend his trip more than he had planned for but still give him time to get back for the wedding. He headed for the hotel and booked a room for two nights.

The next day Alex had purchased all that he had planned to get except for the horse. He had finished lunch and had some time to kill before he could take care of that business. He decided to walk to the dock and check out the activity. Cape Girardeau's dock was a busy place. Andre had told him it was the busiest port between St. Louis and Memphis. There were several boats, a few canoes, a military boat and a bright red and white flat bottom boat several hundred yards out heading in. He could tell passengers were out sitting on the deck with parasols above many heads. He was curious about travelers on the river and liked to watch them coming and going. A couple of times before he had met a few here and struck up a conversation with them. They nearly always had an interesting story to tell about themselves or their reason for passing through. He felt that would be the case with this boat. He might meet some of them at the hotel tonight, but now he had to get on to see the man about a horse.

CHAPTER 23

Grace did not hear any squealing or smelly animals on the Mary Mae because there weren't any. Even though it did transport some cargo, it was built to mainly transport passengers between St. Louis and New Orleans. A large portion of it included a cabin which held bunks for the passengers and two small closets. One held a chamber pot and the other enough space to freshen up and change clothes. A ladder outside the cabin went up to the roof where a railing had been built and adequate seating which could accommodate those passengers who enjoyed being out side.

Most all the passengers were outside anticipating their arrival in Cape Girardeau. The pilot had told them they were very close. This was a relief to everyone as they had experienced a scare earlier in the day and were still a little uneasy. The ever changing Mississippi River had unsettled one of its sawyers only to grab it back in the muddy bottom again. The only problem was that the location where it had been positioned this time happened to be in the channel the Mary Mae had taken around a sand bar. The huge sunken tree was just far enough under the water that no limbs broke the surface to create the ripple in the muddy water to alert the crew of its presence. When the boat had gone over it there was a loud noise as it scraped over the top of several of the limbs. One of them had managed to puncture a tiny hole in the boat. The leak was a trickle, but the pilot knew this could lead to a big hole if not taken care of soon. He alerted the passengers that they would be spending some additional time in Cape Girardeau until the leak could be repaired properly.

Grace, like many of the other passengers was anxious to get to her destination. She had met a couple that were actually traveling to New Madrid as well. She found out they owned a hemp plantation not too far from town and knew her parents. She and the woman were enjoying each other's company and quickly becoming friends.

The two women were in conversation when one of the passengers shouted, "I see it. I see Cape Girardeau."

Grace along with everyone else looked at the dock which grew larger with each passing minute. She was amazed at all the boats and could see people moving about while others appeared to be just standing and watching the activity. They were still close to a hundred yards out when she saw a man in buckskins mount a huge black horse and trot away. For some reason Alex came into her mind. She could see him in his uniform riding away from her. This shocked her as she realized it was the first time she had thought of him since she had boarded the Mary Mae.

She turned to her new friend and said, "I am sorry. What were you saying?"

"The pilot says we need to plan for a two night stay here." Florence said.

When she looked back at the dock the man and the big black horse had disappeared. The Mary Mae unloaded its passengers and their baggage as the pilot was not sure if they would be in Cape Girardeau for more than one night. He had to get the boat raised and see how extensive the damage or potential damage was.

Grace had heard there was an excellent new school here in Cape Girardeau. Now she would have time to visit and see if she could learn something that would help her with her soon to be students. The passengers were taken to their hotel. There were two hotels in town and located across the street from each other. They were staying in the nicer of the two that was now completely filled. Grace was looking forward to a nice warm bath and made arrangements for one right away.

She sat in the warm soapy water soaking and again planning her school room in her mind. She was excited about visiting the school here and decided she would have an early breakfast and arrive before the students in the hope that the teacher would be there and have some time for her. She got out of the tub even though she wanted to sit and soak longer. She was certain some of the others would want baths and the tub would be needed elsewhere. Grace realized she had still stayed in longer than she intended. She dried off, put on her robe and took one of her books out. She wasn't ready to dress for dinner and did not want to go out. The book was interesting, but Grace found she could not concentrate on it. She gave up and put it away. She walked over to the window and pulled the curtain back. There was that big black horse again or at least it looked like it in front of a saloon that was next to the hotel across the street. A young man was walking the horse along with another smaller horse. They were headed down a small alley between the hotel and the saloon. It was not the same man that she had seen riding him earlier. This looked like a very young man and he was short and stocky. The man she had seen was tall and thin like Alex. She assumed they were being taken to the stable and the man was in the saloon. She watched the back end of the big black horse disappear.

Alex was in the saloon, but not for drinking. He had heard they served a good cut of beef steak and pan fried potatoes. That suited his taste. He was thinking about going across the street for a coffee and dessert. He knew that he would most likely be able to engage in some interesting conversation.

Alex decided he was too full for dessert. He was going to take a walk before bedtime instead. There were always guests sitting out on the side porch of the hotel across the street. Some would be rocking while others enjoyed a smoke or chew of tobacco. Tonight was no different, but his desire for conversation had left him and he walked on by. He was thinking about little David and Falling Waters and missing them both.

Grace finished her supper and retired to her room. The tension of the leaking boat had taken more of a toll on her energy than she realized. She quickly undressed and climbed into bed with her book. She did not make it past the second page before she turned the wick down in the lamp and was sound asleep.

The next morning Alex had a leisurely breakfast and lingered over his coffee. He was still a creature of habit and had risen before daylight. He wanted to buy something special for Falling Waters before he left this morning. He had something a lot smaller than a horse in mind. There was no need to rush back, because he knew there was going to be a lot of activity going on in preparation for the wedding tomorrow. He would probably be in the way. He was sitting in front of the hotel pondering a few options and sipping from a mug of hot coffee when he saw a woman hurrying from the hotel as though she was late for an appointment. He could not see her face because of a hat she was wearing. Her head was bent in concentration trying to get her parasol open for the light rain that was falling. She finally was able to open it and continued in a rush down the street.

Grace could not believe she overslept. Breakfast was her favorite meal of the day, but she had to skip it today if she wanted to make it to the school before the students. She had asked for the location of the school from the hotel staff and knew it was on the edge of town. If she hurried she would still have time to visit with the teacher.

When she arrived the teacher was there. She was very cordial and expressed delight in helping Grace as much as possible. She invited Grace to stay after the students had arrived and listen in as long as she would like. Grace accepted her invitation and stayed for a little while. She planned to come back and meet the teacher after school today where they could really talk.

Grace was coming back into town and it was busy with people the way every town is in the morning time. Florence came out of a specialty clothing store and joined her. She was showing Grace her new scarf she had just purchased. As they were standing there Grace put on the scarf, twirled and laughingly said, "I think the color matches my eyes, don't you?"

Florence was laughing too and had moved in front of Grace between her and the street just as the big black horse was starting to pass behind her.

Grace looked over the top of Florence's head just in time to see the profile of the bearded man dressed in animal skins in the saddle also wearing a coon skin hat and moccasins.

Grace gasped and the color drained from her face. Her eyes were huge. The man passed and Grace could not take her eyes from him. She appeared to be frozen where she stood except for her eyes and head that followed the man as he rode further and further away from them. Finally, she took a breath and shouted, "Alex, Alex wait!" She ran toward the man and the two horses for a few steps and called again, "Alex wait!" She knew he could hear her because others on the street had turned around. The man did not stop. In fact he never even turned around.

Florence caught up with her and asked, "Grace are you alright? You look like you have just seen a ghost!"

Grace watched the man and the two horses turn a corner and disappear.

She turned to her and said, "Maybe I did. It wouldn't be the first time."

Florence was watching her closely as the color slowly returned to her face.

Grace said, "I will explain it all later. Right now I need to get some food in my stomach. I feel a might faint."

They walked to the hotel arm in arm. Her friend watching closely as the color slowly returned to Grace's cheeks.

CHAPTER 24

Grace along with the rest of the passengers had finished breakfast. They were now mingling on the veranda while awaiting word of possible departure this morning. Florence had not come back down from her room. Grace had found a rocker situated off to its self and turned away from the group. She did not reposition it as this suited her mood this morning. The man she saw yesterday and just knew for that one second was Alex had affected her more than she realized. The dream that had haunted her night after night for months before it finally began to leave her sleeping peacefully had returned last night. Actually it was not the same dream. Before she had always awakened hearing Alex calling for her. This time she was awakened by her own voice shouting his name along with the tears that had also returned. She knew it wasn't him. If it had been he would have seen her, probably before she thought had seen him. She would no longer visualize him riding away in a uniform when she thought of him. That vision had passed and had been replaced with a bearded stranger in buckskins riding a big black horse and always he was riding away from her.

As the Mary Mae allowed the current of the Mississippi River to take them closer to their destinations the passengers seemed to be enjoying the sunshine of the day. Someone asked how fast they were moving and another passenger estimated about four miles an hour. Florence's husband had spoken with the pilot and been told they should reach New Madrid day after tomorrow if there were no more problems. Grace and Florence had managed to get two seats at the front of the boat on the deck. Grace had told her about her life with Alex and his disappearing.

They were passing by the mouth of the Ohio River where it joined the Mississippi River from the east and both continued their journey to the Gulf of Mexico. One of the things Grace intended to do in the near future was take a trip to the much talked about city of New Orleans. As they watched the mouth of the Ohio River pass by Grace's thoughts went to the many people she knew who had followed on and off the Ohio to reach the Mississippi River and cross its waters to the new land on the western side just as her parents had done. Many of them came to settle near its waters and others came to pass on to new places farther west.

"In just two more days and a whole new world will be in front of you, Grace." Said Florence.

"I know. I really did not realize that St. Charles was so isolated, until returning to St. Louis and now seeing all the traffic on the Mississippi. I have a feeling the hotel is going to be frequented with a lot of interesting guests. After all, I have already become friends with one and I am not even there yet." She said smiling at Florence.

Florence's husband had come up and was leaning against the rail as the women talked.

"Ladies, you might want to think about going below in a little while."

He was pointing to the right of the boat toward the darkened western sky. The Mary Mae was almost around a bend in the river. As the boat cleared the bend and was now on a straight stretch, they could all see not too far ahead of them another flat bottom boat moving south also. There was a canvas covered wagon on the back of it and two animals that were probably mules.

They were all watching the sky that was black as far as one could see to the west. The bottom of the clouds looked like a straight line that hung just above a lighter sky which reached the tree tops. As they watched it looked as though a dark black/brown and green hued mushroom was starting to form from and in front of the cloud. They all gasped as they saw blue lightening flash and then heard an extremely loud clap of thunder. Some of the passengers had begun to hurry to the cabin below. A couple of the men came and joined them also watching the cloud. It was hard to determine for sure which way it was moving as the sky was blue everywhere but in the west. Grace suspected it might be coming their way because of the slight change in the breeze which was now coming from the west.

The pilot ordered the crew to take the boat into shore. He knew from the green hue in this cloud that it held a lot of wind. He did not want to be caught in the middle of the river if it reached them. The Mary Mae headed for the east bank. They were in a wide area of the river so it would take a few minutes to reach it. All of them on deck knew they needed to go below, but were all mesmerized by what was happening.

The mushroom part of the cloud's bottom had started slowly spinning. It began turning faster and faster. A point formed in a cone shape and began to drop from the cloud and go back up in it and disappear repeating this process several times. In less than a minute it seemed it dropped and did not go back up. It worked its way closer to the ground and looked like a giant rope loosely curving from the cloud and now touching the tree tops. It looked so odd against the lighter sky. The rope quickly grew into a wide dark spinning wall below the mushroom cloud. They could all see trees being picked up and rotating in the monster. Grace had heard some of the soldiers talking about these spinning clouds and knew they were in extreme danger.

The lightening continued and now there was no doubt that it was headed toward the river and would cross a little distance in front of them. Grace looked to see if the other boat had made it to the bank yet and was horrified to see that they had just started to turn and were still in the middle of the river.

Grace screamed, "They are not going to make it in time."

The wind had picked up as the Mary Mae crew were rapidly tying it up at the bank. The river was covered in white caps and as the trunk of the mushroom cloud reached the river it was sucking the water up in it along with huge tree limbs and smaller trees.

It seemed to Grace that everything had almost stopped but was still moving ever so slowly. Where they were the trees were swaying back and forth. They could hear limbs breaking and the wind along with the lightening was deafening. Screams from the passengers below could still be heard at times. Everyone still on deck was clinging to the rail to keep from being blown over or off the boat by the wind.

The spinning cloud reached the other boat that was still not even close to shore. They could see the wagon being jerked from the boat along with the animals. Along with all the debris from the forest the wagon and two mules were spinning above the boat in the river. Suddenly the boat itself was picked up and began to spin. The cloud continued its path toward the eastern bank of the river. Shortly before it reached shore they saw the wagon fly from the cloud into the trees. The boat was tossed in the river and the mules dropped in the forest as though hands had opened and released them. The trunk appeared to be lifting off the ground and returning to the mushroom above. It was soon apparent that it was not done yet and dropped again to the forest floor as it continued its journey to the east, before it lifted back up into the cloud and disappeared. The whole thing from the time the rope formed and the cloud reached the eastern bank had been less than ten minutes, but seemed like an eternity.

When the Mary Mae drew close to where the tornado had crossed the river and reached the spot where the boat had been thrown from the cloud into the river some of the crew dove overboard and disappeared in the murky water. One surfaced saying the boat was just under the surface. He went back under. He and another man came up with the body of a middle aged man. The men dove many more times into the river, but found no other bodies with the boat.

When they reached the bank, it was strange and frightening looking. Even from quite a distance away they had seen the trail of destruction left by the spinning cloud. The path of devastation was several hundred feet along the river bank and went that far into the woods. Where the cloud had finally lifted up the mutilation of the trees stopped and the forest stood tall and rising again into the sky with all its green glory.

When you looked out from the deck of the boat it was easy to see that most of the trees were gone or laid over as if they had been trampled on purpose and pushed over in the same direction. Other places they seemed to be broken and limbs lying all scrambled up. The area looked as though someone had come through with a giant scythe and cut a swath through the forest as though they were cutting a field of high weeds and after cutting the path a distance the cutter had just stopped. They could all see broken pieces of the boards that had once been a part of the wagon scattered about near the bank.

While the crew tied up the boat Grace and the rest stood silently staring at the destruction. Mixed in with the broken forest were pieces of clothing, wood that was most likely parts of furniture that had been on the wagon and around one of the tree trunks still standing on top was a wagon wheel. Many of the passengers along with Grace had started working their way off the boat and began threading carefully through the debris.

She was not dressed for climbing over broken trees and huge limbs, but a sense of urgency had gripped her as well as everyone else and she battled the obstacles without any thought except the hope of finding someone they could help.

Grace seemed to be the only one who had gone to the left and was slowly and laboriously advancing along the bank, when she saw something move slightly a few feet ahead of her. When she got closer she could see that it was a small child standing on the bank wet, covered in mud and sand with green tree leaves and twigs stuck to the mud and dangling from her body. Had they not known what had just happened, at first glance she could have been reported as some sort of mysterious river swamp monster. When Grace walked closer she could tell it was a little girl by the remains of a tattered dress she was wearing. The first thing Grace could see that wasn't covered in mud were these huge terror filled blue/green eyes peering through the mud caked face. There was one clump of long blond hair that stuck up and hung out from her head. The rest of her hair was covered in the river mud and plastered to her head. Grace felt like her heart would break at the pitiful sight of her, but at the same time overjoyed to find her alive. She was guessing that her age was around three to four years old from her size.

She did not want to frighten her any more than she already was, so she did not call out to the others. She worked her way over, under and around the broken limbs now covering the bank. The child was obviously in shock as she stood with a fixed stare seeing nothing. Grace very carefully checked to see if there were any broken bones. There did not appear to be any. She led her to the edge of the river and began to wash off some of the mud and debris using her skirt to dry her off as best she could. The dress she had on was in tatters. It was barely hanging on her body by one shoulder. Most of the bottom half had been ripped from the dress. Other than minor scratches and one cut on her back she seemed to be uninjured. The child had not uttered one word as Grace led her back to where the Mary Mae was moored.

She took her on board. Florence helped her clean the cut and bathe her properly. Florence took one of her clean sleeping gowns and cut off the bottom part. She then quickly sewed a big pleat in the front and back neckline to keep the shoulders from falling off. They dressed her in it with a wide ribbon tied around her waist.

Both women jumped as they heard a gun go off. There were no more shots fired and after a few minutes they took the little girl outside the cabin of the boat. A few of the passengers had remained on the upper deck. The others along with the crew were working their way along the river bank while several of the men had walked into the devastation that had once been a living forest. There had been no other passengers of the doomed boat found until now. A man was being carried out and was laid on the bank by the boat.

Before Grace could stop her the little girl ran across the gang plank and on to the shore where the body lay.

She squatted down near his head and placed her tiny hand on his face and cried, "Papa, wake up. Wake up Papa." She began to push his head back and forth still crying, "Papa, wake up. We have to find Mama."

By the time Grace reached her she was crying hysterically. Grace did not snatch her up right away. She squatted down beside her and put one of her arms around the little girl and held her closely. She just held her until she came to the realization that her Papa was not going to wake up. It had been very hard not to pull her away.

She looked at Grace and said, "Why won't Papa wake up?"

Grace then picked her up and carried her to the boat. She sat and held the child and rocked her with her body until the little girl finally slept. Grace laid her in her bunk and watched her sleep for a couple of minutes before going back up on deck. She thought about helping in the search, but did not want to be too far away in case the child woke up.

The men did find three more bodies. They were all men. No sign of the little girl's mother was found. Someone had found a dress that belonged to the child. It was torn, but Florence was able to patch it enough for her to wear it.

As the end of the day was fast approaching everyone had returned to the boat. The pilot decided to spend the night there just in case anyone else had survived and might see the camp fire. The cook managed to set up and prepare a meal after some of the crew had cleared the debris from a spot near the boat.

The little girl had awakened after a short nap and had climbed in Grace's lap. She had not said anything since trying to wake her father up. Grace was able to get her to eat a few bites of food before she drifted back to sleep. Again Grace watched her sleeping awhile before going back up to the deck. Everyone that had not collapsed from mental and physical exhaustion was there quietly talking. Grace sat next to Florence.

"You know that gun we heard was one of the crew. He had to shoot a mule that was found alive, but badly mangled." Florence told her.

Florence's husband spoke up and said, "We found one of the men who was lodged in a tree trunk. The tree had been huge and what was left was now just one tall twenty foot stump with a fork in it. The man had been thrown and wedged in that fork as if a giant had picked him up and placed him there in a sitting position with his legs and arms crossed. Another stump had a chair sticking out of it with nothing broken. One of the four legs was stuck in the side of what was left of the tree looking as though it might have grown there. How did that chair leg push through that tree stump and not break off? Well, ladies I am going to try to get some sleep. You two should as well. I overheard the pilot saying they were going to search one more time in the morning."

Grace and Florence continued staring out into the darkness. They were the only two left on the deck. She was worried about the little girl. Grace did not think she should have to keep seeing the place where she lost her father and mother and possibly other family members. Grace did not know even if she had a brother or sister who might have been on the boat also. However she understood the need to try to find anymore possible survivors. The little girl still was not talking.

"Grace, have you thought of what should be done with the child. She has not left your sight or hardly left your lap for that matter since you found her. You know we will be happy to take her with us and give her a good home. However, each time I have tried to hold her and give your legs a rest she has cried so."

"Florence, I am going to keep her with me. I have figured out a way that might possibly help identify her. It will just take some time. Until then my family will help me love her and take care of her."

They did search the next morning and found no one else. The men surmised that the ones who were not found had probably been lost to the river or buried too deep in the debris to be seen. When the Mary Mae finally pulled away from the bank and headed toward the middle of the river with a deep blue cloudless sky overhead, Grace took a deep breath. She was sure she wasn't the only one.

They would be in New Madrid soon now. She would be starting her new life there with a precious child she had not planned on. Furthermore, this child had literally been dropped from the sky in a dark spinning cloud. It didn't seem real when you thought about it. Reality came back in a rush when the little girl sitting in her lap moved. She suddenly remembered something she had written and memorized in her journal after she had decided to leave St. Charles.

Grace looked over at Florence and said, "Life is one moment after another that comes to pass us by in the relentless journey called time. Any one of these moments can bring unexpected and irrevocable change which may place us on a new path sending us in a new direction we never would dream of."

A crewman shouted, "There it is folks, New Madrid.

End

If you liked this story, it has not ended. The life of Grace is continued in my next book called *Lodgings by Grace*. It will be available soon.

Thank you for reading.

ABOUT THE AUTHOR

As must be with all writer's Barbara is no different in that she has a deep love for books. This love affair began at a very early age and has grown ever stronger through the years.

Along the way she continuously wrote tidbits about her life. Some were humorous and others were sad, but in the early days she learned her writing could bring laughter and tears to the reader. As a consequence, she was always saying to others, "I am going to write a book one day". After having lived in seven states, Germany and now the country of Panama that day finally came. Once she stepped through the "writing door" she knew it could never be closed again.

Barbara Maria Kelly's first book, Comes to Pass is a historical fiction containing romance with a slight touch of suspense and mystery. It is being followed by a second book well underway that continues this story line.

Barbara can be reached by email at barbarakelly55@gmail.com.

79811387R00166

Made in the USA
Lexington, KY
25 January 2018